TRAILS

Adventures of Denny Caraway, Alaskan Homesteader

Warren Troy

PO Box 221974 Anchorage, Alaska 99522-1974
books@publicationconsultants.com—www.publicationconsultants.com

ISBN 978-1-59433-259-3
eBook ISBN 978-1-59433-264-7
Library of Congress Catalog Card Number: 2011942813

Manufactured in the United States of America.

Dedication

I dedicate this book to:

My wife, who knows the life full well

My brother, for his unerring literary advice

All my Alaskan friends for their character, inspiration and lore

Joel "Yog" Naspinski who has always believed

and

many thanks to Sue Henry for her kindness and support.

I didn't come to Alaska to search for great riches,

nor did I come to catch her fine fishes.

I didn't come north to act out deep wishes.

I just came up here to get away

from all those fine-haired sons-a-bitches.

Anon

Introduction

SOMETHING HAD TO CHANGE IN MY LIFE. I FELT LIKE I WAS JUST existing, and had stopped looking forward to what a new day might bring. Even though the things in my life were what most people would appreciate having, a successful, high-paying job, nice home, friends, lucrative investments, there was still something missing, and the empty feeling inside me was getting stronger. It just wasn't clear to me what it was that I needed.

It was January, 1990, and I had just turned 40. Middle age was kicking me in the backside. My one attempt at marriage had gone off the rails, and I hadn't tried to hook up with anyone since my divorce. Sometimes, alone at night, oblivious to whatever mildly entertaining drivel was droning along on the screen, I'd have moments of frustration, sometimes despair, which were getting more difficult to dispel, even at work.

My job, handling public relations for an advertising firm in Reno, had become irrelevant and stressful for me. Burnt out on the constant interaction with people, I had come to dread new assignments and, more than likely, the unpleasant personalities of the people I'd have to deal with, people I wouldn't want to know otherwise.

I was tired of city life in general, with all its excessive noises and smells, as well as the large population. I had to go into Reno to work and to entertain clients. Other than that, I avoided going into the city whenever possible.

The only activities that brought me some relief were fishing or deer hunting in the mountains of Northern Nevada, when I could find the time to get away. But, those trips were all too brief. When I returned, all the things that brought me down were still there waiting for me. I needed a serious change, full-time and permanent. The sun had stopped shining in my life.

My friends were tiring of my attitude. It had become all too obvious that I wasn't happy, and it was rubbing off on those around me. At lunch one day, after listening to me grumble about a new client, one of my fellow workers said, "Jeez, Denny, why don't you just go live all alone in the woods somewhere, maybe Alaska. That should suit you to a T! A few weeks of that and you'll gladly come back to what you've got here!"

The instant he said "Alaska," something clicked audibly in my head, like a light switch going on. Alaska! Somehow that sounded so right. I mean, lots of people had gone there before me for many different reasons. Some probably just to get away from it all. I was determined to explore the possibilities.

Over the next several months, I threw myself into researching Alaska, especially the experiences of people who had lived there, and what they had gone through in the Alaska wilderness, known as the bush. The stories I read about homesteading were fascinating. There was one book about a man in the middle of the 20th Century who'd built an incredibly fine little cabin way out in the wilderness by a beautiful lake. He lived there by himself for many years with little human contact, and loved every day of it. I could tell that what he seemed to take in stride every day was a rough life and an incredible adventure. I wanted to do the same, to literally build a home and carve out a life for myself, a life totally opposite from the one I had now. I considered whether or not I had what it took to live that way, alone in a wild place where survival was a real issue, not a virtual reality. The more I considered it, the more it appealed to me. It was so peaceful in the Nevada high desert, hunting or fishing by myself. Surely Alaska would be an even better place to find sanctuary from everything that was dragging me down.

Done with my researching, I decided I had to give it a go. If it proved too much for me, then nothing was lost and surely some wonderful experiences would be gained. I just had to try. The fact that being middle-aged might be an obstacle crossed my mind once, then was dismissed. I was in good health and had outdoors experience, so that shouldn't matter.

It didn't take as long as I had expected to sell my house and get rid of all the things I wouldn't need up north. I'd gather what gear was necessary once I arrived in Alaska. Selling my investments, liquidating all my accounts and retirement policies gave me a sizeable lump of money to use for my new life. My friends thought I was nuts, disassembling my life like this, but I didn't want to do this half-way, certain it was the right thing for me.

Six months from the time the suggestion to go live in Alaska had been tossed at me, I was ready to go, to cut loose from the unsatisfying life that was making me miserable, to head into the wilderness for a new beginning. Denny Caraway was headed north!

Two nights before flying up to Anchorage, I dreamed about Grandpa Pete, my mom's father. He was the one who'd taught me to fish, hunt, and camp, my own father not being interested in such things. Grandpa had been my best friend, my buddy. He was there for me after my parents died when I was in my 20s. His own death just a few years ago was a great loss to me.

I dreamed that we were standing on the edge of a high precipice overlooking a land full of rivers, mountains and lush, green valleys. As we stood together gazing out upon the amazing panorama, he spoke to me. "No matter what comes, Denny, you just take care of it with what the Good Lord has given you and everything will be fine. I'll be watching out for you." Then it all faded out, though I would remember his simple, direct words.

Episode

1

THE TOWN OF HAZEL, ON THE COAST OF SOUTHCENTRAL Alaska, is located at the mouth of Long Bay. The first white people to settle permanently in the area were Benny O'Mara and his wife Hazel, who anchored their small fishing boat there in the summer of 1949. There were no roads, just a rough piece of coast bordering untouched wilderness. In those days, living in Alaska was only for adventurous, self-reliant, and strong-willed individuals. An ability to live off the land was vital. Alaska was harsh, inhospitable, and dangerous until you figured out how to survive. Even then, it was harsh, inhospitable, and dangerous.

Benny and Hazel were up to the task, building a home with their own hands and working hard to make a living by fishing, mostly for cod and halibut, until the rough nature of the work took its toll on them in their later years.

Though the O'Maras would have preferred retaining the solitude they had originally found there, others eventually showed up and stayed on too. They were people who appreciated the area for the same reasons as Benny and Hazel: for the remoteness, the abundant natural resources, and the wild nature of the place. Many actually looked forward to the challenges that living there presented.

By the late Fifties, a small town had been established. It came to be called Hazel, for the O'Maras had been unanimously accepted as the community's founders and civic leaders.

Over the following years, Hazel's population steadily grew, but it remained a pleasant little coastal hamlet, the number of residents peaking at around five hundred. A road system was eventually built all the way from Anchorage, bringing more people and development with it, which were begrudgingly accepted by Hazel's clannish residents. After all, what choice was there?

When the first signal light was installed at the main intersection in town, Hazel O'Mara was there to see it, but Benny wasn't. He had died when his car slid off the road north of town one icy February morning in 1979, plummeting down the high coastal bluff to the rock-strewn beach below.

Hazel stepped down from her position as long-time mayor after that, but she continued running an eatery called the Log Cabin Cafe, with her daughter Gwen. She and Benny had opened it after they stopped fishing.

By 1990, the town of Hazel was still small and easy going, even though there was now a fast food franchise as well as one car dealership, two boat yards, an ATV shop, and now two traffic lights.

At that point, most of the old-timers who had originally homesteaded the bush country around Hazel had moved away, turned their full-time homestead cabins into weekend getaways, or died.

One of those who'd relocated was George Whiting, who moved into Hazel for the convenience and comfort it afforded him after spending almost thirty years out on his remote homestead. George's old bones could no longer handle the long, rough trail that led out to his cabin, or the hard daily work necessary to live out there. So, he bought and logged several acres close to town overlooking Long Bay, and built a solid log home from the large spruce trees he had cut down.

Even after he had settled comfortably into his new home, George didn't part with his homestead for some time, years in fact, though he never did go back out to the old cabin. Finally, seeing no reason to keep his old bush home any longer, Whiting put it up for sale. After placing a small ad in the Anchorage newspaper, George wondered if there would be anyone who'd want to live the woods life. He would soon find out.

Episode

2

THOUGH I WAS GLAD TO HAVE LEFT NEVADA AND COME TO Alaska, two weeks in Anchorage had me itching to be somewhere far away from the same kind of city life I'd escaped when I said good-bye to Reno. Looking around Anchorage, it was disappointingly familiar in spite of its smaller buildings and fewer people. Even the Alaska store and street names made little difference. It was still the same environment that I had gladly left behind. I knew in my gut that my happiness, and perhaps my personal salvation, was somewhere out there in the wilderness beyond the city limits.

While sitting in a coffee shop, I saw a classified ad in the newspaper that grabbed my attention. It read: "Remote land for sale in Southcentral Alaska, small cabin, five acres. Call George at 244–8911."

Reading that abrupt proposal lit up my mind, and I knew I had to respond.

A few minutes later, I was talking to George Whiting on the phone. I told him my name was Denny Caraway, and that I was very interested in his remote land.

He said that was fine and told me how to get to the town of Hazel where he lived, and that was it. The next morning, I drove south in the almost new Jeep Cherokee I had purchased when I arrived in Alaska.

I tried hard to keep from daydreaming about homesteading while traveling down the bumpy, twisty, asphalt highway, but the incredible scenery along the way proved an even greater distraction.

There is no way to describe the mountains, rivers, lakes, and deep forest surrounding me without using trite adjectives such as "majestic," "awesome," "vast," and "untouched wilderness." The thing is, going down that road none of them seemed overused, only understated. The country defied verbal description. I stopped at every major scenic pullout along the way, not wanting to miss anything. It was a feast for my soul, and I couldn't consume enough.

I had a strange feeling in the back of my mind that I was actually going home. I had never been here, but I didn't question it, just accepted that this was meant to be, a part of my destiny.

George Whiting was home when I arrived at his place that afternoon. Although in his seventies, he looked ten years younger, with a handshake that was firmer than expected.

When George invited me into his beautiful log home, I noticed he was in stocking feet, so I removed my shoes by the door. He smiled at my respectful action, and it felt like I had passed some kind of initial test. He offered me a chair at his rough-hewn wooden table, and a cup of coffee, which I gladly accepted. I told him that the view from his yard of the mountains and glaciers across the bay was incredible. He just smiled again and nodded knowingly. We chatted over our mugs about Alaska in a general way, before getting down to discussing the parcel of land he was selling. Mr. Whiting had a relaxed, peaceful way about him, and was pleasant to converse with.

George described his old homestead for me in detail. Though I had hoped he would have some photos to show me, he spoke with such great detail and clarity they really weren't necessary. He told me about the forests of spruce and birch, the animals living there, and how the changing seasons affected wilderness living. He also spoke of the joys and hardships of the homestead life. When George painted a mental picture of the cabin itself, it sounded like a perfect forest dwelling. I could tell he had loved living there, and that he was still there in his mind. George was an eloquent, colorful speaker, and I was hooked.

He also seemed an honest, straightforward man, different from most of the people I usually dealt with. He confessed to me that he hadn't been out to the place for about five years, so it might need some work. I assured him that wouldn't be a deciding factor.

Before we parted ways, George and I had reached an initial agreement, based on my seeing the land before making a final decision. He handed me a finely drawn map, marking the exact location of the homestead and the way there in detail, starting at the eastern edge of Hazel. Looking at the map, it appeared to be an easily followed route. But then, I hadn't taken the trail yet.

Getting a room at the local motel, I barely slept that night, fantasies of the next day's journey running around in my head. I gave in to them, but eventually dozed off.

The next morning, I purchased enough food to last me several days. I would head out to the Whiting cabin after having breakfast at a homey little place George had suggested, called the Log Cabin Cafe. It was run by a lady named Hazel and her daughter.

Hazel was an older woman, probably in her late sixties, lean, and her silver hair worn in a braid. When I met her, she was wearing a flannel shirt and denim jeans, with a food-stained apron tied around her middle. She had an attractive face, though it had a slightly weathered look, as if the natural elements had been in intimate contact with her for a long time. But it was her eyes that caught my attention. They were a piercing blue and held a steady gaze. I had the feeling she was a strong, determined person who had lived a lot of life and was still going strong.

When she brought my food I introduced myself, and she, in turn, told me her name. Kidding, I asked her if the name of the town was what had brought her there. She just stood for a few seconds, unsmiling, giving me a very direct look, before informing me that the town had been named after her. I smiled, assuming she was making a joke too, but she pointed to a framed black and white photo on the wall, and walked away.

It was a grainy image of a man and woman on a small, old-fashioned fishing boat, each of them holding up a huge salmon. Walking closer to the photo, I studied the people in it. The woman looked to be in her early twenties, and could only be Hazel O'Mara in earlier times. The man was lean and tough looking, a good match for her. The caption, handwritten on the bottom of the photo, stated: "Benny and Hazel O'Mara, founders of Hazel, Alaska, 1954."

Her daughter Gwen looked like a younger version of her mom. She was also lean and fit looking, with dark brown hair and the same clear blue eyes with an equally resolute look.

I liked the two women right away, and wondered if this little Alaska town was fully populated with tough, honest, straightforward people.

After breakfast I began my journey to the old cabin, driving along the narrow blacktop road indicated on George's map. About ten miles out, the pavement ended turning to gravel. To my right, Long Bay presented a magnificent panorama with amazing glaciers and craggy snowcapped peaks on its far side. The bay was about twenty miles long and relatively narrow, perhaps two or three miles at its widest. Numerous coves and inlets showed across the water. Once I was settled on some land, I planned to go explore them all.

I had already arrived at the conclusion that there was no other place like Alaska, and here I was going deeper into its heart.

Continuing up the narrow road, I almost missed my turn near a small pond with a swimming float in the center, but I cut the wheel sharply and made it around the corner. There was the hand-printed sign nailed to a small spruce tree that George had marked on his map. The sign read, "Grizzly Lake." Quite a grand name for such a little spot of water.

The dusty road ran up a steep incline before turning sharply to the right. As I started around, I had to swerve way to the right and slam on the brakes. A man in a rusty old pickup truck was roaring right toward me, raising a billowing cloud of dust behind him, moving at the last minute just enough to avoid me. I saw his hard face, eyes staring straight ahead like he just didn't give a darn, and I made a mental note to keep an eye out for him, as his dust engulfed me.

The Cherokee's right wheels were off the road in a narrow little ditch. After shifting into four-wheel drive, I was able to back up onto the road. My adrenalin subsiding, I continued on for several more miles until a settlement George had described came into view. Just before reaching the cluster of buildings, I had to stop and wait for a mother moose and her two calves to make their way across the road. I sat there, happily taking in my first view of moose in the wild. They weren't beautiful animals, but they were unique, and the mother was definitely large. Her big puffy nose was funny looking. I had read that some people considered moose muzzle a delicacy. I just let that idea go by.

Just past where the moose had crossed, I noted that off the left side of the road were a number of trucks with small utility trailers hitched to them, parked in a clearing in the trees. I wondered if they were owned by people who had some sort of off-road vehicles that they used to hunt or get out to their cabins.

The settlement was located at the end of the road by bluffs that overlooked the bay. George told me the folks who lived in the collection of roughly built houses were the remnants of a group that had settled there in the early Seventies, disillusioned San Francisco Hippies who came to Alaska to continue their dream of peace and love.

George said they had not been easily accepted by the conservative people in Hazel, but were eventually tolerated and considered harmless. They were also a good source of material for jokes and commentary about their personal habits. Besides, the "Sandal Family" as they had been labeled, lived outside town, keeping pretty much to themselves. Now, there weren't many of them left.

I'd noticed that the road had been climbing as I drove, but was surprised to find that the bay was hundreds of feet below the Sandals' place. There was a switchback dirt road, a wide trail really, which led down to the bay from a little parking lot the

Sandals maintained. They charged two dollars for parking. $2 was painted in red on a small bucket with a locked lid nailed to a spruce. I parked the Cherokee, strapped the .44 Magnum pistol's belt and holster around my waist, put on my pack, dropped two bucks in the bucket's slotted cover and headed down the steep trail.

George had explained that people used to drive motorcycles, cars, and trucks up and down the trail, steep and narrow though it was, until a kid on a dirt bike going down met a truck coming up, and was slammed right over the edge, falling a long way before making contact again. It must have been true, because about halfway down I spotted a piece of metal that looked like part of a motorcycle fender imbedded in the bark of a large spruce.

When I got down to the beach, the tide was way out, but the high-water mark at the base of the bluff showed there would be no walking room when it came back in, so I set a steady pace.

The beach ran without a break for miles along the north side of the bay. From sea level, the mountains and glaciers on the opposite side loomed even more majestic, dominating the scene. Interested in everything around me, I had slowed my steps and hadn't noticed how fast the returning tide was heading toward me. Breaking into a trot, I managed to get past the narrowest part of the beach without the tide catching me.

Coming to an area where the bluffs were farther back from the beach, I spied a red-roofed log cabin nestled among some huge old cottonwood trees. There was a corral close to the trail, with several rangy horses inside. I hadn't expected to find horses here. High in an old spruce tree next to the corral was a massive nest with a bald eagle sitting in it. The whole scene just didn't seem quite real to my mind. Alaska was definitely displaying its unique nature.

Farther down the trail, a dilapidated bridge made of two wooden poles topped with plywood spanned the mouth of a creek that ran out into the upper end of the bay. The bridge must have settled over time, because it was barely above the surface of the water. As I walked cautiously across it, it bobbed and jiggled under my weight, the creek actually washing over its surface. I scooted across, managing to stay dry.

Past the bridge, the land was open and flat and covered with lush grasses, but the surface of the trail was bare and hard packed. Scanning the horizon, I saw that the flats extended for miles beyond the head of the bay. There were several large animals in the distance, but I couldn't tell what they were.

To my left was a row of trees that ran along the edge of the flats where they butted up against the steep bluffs, with a clearly visible path leading to them. For some reason, this section of the trail wasn't marked on George's map, but it felt like the right way to go.

About halfway to the trees, I came to a small slough full of cloudy brown water running across the path, with no bridge to cross it. I wondered if it would go dry at low tide, but didn't want to wait hours to find out. The path continued on the other side, so wading across seemed the only option. It probably wasn't very deep. Taking off my boots and socks and holding them overhead, I started across. At first the water was only up to my thighs, but the mud on the bottom was very slippery. Unfortunately, there was a narrow, deeper channel in the middle concealed by the murky water, and I lost my footing on the slick bottom. Down I went, up to my neck, just managing to keep my boots and socks dry.

Struggling to my feet, I clumsily made it to the other side, and sat down on the hard ground. The sudden dunking in the icy water had taken my breath away. Soaked to the skin, cold, and feeling pretty dumb, I was glad to be in the middle of unpopulated country where there was no one to witness the incident.

Opening my pack, I was relieved to see that it was still dry inside, so my gear was okay. Remembering the pistol on my hip, I was going to pull it out to clean it off, but the holster was empty. I had left the safety strap unsnapped and tucked behind the holster in case it was necessary to quickly draw the gun. I knew the revolver was in that freezing slough, and had no choice but to retrace my steps and walk back into that nasty channel.

Feeling around in the muck on the bottom with my bare feet, my big toe bumped into something hard. Taking a breath and completely submerging, I brought a gray, slimy rock up to the surface. Tossing it aside, I continued searching. A few minutes later, I caught my numbed foot on something that definitely felt like a piece of metal. Squatting again into the water, I reached down and brought up: MY GUN! Careful to keep my footing, I returned to dry ground.

Glad to be out of the silt-choked water, I walked over and dropped down by my pack and boots. Shivering, I pulled a roll of toilet paper in a plastic bag from my pack. After wiping off my face and neck, I removed the cylinder and cartridges from the pistol and shook and blew out the water and muck, trying to thoroughly clean the pistol with the paper. It was the best I could do. I wiped out the holster, slid the gun back in, and made sure to snap the safety strap into place.

Sitting there on the dirt, barefoot, wet, and cold, I felt like a kid on a foolish childhood adventure. One slip and I had been transformed from a middle-aged man into a ten-year-old boy. Alaska had just begun to show what it had in store for me.

I got a chill down my back, not from the cold water I had been dipped in, but from the realization that I didn't know diddly-squat about Alaska. No matter how many books I had read or films I had viewed, I was ignorant of its living reality.

Now, the fact that I was totally alone overwhelmed me, and for a moment I contemplated waiting for the tide to go out again, and heading back to Hazel to find someone to guide me out to George's old homestead. I also considered the idea of rethinking the whole plan while sitting in a warm, dry restaurant, a hot meal in front of me, and a stiff drink in my hand.

Serious doubts about my ability to deal with Alaska had formed in my mind. This first journey into the wilderness was barely begun, and I had already gotten into trouble.

Wiping off my feet, I put my socks and boots back on. I realized I hadn't been hurt and my gear was okay. That thought calmed me, and I put the idea of returning out of my mind. I had come here to find a place for myself, and that was exactly what I was going to do. I damned well wasn't going back to Reno. Maybe I was unsure of how I would deal with whatever Alaska was going to throw at me, but if I didn't give it my best shot, I would never know. Recalling my grandfather's words in the dream, I took heart and pressed on.

Hoisting the pack, I continued on toward the trees. It took another twenty minutes to reach them. They turned out to be a long row of old cottonwoods. The trail that ran along them was rough and deeply rutted with knobby tire tracks. People apparently rode this path on motorized vehicles, but the tracks were too close together to be trucks or jeeps. I wondered what kind of machines people used here. After several hundred yards the tire tracks turned right toward the flats, but I continued straight on, following a narrow foot trail.

Initially the path was clear and open, but I soon entered an area of dense vegetation that choked the trail and grew together overhead like a natural roof. It was a little unnerving pushing through, not knowing what lay ahead.

There were some tall, very odd plants I quickly learned to avoid. They looked kind of tropical, having very wide, flat leaves. There were thin, sharp spines all over the stalks and the undersides of the leaves. On contact, the tips broke off under the skin causing painful little wounds that quickly became infected, as I soon found out. I later learned that these plants were called devil's club. What an appropriate name.

Just as I was wishing for the thick undergrowth to end, I came out into an open area that looked almost landscaped, with small clumps of bushes here and there, and grass cropped short like a lawn. To my right, the wide open grasslands revealed several animals, but I still couldn't tell if they were cattle, moose, or what.

Walking through this clearing, I saw what looked like cow pies scattered all over the ground. At first I wondered if these might be bear droppings, having never seen any. But, it would take a lot of bears to leave so many behind. I thought of those animals out on the grasslands and decided they must be cattle, and this was their poop. Still, I picked up my pace. I had that creepy feeling of being watched. I never saw or heard anything to be alarmed about, but the feeling remained. The trail soon became overgrown again, keeping me on edge.

I realized I hadn't looked at George's map since before the incident at the slough. I stopped and pulled it out of my shirt pocket. It was no longer legible, the ink all blurry from getting wet. But, I had studied the map the night before, and over breakfast. Feeling certain I could still find my way, I moved on.

The bluffs continued close on my left with high vertical walls that seemed to be steadily crumbling away, judging from the piles of debris along the bottom. The top edge was fringed with trees and bushes, while numerous roots snaked out through the upper edge of the face.

Breaking out of the undergrowth again, I came into a small meadow about fifty yards across. Right in the middle of it, a big steer stood facing me. But, there were a couple of details that made it obvious this steer was a bull, and he was not happy to see me there. There were several smaller cattle around him, standing with blank expressions on their wide, flat faces. The bull began behaving aggressively, head down, and snorting and pawing the ground with his front hooves. Without thinking, I pulled my pistol out of its holster, pointed it at the bull, and said in as loud and firm a voice as I could muster, "Hey, don't even think about it!"

The bull stopped his hostile moves, and stood glaring at me. He seemed to be considering my attitude and the object I was pointing directly at his face. Jerking his head up with a final snort, he turned and walked away, moving off into the bushes followed by the steers. I stood there waiting for something else to happen, thinking how weird this was. Yeah, maybe an angry bear or even a hungry wolf might have hassled me, but a pissed-off bull? I started hiking again, wondering what was next.

George's map had indicated a trail running up the spine of a steep ridge behind some deserted structures that were supposed to be nearby, but he didn't show exactly where that ridge trail started. He had just drawn a little arrow and written, "Go this way," on the map. Working my way through more heavy vegetation, I came to a larger piece of open ground, and on the far side part of a wooden wall and roof were visible. After another minute, I was at the old shacks George had referred to. Though I still had to find his cabin, I felt good about having come this far.

Drinking some much-needed water from my canteen, I studied these three old shacks. They had survived, but were in miserable condition. I was expecting to see log structures, but the frames were just two by fours and the wall coverings were thin plywood, much of which was now missing. I didn't see any insulation. Judging from the old fire rings, people regularly camped here. I wondered who had built these derelict structures, and what had caused them to leave.

Tired and hungry, I found a smooth, grassy spot by one of the shacks, sat down with my back against a wall, and took out one of the deli sandwiches I had bought in town. It tasted wonderful after my long hike. With the warm sun shining on my face, I soon dozed off, the half-eaten sandwich still in my hand.

A loud whinnying startled me awake. There were three people on horses lined up right in front of me. I just sat there staring at them. One of the riders said hello, then suggested I shouldn't fall asleep out in the open like that, as there were lots of bears around and it was better not to lure them in with food smells, especially since I was holding the sandwich in my hand.

I could tell, in spite of the man's friendly tone, that I hadn't made a very good impression on him. I nodded my agreement at the suggestion, and asked him if he knew where the trail up the ridge might be. The horseman shook his head, wished me good luck, and they all rode away. Quickly finishing my sandwich, watching for marauding bears as I chewed, I slipped my pack on again and started looking for the trail.

But, it was not right behind the old ruins, and I had to wander through the woods for a while before I located it. Crossing a narrow creek bed, I finally found it behind a patch of heavy bushes surrounding another big, old cottonwood tree. The footpath started up a slope onto the narrow spine of a steep ridge closely bordered with trees, bushes, and more devil's club growing on both sides. The soil on the lowest part of the trail seemed strangely chewed up and loose. It looked pretty unstable to me, but I took a deep breath and started climbing, hoping it really was the right trail. As soon as I started up, I knew this was going to be another extraordinary event.

The acute angle of that first slope and the trail on the narrow ridge spine had me literally on all fours at times, grabbing whatever I could to pull myself up. In no time, I was sweating and breathing hard. I had thought I was in pretty good condition, but now that seemed to have been a foolish assumption. Alaska was again putting me to the test. The silt left inside my clothes from the dunking I had taken earlier was chafing me in sensitive places. If I'd had any ideas that this would be a fun hike, they were now totally removed from my mind. This was getting serious. Having to watch where I placed every footstep, I kept on climbing.

At one point, where the trail leveled off briefly so I could stand upright, I saw through a break in the bushes that I had climbed hundreds of feet. Looking down, I noticed that just in front of my boot toes there was an almost vertical cliff. Hugging the inner side of the trail, I continued on. Some portions of this precipitous route were less than two feet wide and uneven, with a clear drop-off on either side. Judging from the packed surface of the trail, it was well established, causing me to wonder who would use such a dangerous course on a regular basis, and why. But, I just looked straight ahead and kept pushing up the trail, wondering how much farther I had to go.

Just as my aching legs were begging me to stop, I saw a stunted, twisted spruce tree growing out of the inner side of the trail. One of its branches ran low and parallel to the trail, and I sat down on it for a rest. Judging from the way the bark had been rubbed off the top of the limb, others had rested here before me. I noticed that the name Bob was roughly carved into the trunk of the tree.

Incredibly thirsty, I reached for the canteen in my pack's side pocket, but it slipped out of my fingers and rolled over the edge of the trail. It seemed to slide, bump, and fall forever. As I listened to it going away, I hung my head and sighed. A lone drop of sweat dripped off the end of my nose onto the dirt. Time to move on.

I stood on tight legs and continued climbing, but not for long. Barely twenty-five yards farther, I reached the top of the ridge, walking onto level ground. Pushing past some tall bushes, I was greeted with the sight of a long, narrow, one-story building, sheathed in wavy-edged slabs of wood. It had two small windows on the side facing me, and a rusting metal roof. A slightly tilted chimney pipe emitted a thin ribbon of smoke. There was a lush, young garden next to the house, and a well just beyond it. I walked forward to knock on the door, but it opened before I got there.

A short, but very wide, frowning man with a thick, unkempt beard stepped out. He was dressed in faded and torn brown canvas pants, a red plaid flannel shirt with both elbows out, wide suspenders, and tall, brown rubber boots that had seen better days. A shapeless cloth hat was perched on his head. I couldn't help thinking of some somber gnome from a book of old tales. In a deep voice, he asked me what I wanted.

I tried to say hello, but my dry throat didn't oblige. A raspy growl came out instead. The man just stood looking at me. I managed to explain what I was doing there. When I mentioned George Whiting, his aspect changed, and he seemed to relax. He asked if I wanted a drink of water and I nodded enthusiastically.

Leading me to the well, he dropped the bucket in and hauled it up again full of icy-cold, sweet water. Scooping some out with a dented metal dipper, he handed it to me. I could feel the cold water running all the way down my throat and hitting my empty stomach. It had a slightly silty flavor, but I loved it.

I told him my name was Denny Caraway, and he introduced himself as Monty Leer. Monty told me he was just heading to town to meet his wife, but that I was welcome to rest a while at his place. Before he left, Mr. Leer told me how to get to George's old homestead, which was only about two miles away. It sounded easy enough.

He said if he didn't have to meet his wife, he would be happy to guide me to the cabin. Smiling, he said, "But my wife is not someone you want to keep waiting."

I mentioned how difficult it had been on the steep trail I had just come up.

He agreed it could be rough until you got used to it, but that he climbed it regularly to get into his place in late spring, summer, and fall, until the winter snows made traveling the overland route the easier way to go.

Having said that, Mr. Leer walked over and pulled an empty pack from inside the door, along with a long barreled pistol in a worn leather holster. It was the same model as the one I carried. Shaking my hand and wishing me luck, he headed toward the ridge I had just climbed. I called out to him, "Who's Bob?" Monty looked at me a moment, smiled again, and said, "Bob is the tree." Then he was gone, headed down to the bay.

It was great meeting Monty Leer. He was the first Alaskan homesteader I'd met who was still living the life. I hoped I would get to visit with him again.

Standing there alone, I realized how tired I was. Taking a break sounded fine to me. Pulling off my dirty boots and sweaty socks, I left them on the wooden steps before going inside.

The interior of Monty's home was the complete opposite of his scruffy appearance, being neat, clean, and organized. I decided his wife must be very tidy, and probably demanded the house be kept in order. Laying my pack on the linoleum flooring in the kitchen area, I had a look around. There were a lot of books on home built shelving. In fact, everything in the place, except for the couch and several stuffed chairs, was handmade, not fancy but sturdy, which I found very appealing. The interior walls and ceiling were all wood. On the floor was a bearskin rug, clawed paws, toothy head and all. What must have been a beaver hide tied onto a round wooden hoop was on one wall across from a set of moose antlers on another. There was one large window on the back wall, and the view through it was like a classic picture postcard of the Alaska woods. This was definitely a homesteader's home the way I imagined it might be, except for its large size.

In my dirty clothes I didn't know where to sit, so I just sat on the floor, my back against the couch. I must have nodded right out. Sometime later, I awoke to someone nudging me in the hip. It wasn't Monty Leer.

This man was taller, leaner, and more neatly dressed. Clean-shaven, about five foot nine, he was wearing the same type of canvas pants, with a blue flannel shirt and the same brown rubber boots Monty wore, but his clothes were clean and in whole condition. I had to find out about those boots. On his head was a baseball cap with the word STIHL embroidered on the front. He also had the same type of .44 Magnum pistol in a holster on his hip. I decided this must be the basic uniform for living remote in Alaska.

His personality was different from Monty's. Mr. Leer was friendly enough once he got to know you, but he had a generally serious demeanor, while this fellow was all smiles and hellos, a few too many in fact. His eyes never stayed still, flicking back and forth even when he was talking directly to me. My gut told me to be wary around him.

I introduced myself, and told him I had met Mr. Leer and he had offered me the use of his home to rest up.

Giving out a loud barking laugh, he said, "Mr. Leer?" stuck out his hand, and told me his name was Bucky Waters.

I shook it, noticing that though his hand was rough and calloused, the shake had no firmness, no feeling to it. That made me pull my hand back a little too quickly. His eyes stopped moving momentarily, and his smile flattened out, but he quickly recovered his friendly façade. Waters went to the kitchen area and started heating water on the small gas range. I silently watched him as he moved around like he owned the place. I concluded that he must know Monty Leer and his wife well. The hot cup of strong tea Waters handed me a few minutes later was, at that moment, a perfect drink.

As we sat at the Leer's table, Waters kept up a steady line of conversation laced with lots of questions regarding my whos, whats, and wheres. I quickly realized he was trying to draw me out to find out what he could about me, and I carefully worded my responses, keeping them vague. He finally gave up.

Finishing our mugs, Waters said his place was about a mile from George's old homestead, and that he'd take me there "if you think you could make it."

I just nodded. There was a condescending tone in his voice I didn't appreciate.

Stepping outside into the cool afternoon air, I discovered there was only one of my socks on the steps. As I stood wondering where the other had gone, a squirrel chattered from a nearby tree. Looking up at the owner of that cranky voice, I saw that the darned thing had my sock with it on the branch.

Seeing what had occurred, Bucky said, "I guess he'll have a nice soft nest and you'll have one cold foot." He gave me a wide, toothy grin that I found very irritating.

I pulled another pair of socks from my pack, putting them and my boots onto my blistered feet. I was stiff and sore all over. Likeable or not, this character had easily read my exhausted condition.

We started hiking away from the house, going into the woods along a well-worn path with roots extending across it. I had to watch my step as I tried to keep up with Bucky, who was making good time ahead of me. Heading down a short slope, we hiked across an area consisting of a series of low, narrow, wooded ridges with little swampy draws in between, before coming to Waters' homestead on top of one of the ridges.

His "cabin" looked like three or four sections of differently designed homes joined together, as if he wasn't sure how he wanted it to look. It had a large picture window in the front wall with several sliding windows on the side, in contrast to the small, square, solid windows at Leer's place. The structure even had a number of different types of roofing. It was pretty strange.

Instead of the forest that had presumably been there originally, the land around his home had been completely cleared. There was a big vegetable garden, and what looked like some kind of berry patch, maybe strawberries. There was also a greenhouse and a large, unfinished outbuilding.

Lots of equipment lay around in various states of disrepair, including several broken snow machines and a couple of old chainsaws. In contrast, there was a small, new-looking tractor by the side of the outbuilding. I wondered how difficult it had been to get it to his homestead.

I couldn't tell what the inside of his home was like at that point, because he didn't invite me in. We just walked a short distance behind his place onto a wide, cleared trail. He pointed toward a couple of fifty-five-gallon barrels several hundred feet from where we were standing, and told me to walk to the barrels and turn left onto the trail that crossed there, and that would take me to George's old homestead. Turning around he walked away, and that was it. It was obvious to me that not all the people I would meet here in the Alaska bush would fit my concept of a traditional homesteader. The contrast between Leer and Waters certainly proved that.

It was also obvious to me that I was probably the most inexperienced person in this part of Alaska. I found consolation in the fact that while I didn't know much about where I was or what I should do, at least I had chosen the right gun. That would have to do for now.

Shifting the pack on my back and adjusting my holster, I headed toward the trail he had pointed out, turning left onto it as I had been told. It appeared to be an established path, but not recently used, judging by the grasses growing in it. I followed it for about a mile, through some of the prettiest country I had seen so far. The forest consisted of mostly large spruce with some smaller birches in among them, and a lot of low bushes. I saw wild flowers in abundance as I walked along. Sunlight filtering through the trees gave the place a peaceful atmosphere.

Several times, I came to an area where someone had cut down a tree, and processed it for some purpose I didn't understand. What had been done to the trees stirred my curiosity. There were long, half-round strips of bark-covered wood lying around that appeared to have been cut from the outside layer of the trunks. I wondered why.

Hiking along the slightly uphill path, I came out of the trees onto the edge of a long, narrow expanse of tundra. The trail ran straight across it. I hoped this was the tundra George had marked as the one near his cabin site.

Heading across the one hundred yard stretch of squishy muskeg enjoying the light breeze blowing steadily over it, I was surprised to see what looked like a pair of small shorebirds fly up right in front of me, shrilly expressing their irritation at being disturbed. They repeatedly strafed my head until I was well past their territory.

Entering the woods on the far side of the tundra, I hadn't gone very far when I spotted a small cabin in the trees to my left. It must be George's old home. Forgetting my tired muscles and blisters, I eagerly trotted to the little structure, full of excitement over finding it.

But upon closer inspection, my feelings of satisfaction at discovering the place faded. The cabin was in sad shape. The roof was sagging in, the only window was broken, and the door was hanging by one rusty hinge.

Walking through the tilted door, the view inside did nothing to raise my spirits. The interior looked as if looters had ransacked it. There were books, bottles, cans, and cooking gear scattered all over. A little handmade wooden table lay on its side like some long-dead animal. Slipping my pack off, I sat down on the one chair in the place and continued to survey my surroundings. It was an awful mess, not at all what I had expected from George's description. But he hadn't been there in years, and the untended cabin had suffered the consequences of that neglect.

I stepped outside again to explore the property, and to momentarily forget the cabin's condition. I looked for the land's corner markers. It took a while, but I was finally able to find them all. They helped me get an idea of the parcel's general shape and location.

The piece of land George had settled on was high enough above the level of the tundra to be dry and good for building. He had limbed trees to head height all around his cabin, giving the area a groomed look, but after five years they needed trimming again. The ground was covered with ferns, mosses, and tiny, leafy plants. It was pleasant and parklike.

Going back inside, I turned the table upright and sat there as I ate the other sandwich I had brought. As soon as I was done, despite being bone tired from my hike I set about straightening the place up, putting all salvageable items like books and kitchen utensils on the shelves along the back wall, and the usable pots and pans on nails already driven into the wall logs on either side of a narrow, wooden counter. The worthless things I put in a pile outside the cabin next to the door. One item in the pile was an empty blue and white box that had held something called Pilot Bread, but it looked like big crackers judging from the faded picture on the box. I'd have to find out what these were.

There were a lot of food cans, but they were all empty and crushed, with holes in them. They must have been worked over by bears. Several of the pots had dents and punctures in them too. On the floor was a mound of dirty white stuff lying on a mangled box that apparently used to be powdered milk, but wasn't anymore. It was surprising that animals hadn't licked it up. Taking a worn down broom from a corner, I swept up all the debris from the floorboards.

The sheet metal stove, which would double for heat and cooking, had a light film of rust all over, but seemed to be solid. The stovepipe had been knocked apart, but only took a few minutes to reassemble.

The cabin was about sixteen feet square inside, which seemed more than adequate for me. I set the little table against the wall with the window in it. After several hours of cleaning, the cabin looked so much better that my spirits were up again.

There were some rusty tools in one corner, along with a bag of nails and some screws, also rusty but usable. I reattached the upper hinge to the door and put a piece of heavy, clear plastic sheeting I found over the broken windowpane. Though it wasn't particularly cold out, I gathered some small, dry branches and made a fire in the stove. The one-gallon container of water in the bottom of my pack that I had regretted carrying as I was climbing up the ridge trail, was again a good idea now that I was here. There was supposed to be a spring box somewhere behind the cabin, but I didn't know what condition it was in.

Rinsing out a small sauce pan with bear dents but no holes, I poured in some water and heated it on the little wood stove. As I quietly sat there, the crackling and popping of the burning wood were sounds that I found very soothing. When the water was boiling, I mixed in a packet of powdered cocoa, and on a whim, tossed in a spoonful of instant coffee. Sipping it slowly, I enjoyed the flavor, and decided it was a hearty drink, just right for enjoying in a log cabin.

With the door closed and the window covered over, the cabin felt pretty snug, even though there were lots of little gaps in the chinking between the wall logs. The wooden chair was solid, so I leaned back against a wall and allowed the feel of the place to sink in as I carefully scanned the interior. The roof needed some propping up, but wouldn't be too difficult to fix. I'd have to put a pole under the middle of the top roof log, trimming it until it was just the right length to hold the roof level. In the corner of the cabin with the other tools was a really heavy duty jack, the largest I had ever seen. It looked like a bumper jack for a semi truck. I could use it to set the roof right. When I was outside, I'd looked up at the roofing and it seemed in good shape, with no visible holes or tears.

By the time my drink was finished, I had decided this cabin would be fine to start with, but that I would build a larger frame cabin a little farther into the trees as my permanent home. I would spend a couple of days looking for a good building site on the five acres. I also wanted to do a little exploring before heading back into town to conclude the deal with George. His price seemed reasonable, and I was certain this was the place I had been hoping to find.

In the middle of that thought, there was a raucous noise outside the front door. There could only be one source for the grating sound. Opening the door, I saw a blue jay sitting on a crude, wooden bird feeder, a short piece of plank nailed onto a spruce pole set in the ground. Seeing me, the bird increased its complaining. I had the feeling it was condemning me for the empty feeder. I wondered how many times the jay had come over the years to find no one home and nothing to eat. George had mentioned how they would show up every day, sometimes eating out of his hand. Apparently they hadn't given up yet. I didn't know how long jays lived, so this might not be the one that had come to George's cabin when he was here.

Apologizing to the bird, I went in and took a bran muffin from my pack and broke off several pieces. As I approached the feeder, the jay flew up to a higher branch, waiting for me to leave the food on the feeder and back away before coming down to eat. While it was eating, another jay came down to eat too. It was smaller, and I figured they might be mates. Finished with their treat, they took off, continuing the rude noises as they flew away.

I threw a few more sticks into the stove and began cooking. The long, difficult walk had given me a major appetite. While I prepared my luxurious meal of Spam and beans, sitting back while the food was bubbling along in a small cast iron skillet, I had a powerful feeling that being in this little cabin surrounded by wilderness was filling me with what I had needed for so long, a sense of "rightness," of being where I ought to be. The frustration I used to feel when I was alone was gone. Being by myself in this remote place made all the difference. I was a lucky man to have this chance, and planned on doing whatever was needed to make it work. I was determined not to blow it. The doubts I had down by the slough were gone, and they wouldn't be coming back. I'd see to that.

I enjoyed my Spam and beans, eating every last bit and licking the plate clean. I decided that if I was going to have this kind of appetite living out here, keeping a good supply of food would be essential. I wondered how I would do taking wild game for meat. It would probably be different than deer hunting in Nevada.

I went out to have my first experience with an outhouse. I had never used one before, except for those cinder block bathrooms at rest stops, which weren't quite the same. After I'd sat in the little wooden privy for a few minutes, the lack of a door making it a scenic experience, a moose walked through the trees just a few yards from me. It was a big bull with a huge rack of antlers. This guy was high and wide, and I was kind of glad he didn't notice me sitting there.

I was glad too, that I had packed in some toilet paper, because there wasn't any at the cabin. I needed it at that moment, and not for drying my pistol. My pistol! I hadn't looked at it since the dunking at the slough.

Going back inside, I pulled the .44 out of its holster and found there was very light rust on the gun. Not good. If I was going to live out here, I'd better learn to stay on top of caring for my equipment. I had seen a little old can of household oil near the tools. It was still usable. Rummaging around, I found an old toothbrush too. I set about cleaning and oiling the revolver. I stripped it down completely to do it right. There was a lot of damp grit inside, but after an hour of work, including figuring out how to put it back together properly, the revolver was in good condition again. I'd better make sure to keep it that way.

A wave of fatigue swept over me. My day was done. Lying on my sleeping bag, I felt at ease, but didn't fall asleep right away. I lay there listening for sounds in the forest, but everything was still, not even a cricket chirping.

But then, I heard a strange schussing sound, barely audible. Listening intently, I realized it was the sound of the blood pumping through my veins. For some reason, after knowing that, I dropped off into a peaceful, dreamless sleep.

I awoke in the morning to the same stillness. I wasn't used to such silence. It was a calm, peaceful moment. No alarm clock, no news noise on the radio, no rushing to work. Yeah, I could get used to this.

Hearing a bird calling, I opened the door, and was greeted with the kind of natural scene I had been hoping for ever since I decided to come to Alaska. Nothing but trees, blue sky, mountains in the distance, and a bird sitting on a branch pecking at the bark. The quality of the air was clean and pure. There were no mechanical noises, no fuel smells, no phone poles and wires. What a wonderful place this would be in which to spend the rest of my life.

Going outside to relieve myself, I smiled as I stood there adding my share to the water table. Try doing that in the city! The jays came swooping in, their raucous cries shredding the quiet morning. They flapped their wings and screeched at me while standing on the feeder demanding food. Apparently, I'd have to keep these birds well fed if I wanted any peace at all. A portion of my last muffin quieted them down, at least temporarily.

I fixed myself some breakfast: the rest of the bran muffin, some oatmeal, and a cup of instant coffee.

Walking out behind the cabin, I searched for the spring box. It was just a short distance away, but unfortunately a spruce tree had fallen across it. There was some water running out from under it between the broken boards. Scooping some up in my hands, I splashed it onto my face and neck. The coldness of the water was invigorating. Drinking some, the taste was almost sweet, it was so pure. Once I brought in supplies and equipment, clearing the fallen tree and rebuilding the spring box would be one of my first tasks.

Strapping on my revolver, I took a walk following the main trail. I felt refreshed in spite of my rough journey the day before. I crossed several other trails, and following one, I found an unfinished cabin foundation about a half-mile away. Someone must have decided it was too much work or had gotten scared and given it up, leaving a shovel and mattock behind, their handles now ruined, the metal rusting away. Near the shovel was a small rusty mass that was once a pile of nails. I hoped my own cabin building would be more successful. I thought about hiking to Bucky Waters' place, but since he hadn't been inclined to invite me in, I dropped the idea.

I settled back into George's cabin in early afternoon. An hour or so later, there was a knock at the door and there stood Waters, that now-familiar, big, toothy grin all over his face. I invited him in and offered him some of my instant coffee, which he accepted, but only after mumbling something about real coffee usually being the thing to offer a guest. I let that pass.

Bucky said he had come by to offer me his services in getting set up out here, hauling things in, and making repairs and improvements. Out of curiosity, I asked him what he would charge.

There went that oversized grin again. "Oh, well, it won't cost you any money, but maybe you could help me out with something sometime. Homesteaders do that for each other as a rule."

As soon as he said that, I knew this guy was slick. I wondered how much time and effort it might cost me for his "help."

Telling Waters I wasn't even sure I would buy the place, I added that if I did decide to take it over, I'd probably be able to handle things for myself. I smiled as widely as I could. When I did that, his face darkened and his grin went away. But as before, he recovered quickly.

Bucky walked to the front door and tossed out the rest of his coffee, came back in, and set the mug on the table. Still smiling, he said, "Well, can't say I didn't offer." Without another word, he went out the door and disappeared.

I knew now that my initial instincts when I met him at the Leer homestead had been right. The man rubbed me the wrong way. I figured it would be best if I made every effort to keep to myself and deal with the neighbors only when necessary, even Monty. After all, I had come here to avoid the obligatory interactions with people that had become so distasteful.

I'd done what I could and learned what I needed to know on this first trip to the homestead. I'd pack up in the morning, head back to town and conclude my deal with George, after which I'd find a place to live in Hazel while I was getting set up on the homestead.

The evening passed peacefully. Very early the next morning, after a simple breakfast of oatmeal and a mug of that delicious cocoa-coffee mix, I shut down the stove and refilled my pack, including several of the old books I thought George might like to have. I secured the cabin, nailing a board from the broken spring box across the front door and two over the window. Putting on my pack once again, I returned the way I had come in several days before. Waters wasn't home when I passed by his place, which was fine by me. Monty wasn't at his place either, but I had a long, cool drink from his well, then took my empty plastic one-gallon water jug and half filled it, wishing I had a canteen.

Going down the ridge trail I made good time, but had to check my speed on the steepest sections to keep from sliding out over the edge. When I got back down to the old shacks, a few feet away from where I'd had my sandwich was a good-sized pile of bear poop. It couldn't have been anything else.

The rest of my hike back to the Jeep was uneventful. Luckily, that ornery bull wasn't around. I felt more comfortable on the trail this time, but stayed focused and paid attention to everything around me. Every turn in the trail or patch of thick undergrowth could hold something to deal with, and I had to stay alert.

The steep, winding trail going up to the Sandals' parking lot wasn't as difficult to manage as I'd anticipated, not after climbing that crazy ridge up to the Leer homestead. But I had to admit that when I got to the parking lot, the Jeep was a welcome sight.

I drove back to town and went right to George's house to complete our deal. He was glad to see me, and wanted a full report on what I had found and how I felt about the place. I guess he sensed my weariness, apologized, and suggested I refresh myself first. That sounded really good, so with his blessing I took a hot shower, but I didn't feel like shaving, which I usually did every day.

I felt renewed, and was happy to relate the details of my journey. I figured there was no reason to let George know how rundown the place was, and told him it was in surprisingly good shape. He was obviously pleased, judging from the smile on his face.

I made out a check in the full amount for the homestead and handed it to him. After we went through the simple paperwork necessary to transfer ownership, he instructed me on how to get the deed put in my name.

When I started to leave, George said there was no reason for me to pay for a motel when he had plenty of room, and I was welcome to spend the night. Enjoying his company as I did, I took him up on his offer. When I told him how much I appreciated his kindness, he smiled and told me that as far as he was concerned it was the way people should treat each other. He said he remembered when Alaskans always offered a helping hand, but things had changed.

He cooked up a terrific stew that night, and it wasn't until he told me it was moose meat that I thought it was anything but good beef. "Someday," he said,

"You'll know what it's like to bring one down yourself, process the meat, and use it for all sorts of good meals." Smiling, he said, "If you leave some scraps of meat in the feeder for the jays, they'll never leave you alone."

As I was getting ready to leave the next morning, George came out of a back room with a rifle. It wasn't new, the finish on the metal and wood worn off in places, but it looked well maintained and ready to use.

In a quiet voice he said, "I used this .30-06 all the years I homesteaded. It's an old Winchester Model 70 and it never let me down."

When he asked me if I had a rifle for hunting, I told him not yet, just a .44 Magnum revolver for protection.

With a resigned look on his face, he extended the rifle toward me. "I want you to have this, if you wouldn't mind using an old gun."

I was a little overwhelmed by his offer, and just stood there, not knowing what to say.

As if reading my mind, he said he'd be pleased if I took the gun so he'd feel as if he was still out there in some small way.

I couldn't refuse after that, and told him I'd take good care of it.

George nodded and suggested I just bring him a little moose meat once in a while.

I told him he'd get some from my first moose, and we parted ways.

Episode

3

THE FIRST THING THAT NEEDED TO BE DONE NOW THAT I WAS committed to this new life, was to find a temporary place in town to work from until I could start living full time on the homestead. Picking up a copy of the local paper, the *Hazel Bugler*, I went to the Log Cabin Cafe for a late breakfast, after which I sat and perused the little classified section for a place to rent.

When Hazel O'Mara's daughter, Gwen ,came to remove my empty dish, she asked what I was looking for in the want ads.

I explained the situation to her, and she suggested I go to see Harry the Clammer on the short dirt road that ended at Halibut Slough, on the coastal side of town.

"Harry has some small cabins to rent. He doesn't charge much and you'll know why when you see 'em. But, since you only need one for a short while, they might suit you."

What Gwen had implied was obvious once I got there. Harry's rentals looked a lot like rundown shacks, because that's exactly what they were. But, I went and knocked on the door of the ramshackle structure farthest back from the road, the one with the hand-scrawled sign that read "Rental Office - H. Frolich Prop." The pungent smell of cooking seafood wafted out when Harry opened the door. The air in his place was hot and steamy from a big batch of clams cooking in a huge stock pot on a wood-burning cook stove.

Introducing myself, I told him what I needed: a place for a few months.

Harry said that was as long as anybody ever wanted to stay in his "beach cabins," so no problem. Handing me a worn key, he told me to go look at the first cabin by the road.

It was one of a cluster of small dwellings he'd built and had been renting for years, with a minimum of maintenance. Despite the general aspect of shoddy construction, the little hut would hopefully be protection from the rain and wind. It was a prime example of recycling and improvisation. Harry had installed a salvaged boat toilet, using a large blue plastic water barrel and a small bucket for flushing. The barrel of water was also for washing. A short hose connected to an outside spigot dangled from a hole in the wall, and was used to refill the barrel.

An old, chipped, white enamel sink in a rough wooden counter on the back wall of the shack had a five-gallon bucket under its short drainpipe to catch dish water, which was also poured down the marine commode. The tiny refrigerator must have come from a junked RV, and the four windows in the place were all of different sizes and types.

A small, pot belly stove was set up to use coal, which was collected off the nearby beach. The coal originated from a large seam located in the coastal bluffs. As wave action eroded the bluffs, coal fell out of the seam and was moved around by the water, scattered all up and down the beach. Harry told me his renters had to gather their own coal, but the stuff was plentiful and more fun than work to find. People hauled it with ATVs and pickup trucks, cruising far up the hard-packed beach at low tide, picking up the "float coal," being careful to get off the beach before the incoming tide could trap them against the bluffs.

Harry was called The Clammer because that was how he made his main living. He used a large, very rough-looking skiff to reach his clamming beds. It had a homemade plywood cabin built on the bow, and was powered by an ancient two-cylinder diesel engine. The boat was coated in the same garish green paint covering most of the shacks. In fact, the boat looked like a floating version of one of them. He ran it on open water that could be dangerous to navigate even in a solid new craft, much less an old leaker like Harry's, but he always made it back, usually with a good load of tasty steamer clams which he easily sold around town. I bought a couple of small batches of them while I lived there and they were delicious.

All his possessions were obviously a direct extension of Frolich himself, with his frayed, patched clothing, unkempt beard and hair, and bad teeth. But, he seemed to continue functioning nonetheless, just like all his hovels and that gaudy green skiff. Though in the past I wouldn't have considered living in the shack, it somehow seemed perfect for me in my present situation. So, I handed over a month's rent and took temporary possession of the humble abode.

Though I wasn't worried about staying there myself, I didn't feel comfortable about using it to stash all the new gear I would be purchasing. The door lock was worn and the two windows that opened didn't latch. So, renting a storage shed would be a good idea. Deciding where to rent a space was simple, since there was apparently just one storage yard in town.

The old-timer who owned the storage spaces, Mr. Harmon, had been living in Alaska since the early Fifties. After we concluded our business, he invited me into his office, where I spent some time talking with him, actually mostly listening. Like George, he was a real storehouse of information, a cache of fact and lore about Alaska and, more specifically, Hazel and its surrounding area, where Harmon had settled back in 1956. When I mentioned I'd be living out in the bush, his face brightened, and he offered me a cup of coffee, then began sharing his wealth of knowledge about the local area.

It was several cups and a couple of hours later before he tired himself out talking about the place he obviously loved, Alaska. He told me he had been a homesteader "up the bay" before the big earthquake in 1964 altered the land by lowering it, ruining his cabin in the process. I was determined to find his old place, once I was established on my own homestead.

Mr. Harmon grumbled about how modern conveniences had made life too easy, so the tough, self-reliant kind of people who used to come in Alaska had been replaced by "typical folks," as he put it. It was clear that he didn't see value in the things most people took for granted that he thought of as luxuries, not necessities.

Listening intently to him, I absorbed lots of worthwhile information about living out in the bush. Though I wanted to live a simpler life, I appreciated modern devices like chainsaws, which would make things easier, but not easy.

The first morning after moving into the beach shanty, I headed out to begin purchasing the necessary gear and supplies for the homestead. Though I had a long list to work from, I was sure I would add to it as time went on. Figuring Anchorage was the best place to find everything I needed, and probably at better prices, I cranked up the Jeep and headed north.

Driving up the highway, I began thinking about the town of Hazel. It was my town now, and would probably become the source for most of my supplies, as it would be foolish to make the long drive to Anchorage every time something was needed. Being a small community, Hazel would benefit from any revenue it could glean. I realized that supporting the local businesses would be the right thing to do, even when they didn't have something in stock and would have to order it. It was a mindset I had never gotten into when living in the city. Any store having what I needed at the lowest price was where I shopped. There was no intimacy, no loyalty, only finding the best deal. Living near Hazel would change all that. My mind made up, I turned the Cherokee around and headed back to town.

Driving was good for me. I could always let my mind run free out on the road, like now, considering and planning what needed to be done on my homestead land and how to build my new cabin. I had purchased a book on basic house building before leaving Reno, and it looked like a simple, straightforward process. An insulated frame cabin seemed to be the best way to go. I'd also read several books on log cabin building, and they all cautioned that building a log home was very work intensive, and that the first one a person built usually didn't come out quite right. Log cabins weren't insulated, only retaining heat in the logs, which needed to be of large diameter, and therefore very heavy for one person to handle.

I knew I would have to get out on the land and actually start building to find out how it would go, but thinking about it made the whole idea more of a reality. I couldn't wait to get started.

Back in Hazel, I went for lunch at the Log Cabin Cafe. There were several other restaurants, but the Cafe drew me, partly because of Hazel O'Mara and her daughter themselves, but also because Hazel made a great hamburger. They were big, juicy, and messy, the way a good burger should be, with thick slices of tomato, and onion if you wanted, and just enough lettuce. She never made cheeseburgers. For some reason, she thought it wasn't proper to put cheese on a burger. I didn't understand why, but that was Hazel, and I never heard anyone belabor the point. She also baked her own hamburger buns, which had a nice chewy crust and didn't fall apart as you ate. The fries were hand cut too, with the skins on.

My eating habits and appetite had changed since I had come to Hazel and gone out into the bush that first time. I was being more physically active than I'd ever been, which probably explained it. I needed more food than I usually ate, and what I did eat was changing. I seemed to be craving meat more than usual. Instead of filling a plate from a fancy salad bar, I was more interested in "standard" vegetables, like onions, tomatoes, potatoes and corn. While my food was getting more basic, I seemed to appreciate the flavor more.

I had to get used to the coffee at the Cafe, because it was a lot stronger than what I usually drank. Hazel added a little cinnamon to it, and I eventually looked forward to a cup or two with a meal when I first came into town from the cabin, or just before I headed back. I had never really thought of coffee as a drink to savor until I had Hazel's brew. Coffee was just "go juice" before that.

After lunch, I headed to a store called Ed's Saw Shop. Not sure what I needed, I spoke to the clerk, who turned out to be Ed, the owner. Once I explained what I was doing, he was happy to help me with my choices. I ended up getting a midsized chainsaw for general woodcutting, and a larger saw for milling my own lumber.

Ed had strongly suggested that because of the difficulty and expense of buying ready-made boards from the lumberyard and hauling them out to the cabin, milling my own was the only way to go since I wasn't building with logs. "Besides," Ed said, "If you really want to know what homesteading is all about, making your own lumber will do it." He had built a number of remote cabins, and was able to answer all my questions.

I bought several different oils for the saw chain bar and motor, files, and a chain sharpener. I also picked up a splitting maul, wedges, and a good short handle axe. I really got off on all this. It was new and exciting to me, and I was more than ready to start building directly from trees.

I saw that Ed also had a selection of work clothes in his store, including the canvas pants that I had seen many men and more than a few women wearing, so I bought two pairs.

Ed told me to get them one size too small, because they would soon fit comfortably once I started "sweating under the trees." It turned out he was right.

Something in the corner behind the pants rack caught my eye. I saw a row of those brown rubber boots both Monty and Waters wore. I asked Ed if they were good, and he laughed, telling me I shouldn't ask that too loudly, since everybody knew about the boots. All the "skookum" fishermen wore them, as did many people living in the bush, because they were so tough, and you could even get them insulated. Like the pants, they weren't cheap, but Ed was right about their quality. I would end up wearing that same pair of boots for years.

He offered me one piece of advice I never forgot: that I should "always buy the best quality gear you can afford, and take proper care of it. Living out in the bush, your life might depend on it someday."

I knew he was right, and all the things he sold were top quality. He told me he wouldn't sell junk goods that might threaten a person's survival.

Since Ed didn't have one in stock, I would go to another store he had recommended to buy a milling rig that would clamp onto the bar of the larger saw I had purchased. It would enable me to build my new place. A chainsaw mill was a vital piece of gear, actually the heart of the matter. It could be adjusted to cut boards of different thicknesses, while the length of the bar on the saw and the power of its motor determined how wide a cut you could make.

Thanking Ed, I headed to Long Bay Supply to get the mill, with this parting reminder from him, "Remember, Mr. Caraway, take care of your equipment and it'll take care of you. Out there it's a matter of survival."

When I got to Long Bay Supply, through the front window I saw Bucky

Waters engaged in an animated conversation with the clerk. I stood outside and considered leaving and coming back later, but Bucky spotted me and came out to where I stood and started talking:

"Listen, Denny, I'm in a bind. I have a couple of small building projects to do here in town which is my main way of making money, and this sum bitch won't extend me any credit for supplies even though I've been coming here for years. I know we don't know each other well, but if you could front me a hundred bucks, I could get it back to you in about a week or so when my jobs are done."

He stopped his nervous banter and waited for me to respond. He was so upset that his eyes were twitching back and forth like tiny caged animals looking for a way out.

I decided to help him this time and see how it turned out. No great harm done either way. Opening my wallet, I found a one hundred-dollar bill and held it out to him. I barely saw his hand as it snatched the bill from my grasp, and without a word of thanks he stormed back into the store and slapped the money down on the counter. I walked in behind him to look for a chainsaw mill and observe what was happening. The clerk slid two full paper bags over to Waters, who grumbled something about going elsewhere next time he needed something, then walked out of the store without acknowledging my presence.

Going up to the counter, I asked the man, who was still shaking his head, for the mill I needed. He had the right one in stock, and even gave me some extra clamps for holding the adjusters tight, because, according to him, they would break after a while. I paid him, said thanks, and started to leave.

He must have seen me give Waters that hundred, because he said to me, "It isn't any of my beeswax, but if I were you, I wouldn't lend Bucky too much money, unless you can spare it permanently."

I nodded, and he said, "Just a friendly tip from a guy who knows."

Partly to change the subject, I told him where I was going to be living and asked him what he might suggest for a good vehicle to get out to my land.

He said I should get a small, lightweight "wheeler," an ATV.

I didn't know what an ATV was, but he explained them to me. After that, his suggestion made sense.

Dropping off all my new gear at the storage shed, the next thing I needed to do was to locate an ATV to carry myself and supplies out to the land. Looking at some in the ATV shop in town, I was surprised at the cost. They were pretty spendy and also seemed bigger, heavier, and fancier than I thought was needed. I wanted to have a light, simple machine as had been suggested, and decided to look for a used one. Maybe I'd get lucky.

I sat in the Jeep and looked through the classified section of the *Bugler*, and also a penny paper which was distributed through the several small towns further north up the road as well as Hazel.

I found an ad for a small ATV described as being in "great" shape, so I called and arranged to go see it that afternoon. I wanted to jump on any opportunity that would help me get out to my five acres.

When I went to look at the little wheeler, my first impression was that it was just what I needed. It was clean, small, and light, and sounded healthy when the owner started it up, which he did with ease. It wore fat, low-pressure tires and felt good to sit on, so after a short test ride I bought it. With a little help from the owner, it slid easily into the back of the Cherokee.

On the way back to Hazel, I felt like I was now ready to make supply runs to the homestead. Once that was done, I could start living there and begin building my new place. I felt confident and full of "pee and vinegar," as my grandfather would have said.

The one drawback to my new little rig was that it had nothing to pack supplies and gear on, so I bought some plastic pipe, adhesive, brackets, and screws and made my own, front and back. They didn't look great, but were definitely sturdy.

The previous owner had said it was great off road, but apparently only if I had nothing but smooth trails or dirt roads to travel on. My initial excitement and ignorance on purchasing the ATV masked the reality that would soon become all too obvious.

I hadn't gotten directions from George for taking the overland trail to the cabin. I guess successfully making that initial hike to the cabin had me feeling pretty cocky, and confident I could run the overland trail with the simple little map drawn for me by a man in Hazel's main bar, The Bear's Den, where I had stopped for a beer.

He said he had been all over that part of the country hunting and snow machining, and had even been to George's place a time or two.

I mentioned Monty and Bucky in passing.

When Bucky's name came up, the guy gave me a funny look and asked what I thought of him.

Put on guard, I just said I didn't really know him well.

He suggested I keep it that way.

Noticing a couple of people looking our way, and suspecting they had been listening to our conversation, I finished my beer, thanked the guy for the map, and left.

The next morning, the first part of the journey took me out the same roads I had taken to walk in to the homestead. But this time, when I came to the parking lot with the trucks and trailers, I pulled in and parked the Jeep. After working the wheeler out of the back of the Cherokee and loading my homemade racks with the supplies, I started it up and headed out the trail.

Right away, things went sour. Riding across the difficult terrain, swampy and muddy in some places, rough and rocky in others, revealed the failings of the dinky wheeler. It had very little ground clearance, no suspension, and only two-wheel drive, with a small, underpowered engine.

Every time I hit a muddy area, the wheeler would slow to a crawl. It was necessary to get off and walk alongside to get it to move along. The smooth-treaded tires offered no traction, and the little single-cylinder engine couldn't handle the weight of me and the supplies over the slick, sticky goo beneath its wheels.

I could see that many others had gone this way before me, turning much of the trail to miserable slop. Never having been here before, I followed the most visible track, which was also the messiest. It got to be an enormous task, and I was grateful for every relatively dry stretch, which didn't occur often enough. In spite of the cool temperatures, I was soon soaked with sweat and half-covered with mud.

Several times, I stopped to talk with people I met on the trail. They were all on newer four-wheel drive ATVs, but were familiar with the little bugger I was struggling with. Most of them admitted they had once owned the same model, but had long since upgraded to something more powerful and trail worthy, which I intended to do as soon as possible.

I told them where I was going, and while they knew part of the way, the first half that was commonly used to get up to Ptarmigan Lake, none of them had knowledge of the last part of the trail I needed to follow. Thanking them, I continued on my way, slowly.

After managing to make another mile or so, I came to a long stretch of relatively dry ground that had lots of puddles of varying sizes. Running through a couple of the little pools weren't a real problem, but the next one I hit changed everything. As soon as the wheeler connected with that particular bit of standing water, the puny rig sank in up over its tires and stopped dead, mired in the mud on the bottom.

There I was, sitting up to my knees in brown water. The machine wouldn't budge. Even with me standing next to it, working the throttle lever and pushing on the handlebars, the thing wouldn't go backward or forward, so I shut it off and just stood there a few minutes in silence, my mind a blank.

Sloshing my way onto dry ground, I stood staring at my stuck ATV, trying to figure out what to do. Looking far to the right and to the left, all I saw was wilderness, endless tundra, and trees. I was fully aware at that point, that I was in the middle of the proverbial nowhere.

I decided to wait for someone else to come along on a big modern ATV to help pull out my sunken machine. But after an hour, no one had shown. Feeling the need to do something, I stepped back into the quagmire and started removing and tossing all my gear onto dry ground.

Taking the axe I had brought, I found a very small, dead spruce tree, whacked it down, removed all the small branches, and chopped off a six-foot length. Slipping one end under the middle of the wheeler's frame, I pried up as hard as I could, but the pole just dug deeper into the muck. I jammed the spruce as deep as I could into the bottom until I hit something hard, probably a rock. Pressing down on the pole, I pushed with all my weight as hard as I could until the pole cracked and I fell to the ground. But the wheeler was still held prisoner in the gumbo mud. I felt a sharp pain in my groin when I stood up. I had strained something, and decided to stop my efforts.

Staring at the mired rig, I realized I should have done as a kid at the hardware store had suggested to me: buy a little hand winch called a "come along," and some rope, in case I got stuck.

I had known better though, that I wouldn't need it with such a small, light vehicle. Yeah, right.

Now, there was only one thing left to do. I had to get back to my Jeep, drive to town, and return the next day with a come along and rope. At least the long summer daylight hours would keep me from being caught out in the dark.

Putting all the goods into one tight pile, I spread my rain poncho over everything, and peed around its perimeter, because I had read it would keep animals away.

Taking only my jacket, hat, canteen and pistol, I started hiking back over the swamps the way I had come. It was only about four or five miles to the trailhead, so I figured it would be a simple thing to do. Walking, I could avoid the messiest parts, making it a whole lot easier. But I had never walked on muskeg. Very quickly, I learned how strange and difficult that could be. One step might be level, while the next could sink in six inches or land on an unyielding mound. After the first mile or so, my muscles were complaining about the strenuous treatment they were receiving, but I continued walking.

Halfway back to the Jeep, I approached a small point of runty little spruce trees extending out onto the tundra from the thick woods to my left. When I was about twenty-five yards from it, two small bear cubs came running out of the forest. Just as they reached the end of the point, one of them stopped, stood on its little hind legs looking in my general direction, and let out a loud bawling sound.

I heard the sharp sound of branches snapping, and here came the mother bear running out to the cubs. Woofing them back into the trees, she ran back and forth, obviously looking for what had scared her kids.

I thought the sound of a human voice would scare her off, but I was wrong. When I yelled, she headed right for the sound of my voice. I pulled my .44

Magnum pistol out, and aimed it at her, but it felt like a toy in my hand. Thirty feet away, the bear stopped, remaining on all fours, huffing and popping her jaws. Suddenly, she got quiet, just staring at me. I saw her tense up, and knew she was going to charge. On impulse, I pointed the pistol toward the ground right in front of her front paws, and fired off a round. The shot sounded like a clap of thunder and hurt my ears, but the bear had been spooked off, gone in an instant.

I stood there watching and waiting, adrenalin pumping through me, but she didn't come back. I noticed the pistol was pointed right at my foot. Holstering the gun and walking farther out on the tundra, I continued walking to the Cherokee. My skin was tight all over. I decided that being in wild Alaska was going to be a constant testing of my ability to survive, a continuous series of potentially life-threatening situations to overcome.

Somehow, that didn't worry me. The danger past, I felt a surge of excitement run through me. It really had been an incredible moment. I almost looked forward to the next episode in this unending adventure.

By the time I made it to the Jeep I was calm again, though feeling different than I had before the bear incident. Driving back to my beach shanty, I had time to think over all that had happened. It was oddly amusing that while face to face with the angry mother bear, despite the possibility of being mauled or killed, I couldn't help but appreciate how beautiful she was, with her long brown fur moving in the breeze. I also envied her power and energy, while my own weary muscles cried out for a good meal, a hot shower, and a night's sleep. Buying a pizza when I got back to Hazel, I took a motel room instead of going back to my shack, because I really needed a hot shower. But by the time I had eaten a couple slices, I was down for the count. The shower would have to wait.

The next morning, feeling surprisingly refreshed in spite of numerous sore muscles, I bought a come along and rope, put them in my pack, and drove out to the trailhead once again. Not stopping to think about it, I hiked back out to the muck where the little wheeler sat silently waiting. The trip was uneventful, so the .30-06 slung on my shoulder was unnecessary, though comforting to have along.

When I got to the ATV, I saw that the poncho had been pulled off my supplies. The soft food, the bread, butter, and bacon were gone, their torn-up, empty packages scattered about. The canned goods were all punctured, crushed, and empty, just like the ones I had found in George's cabin. I saw big paw prints on the muddy ground and deposited in the middle of it all was a mound of bear poop. So much for the scary urine theory.

Hooking the come along to the front of the wheeler's submerged frame, I attached the rope to the hand winch's short, braided metal cable, tied the other end of the rope to the nearest good-sized tree, and started cranking. When the cable was tight, I gave the winch handle a few more hard pulls. There was a sucking sound, and the wheeler moved forward a few inches. It was working! Tightening the rope and cable set up again, I repeated the process and gained a few more inches. After doing this numerous times, the little ATV, with a final jump forward, was freed from the grip of the super mud. Feeling a real sense of accomplishment, believing I had taken another step toward becoming self-sufficient, I started it up and, walking alongside, ran it onto drier ground.

After repacking the smaller load of cargo back onto the machine, I continued along the trail, hopefully toward my destination. I soon came to a very large, boggy area, with lots of surface water, and I could see no way to get around it.

Struck with the thought that maybe it would be smart to get better directions, as well as a stronger machine and some more food to take with me, I turned around and headed back. Nothing was to be gained by being foolishly stubborn.

As I rode, I noticed a lightly used trail running out to my left, and thought that it might lead me around the huge swampy zone, but let that idea go and kept on the trail back to my Jeep. The trip back to the trailhead was certainly easier than the ride in. This time I was careful to avoid the worst places, and ride around anything that appeared treacherous. Driving back to town in the Jeep, the smooth surface of the road felt wonderful after humping that hard-framed little wheeler over the muskeg.

Resting in my little shack that evening, I planned on buying one of the larger ATVs that I had thought excessive the first time I checked them out. Now I knew they were the best bet, with their larger engines and four-wheel drive.

I also needed to find someone who actually knew the way out to George's cabin. Perhaps I could find Monty in town or even Bucky Waters, though he would be my last choice. One way or another, I would find the way to my land. If I had to do it on my own, I'd do whatever was necessary to get there.

I knew I was greenhorn, a cheechako as Alaskans would call me, but necessity was forcing me to learn how to survive by my own resources. I already knew that nothing I wanted to do here was going to be easy, but in my gut I sensed that whatever was required to make a life for myself would be worth the effort. So far, I had managed to get through. I wished my grandfather was still around to give me his sage advice, but I would have to be content in believing he was watching over me. With that thought, I dropped off to a sleep filled with dreams of endless swamps and woods so tight with trees that I couldn't get through, with my cabin just beyond.

I woke up about ten the next morning, and felt like I had wasted half the day. I rushed through washing and dressing as if I were late for work. But, I slowed myself down, realizing that nothing I was going to do that day or the next needed to be rushed into. There was a lot to do, but it would all get done. There was no deadline or time limit. Putting on my boots, I went to the Log Cabin Cafe for a leisurely breakfast.

An hour later, comfortably full, sitting back with a cup of java, I noticed a very large guy with a big, bushy beard, staring at me from a corner table. Finally, I smiled and nodded at him. He came and sat at my table. Shaking my hand, he spoke in a deep gravelly voice.

"I take it you're the new guy in the woods, yes?"

"Well, I bought George Whiting's old homestead, if that's what you mean."

"I know, I saw George at the market a couple of days ago, and he told me about you. He suggested we talk about giving you a little help."

"I appreciate that, but I can handle things on my own."

The man sat staring at me for a moment after my remark, a barely visible smile on his face. "Where are you going to keep your vehicles when you're either in town or on the 'stead? If you leave them at the trailhead, chances are they'll get vandalized in time. I was going to offer you a place to park them when they're not in use. We've got forty acres of land and let a few other folks living remote do the same. But, if you're not interested ... ."

Trapped by my hastily spoken words, I had to give in to his understanding of the situation, and my obvious lack of the same. "I hadn't thought about that. Yeah, that would be very good. How much would you want for letting me park on your land?"

"Nothing, just doing a favor for a new neighbor. Have you got an ATV or a snow machine? What do you drive?"

"I've got a Jeep Cherokee, the blue one out in the parking lot there, and I'm going to be getting a new ATV today to replace the little one I already have. I'll also be getting a snow machine before winter starts, I guess."

"That's fine. Let's say it's all set. My name is Walt and my wife's name is Mary. I'll let her know you'll be parking your rigs with us."

Walt wrote down directions to his place on a napkin, shook my hand again, and left.

Here was another Alaskan offering help without asking for anything in return. I was actually a little stunned by the generosity I had already received from people here. It wasn't what I was used to. I figured that when I was able, I'd help people out too. My life was changing in ways I hadn't anticipated before coming here. This was truly a new start for me.

Looking at Walt's written directions, their place turned out to be located off the side road by Grizzly Lake on the way to the trailhead. It couldn't have been better.

Going to the ATV dealership, I went in to look at their machines again. Not only did I purchase a new ATV, a four- wheel drive unit with a larger, stronger engine and nice big cargo racks, but after explaining where I'd be living and what I'd be doing, Sam Bowen, the guy working there, handed me a pamphlet showing the brands and models of snowmobiles he stocked in season.

He pointed out a basic workhorse model set up for hauling cargo sleds, but was lightweight and reliable. I ordered one from him in advance, and he promised to have it for me by fall. I wanted to give him a deposit on the snowmobile, but he said not to worry about it, he'd hold it for me. He'd also have freight sleds available too.

Sam asked me if I had a trailer to haul the machines. When I said no, he told me he owned a used one he was replacing with a newer one, and would sell it to me at a good price. I bought it sight unseen, showing him good faith as he had done toward me.

I had ample money, but hadn't anticipated all the things I would need to establish myself. The simple life I was pursuing was getting more complicated.

Episode

....

4

LIFE COULDN'T BE BETTER. HERE I WAS, SITTING WARM AND DRY in George's old cabin, listening to a steady rain making soft drumming sounds on the roof, and musical drippings from the eaves.

I was kicking back after finishing the basic repairs needed to make the cabin solid and livable. I'd probably make changes and improvements when the need arose, but for now, its condition was acceptable. Putting the place right had been an enjoyment for me, not a chore.

I had chinked the open gaps between the wall logs, and replaced the broken window glass, somehow having managed to transport the new pane without breaking it. There was now a third hinge on the front door as well.

It had been easier than I'd anticipated to level and brace the sagging roof. Bringing the top roof pole up to level using the heavy duty jack and a piece of two by six I'd found behind the cabin, I fitted a dry, six-inch diameter spruce pole tightly between it and the floor. When I released the jack, the pole was jammed into place. My fix had worked perfectly. The support pole would also serve as a hat and coat rack once I fitted some pegs into it. I liked the way it looked standing there in the middle of the cabin with its natural knots and bumps.

Resting on my pallet made of a foam pad, blankets, and a sleeping bag, I felt peaceful and familiar with the place, even though my life here was barely started. The cabin's atmosphere reminded me of George and his easygoing personality.

I wondered if living this life for many years had been responsible for his mellow attitude, and if my being out here might do the same for me.

I now knew how to get to my land, thanks to Ed, the saw shop owner. I'd been able make the necessary supply runs so that I was finally living out here full time. Now I would find out for certain if this life would suit me.

After purchasing my new wheeler, I had gone to Ed's Saw Shop to buy a flannel work shirt. As I was leaving, I turned and asked him if he might know anyone who could guide me out to George's homestead on the overland trail.

Ed studied me for a minute, then asked if I could wait a couple of days until Sunday, his one day off. If I could, he'd be glad to take me out there himself. Ed said he'd visited George at his homestead a number of times over the years. He'd traveled through this country hunting, fishing, and building cabins, and was very familiar with it.

Telling him that Sunday sounded good to me and thanking him for his offer of help, I headed back to my little hovel, a knot of excitement in my gut.

Sunday took a while to arrive, even though it was only a few days away. I was impatient to get out to the homestead, and learn the trail so I could go it alone the next time. Though Ed was obviously a good man, I would rather have found the way myself, but that might turn into a real fiasco.

Not wanting to run my brand new wheeler out on the trail without giving it some break-in time, I rode it from Harry's cabins down along the beach. The tide was way out, so I headed north, running the ATV's speed up and down to work the engine. I was really enjoying this nice machine. The good suspension made it downright cushy, and it was pretty quick, even though it was new and tight. But I forced myself to take it easy. I ran about ten miles up the beach and back again. I could have gone farther and maybe gotten caught by the tide on the way back, but there was a big bear roaming the sand ahead of me, probably looking for clams or something. Figuring it best not to disturb him, I turned around and headed back.

On Sunday morning, the skies were clear when I met Ed at the trailhead parking lot just off the dirt road. He had a nice wheeler, set up with special cargo boxes on the front and rear racks. There was a five-gallon fuel can in the back one. Ed told me it was there, "Just in case I feel the need to keep going."

When we took off, Ed turned right instead of left, taking a different trail than the one I had used when I made my failed run. Ed told me it was a couple of miles longer than the way I had gone, but an easier trail. The route we took appeared to have had little use, with no deep tracks or bogged-out patches.

Ed didn't fool around, setting a steady pace, making me work to keep up, even on my new wheeler. I needed to step up my riding ability, but I soon got into the rhythm of the ride.

Glimpsing a wide, deep canyon several times beyond the brush to our right, I recognized it as Wolf Creek Canyon, from the topographical map Ed had shown me before we hit the trail. It was the mouth of Wolf Creek that I had crossed on the pole and plywood bridge during my hike along the bay.

If the canyon didn't exist, the distance to the cabin would have been cut in half and been easier to travel. But it was very deep, with extremely steep walls, and virtually impossible to get across. As it was, we had to ride all the way up the west side of the canyon to a location upstream from where the canyon began. At that point the creek was narrow and shallow, so it was easily crossed.

As we rode, Ed occasionally stopped to reveal some interesting facts he knew about the area from his own experiences. I found myself wishing he had been with me on the hike in, and I was glad to be traveling with him now.

I was very satisfied with my larger, four-wheel-drive ATV. It was handling the trail with ease, and having suspension, was a lot more comfortable than the little hard-framed rig. It was capable of carrying much larger loads, too.

After riding across several miles of spongy tundra with stunted spruce trees scattered about, we turned in the general direction of Long Bay. Just past a big patch of chest-high willow bushes, the crossing point over Wolf Creek came into view. There was a flimsy looking slab bridge over the creek that Ed zipped across without even stopping. Having no choice, I held my breath and did the same.

The trail on the other side of the creek ran near the rim of the canyon. It wound through an area forested with spruce, birch, willow, and alder. We had to run at very low speed because of the numerous roots and rocks in the path. The trail eventually turned away from the canyon into more open, swampy country.

The alternating stretches of wooded land and open tundra seemed endless, but we finally came out of a section of trees, and there we were at the upper end of the tundra bordering my land. It seemed so simple now. All my concerns about finding a way out here were dispelled by this journey with Ed. Seeing where I was, I increased my speed, not slowing until I was right outside the little cabin.

Ed pulled up alongside my ATV. We smiled at each other and shook hands, as if we were wilderness explorers who had discovered a long sought-after site. The spell was broken when Ed said, "I bet that new wheeler is easier on your butt."

After building a fire in the stove and getting warmed up, we made grilled cheese sandwiches and heated a can of beans on the flat top of the stove. Ed and I wolfed the food down, our appetites whetted by the ride in. We rested for a while, discussing the ride and the country we had crossed.

Eventually, and with what sounded like regret, Ed said he had to head back to town. He told me he had lots of things to do, and I didn't want to hold him back.

It would have been good to walk my land with him and maybe get a few suggestions about where and how to build, but I didn't want to take advantage of his good nature. He had done enough. We topped up the tanks from the five-gallon gas container and headed back to town. I wanted to stay at the cabin now that we had arrived, but figured it was the proper thing to run back out with Ed. Besides, the ride would reinforce my familiarity with the trail.

The return ride was just a reversal of the first, but this time we had the experience of seeing a large gray wolf crossing the tundra ahead of us. It emerged from the trees, taking long, gliding strides that carried it quickly out of sight into the woods on the other side of the muskeg. It hadn't given us a sideways glance, but I sensed it was totally aware of us.

Ed told me that wolves were scarce in these parts, though there was supposed to be a small pack way up the head of the bay on the far side. He suggested I shouldn't mention seeing it to anyone, and explained why:

"Sure as shootin' someone will come hunting for its hide. I've got nothin' against pelt hunters making their livelihood, but I think wolves are special animals, so I'd appreciate it if we kept this between us. A few years ago, it might've been me taking the skin. "

I told him I'd keep it to myself, and we continued on.

At one point, Ed bent down from the wheeler and picked a little bunch of funny-looking leaves from a plant under a tiny, stunted spruce tree. Handing them to me, he said it was called Labrador tea, and I should drop about as much as he had picked into a mug and fill it with boiling water.

When I first tried it, I found I did like the herbal flavor even though it had a resinous aftertaste. It was a soothing drink at the end of the day.

Back at the parking area, after loading our ATVs onto their trailers and warming up our vehicles, I thanked him and offered an open invitation to come out to my place any time. I tried to give him some money for the gasoline and his help, but he just smiled and said it wasn't necessary, and that he had enjoyed making the journey with me. We shook hands, and headed back down the dirt road toward town.

When I walked into my shanty, something didn't seem right. I looked around and saw that some of my personal stuff was not quite as I had left it, though nothing seemed to be missing. I walked to Frolich's place and asked him if anyone had been in my rental while I was gone. He gave me a funny look and said he hadn't seen anyone, no one at all.

Believing that Harry had gotten nosey, I bought a good hasp and lock to put on the door, and made sure the windows were blocked with sticks so they couldn't be opened. After that, Frolich was pretty cool toward me whenever I saw him. I figured the sooner I got out to the homestead, the better.

It took me a dozen trips through the next six weeks to get all the basic supplies and equipment out to the cabin. The tough clothing I'd bought was already looking worn, and I now blended in with the locals. An elbow was out in one of my flannel shirts, and it would remain as it was to remind me of my hard work. I had lost about ten pounds, and my once snug pants now fit me perfectly. I was a lot tougher than when I'd first arrived in Hazel, and felt confident riding the trail after repeatedly hauling stuff out to the cabin. The ride itself was never really smooth, and rarely without minor incidents.

Soon enough, the time came for me to make the last supply trip out to the homestead. I had purchased everything on my list of necessities plus a few more items I thought might come in handy. There would be no return trip to town now, until a restocking of expendable goods or the need for some additional piece of equipment was required. I would be staying out at the cabin full-time, and was more than ready. Even the little town of Hazel had become too busy for me.

After parking my Jeep at Walt and Mary's place, I packed the supplies on the ATV, rode to the trailhead, and headed in.

I was out on the first long tundra I had to traverse, when I stopped and shut the machine off. Sitting there, I closed my eyes and drew in a big breath of the sweet, clean air that surrounded me, hopefully for many days to come. At that very moment I had an idea of what perfect was: the chance to have many unique and wonderful moments living a life most people could only dream of or try to comprehend. And here I was, on my way to live just such a life. Starting up the wheeler again, I continued my journey.

Episode

5

I WAS FINALLY LIVING IN GEORGE'S OLD CABIN, WELL STOCKED with provisions and gear. Now I could set to work building my new cabin. Living remote and alone in the forest was going to be unlike anything I had ever done, but I had been correct in believing that this life was the one for me. It just felt completely right.

I had quickly learned while running supplies, that transporting anything into the bush, large or small, is a major event and not to be taken lightly. There is a finite amount of materials that can be carried at one time by wheeler or snow machine and sled. So, the advice I had been given about making my own lumber with the chainsaw mill instead of hauling in boards from town made good sense.

The method for making lumber from trees with a chainsaw mill was a simple process, but long, hard work. I had to cut the trees down, limb them, and cut the trunks into the right lengths for the purpose the boards would serve, joists, rafters, floorboards, etc. I had to make a guide rail out of very straight two by fours brought in from town to make the initial squaring cuts on the lengths of trunk, after which I'd adjust the mill to cut the boards to correct thickness.

It all sounded so simple, until I actually attempted to do it. The first few boards came out shaped like parallelograms instead of rectangles. Having to go through so much to make lumber, I was determined to do it right. I found that the adjusting marks on the mill were a bit off, and I had to fudge with them a little, one side to the other, to get it right and make squared boards. Once I had that figured out, I began producing proper lumber.

The big chain saw I had bought for milling was very powerful, and the noise it made overwhelming. Earplugs would be my next necessary purchase. At least I didn't have to cut all the boards by hand like the old-timers.

The first spruce trees I cut down and milled were close to my homestead. I made sure to cut trees outside the borders of my land. I didn't want to alter the area right around the cabin. So, transporting those first boards, which I would use for the foundation framing and the floor platform, was easy, and I could get right to work on those parts of the structure. Once I started traveling farther away from the homestead to find suitable trees, hauling boards got rougher.

At first, I tried tying several boards on the rear rack of the ATV, letting the back end of them drag along the ground. But the trails were often narrow and twisty. The longer boards would sometimes jam up between trees, either yanking them off the rack or breaking them. Sometimes they just slipped off the back of the wheeler, and I'd have to stop and hitch them up again, which happened all too often.

Needing a better way to haul boards, I drew up some basic plans and had a guy in town weld up a low, narrow little trailer for me made out of lengths of angle iron with a solid axle underneath. I put on some ATV wheels and soft, low-pressure tires like the ones on my first wheeler. The trailer helped to some degree, as I was able to carry more boards and fasten them down more securely. But, the trails on the wooded ridges were so rough that the trailer frame kept bending and sometimes breaking from the bouncing and bumping, even with a moderate load on it.

Near the end of that first summer, Waters had come down the trail and saw me standing by my little trailer which had broken down again, the weld holding the axle breaking on one side. The look on his face told me he wasn't particularly sorry to see me struggling to get along on my own. After several unproductive but pointed remarks about my predicament, he suggested I mill all the boards I could in the summer and stack them up right where I cut them. After replacing the rubber tires on the trailer with a pair snow machine skis, I could easily run the lumber up to the new cabin site on the smoother winter trail. I told him that I didn't think it would be very practical to build in the winter because of the short daylight hours. Waters just stared at me for a moment, shook his head, and left. I hoped my putting him off like that might cause him to leave me alone, at least for a while.

Waters was an unpleasant man, but he had been living remote for a long time. I would actually follow his advice because it made sense. The winter trail was likely a lot easier to haul on with a nice layer of snow to smooth out the bumps. I just didn't feel like agreeing with him. So, for a large part of the summer that remained, I concentrated on milling boards, stacking them on site to be moved after snowfall, which I figured would come soon enough. But, I finally just had to get back to building.

It felt great when I had the foundation and floor platform done. I had taken my time and done a good job, the difference in measurement diagonally between the four corners less than an inch. I had never built anything like this before. In fact, I had only helped a friend build a storage shed from a kit once, and built a dog house when I was still a teenager living with my folks. But, I had what my grandpa called "good hands" when I did have something to work on.

I'd studied a basic house building book I'd bought back in Reno, and used it as a reference during the building process. It was kind of exciting when it came time to start assembling the walls. I had initially milled enough wood close to my land for at least two of the outside walls, as well as the foundation and platform. I could have continued milling the lumber I needed for all the main walls, but I wanted to get something up, so I went ahead.

It was late August, and fall would soon be cooling everything down. I was surprised at how warm the summer had been, getting well into the high seventies according to the little thermometer I had attached to the outside wall by the old cabin's door. The maddening bugs were mostly gone, but I kept a smoky fire going in a cut-down drum set on stones on the cabin platform to keep them at bay. Now that chill weather was coming in, I could also stop once in a while and warm up over the fire.

I had bought a new handsaw when I realized I couldn't make a precise cut with the chainsaw. But the handsaw, good as it was, really wore my arm out with all the cuts I had to make. I was actually more interested in getting the work done than I was in being an authentic old-time homesteader, so I made a special trip into town and went to Ed's Saw Shop where I had bought my chainsaws.

When I told Ed what I needed, he sold me a small generator powerful enough to operate a circular saw. He said the generator was very quiet and efficient. I figured it should be, considering what it cost, but I wanted a good one. When I started using it with the Skil saw I had also bought, it was really wonderful, allowing me to make clean, straight cuts and speeding up the process. It was also a lot less tiring to use.

Following what I'd learned in the building book, I framed the front wall of the cabin out of two by six boards. Measuring carefully, I cut all the boards to proper length and put together the wall framing with openings for two windows and the front door. The first cabin wall lay flat on the platform, ready to be raised.

As the book suggested, I nailed a couple of short boards against the side of the platform so the wall wouldn't slip over the edge as I lifted it. I knew the wall would probably be heavy, but it turned out to be much heavier than I had expected.

Going down to the old cabin, I brought up the heavy utility jack George had left there, and used it to partially raise the wall, high enough so that I was able to lift it the rest of the way myself, walking my hands along two center studs until it stood vertical on the edge of the platform.

The wall was able to stand on its own once it was up. It was positioned along one side of the platform, but was about an inch off the edge at one end. Don't ask me why, but instead of holding onto a wall stud as I tapped that end with a hammer to get it aligned, I just started kicking it with my boot. It shifted over until it was just about there. All it needed was one more bump.

The instant I gave the wall that one last little kick, it started to fall over, but not toward me and the platform. Instead it tipped outward, and away. I knew I couldn't stop it. All I could do was stand and watch it go. The top of the wall hit the ground, but it wasn't over yet. The surface of the platform was about four feet off the ground, and when the wall hit the ground, it flipped one more time.

The short boards I had nailed on the platform had kept the wall from slipping, but they were barely over the top edge of the floorboards and did nothing to stop the framing from going over. There I stood, thinking dark thoughts as I looked down at this twenty-four foot long wall lying flat on the ground, slightly tweaked, but still intact.

Deciding I'd done enough, I walked to the tool storage box, took my tool belt off, dropped it in the bin, put the other tools inside, and closed it up. I climbed off the platform, shut off the generator, and pushed it under the platform. I went back to the old cabin and stayed in the rest of the day.

The next morning, I went back with my come along and rope. I attached it to a tree behind the platform, and hooked the end of the rope to the middle of the fallen wall's top board. I took three long two by six boards and laid them up against the edge of the platform to use as ramps. Working the come along, I slowly and carefully winched the wall up along the boards and over until it lay flat on the platform again.

I nailed four longer boards vertically on the side of the platform to. I repeated the process of lifting the wall, and once it was upright and square on the edge of the platform, I drove twenty penny nails through the wall's bottom plate into the platform, using more than I actually needed. With my long level, I made sure it was straight up and square before nailing an angled board on at either end to hold it in place. The first cabin wall was done.

Standing on the platform facing the new wall, I looked through the main window opening. I could see how it was going to be when everything was done. Squatting down pretending to sit in a chair, I could see what the view would be. The trees with the tundra behind them and the peaks across Long Bay presented a terrific scene. The cabin was somehow alive now, even with just one raw wall up. It would be great when they were all standing, and covered with a solid roof.

I spent some time assembling the east wall, after which I called it a day. It was still early, but it seemed like a good stopping point. Just before leaving the worksite, I wondered if I should do a little more. Working for myself with no constraints on my own decisions and answering to no one else was a new thing for me. Letting it go, I headed home. The rest of that afternoon and evening I spent reading in the cabin, losing myself in tales of old Alaska. It was funny, here I was actually homesteading, but still enjoying stories about people doing the same thing, only at an earlier time.

The next day I was eager to do more building, but by the time I had almost finished the shorter east wall I had run out of lumber, so it was back to milling more boards.

I found several more usable, but smallish trees near my land, and processed them, but I had to go farther afield to find more good ones. I decided to look for ones sized nearer the full capacity the mill could handle, which was a tree about twenty-four inches in diameter at the base. Luckily, I found two standing next to each other in the woods south of the cabin on my side of the tundra. They were both dead from bark beetles and looked like they had been standing dry for a while. There was no green left on any branches. It took half a day to cut a trail to them so I could begin milling.

These were really good milling trees, and I had gained enough experience that I could drop them right where I wanted them to lie. They were both about forty to fifty feet tall, so that would give me two solid twelve-foot lengths for two by lumber and one length of eight foot one bys from each tree.

When I dropped the first one, it fell perfectly, landing along the slightly up-hill piece of land it had grown on. I started limbing it from the bottom to the top. Cutting off all the branches from a large spruce like this took a while. There were lots of branches, the lower ones big enough to need cutting in two before removing them right at the trunk. Reaching a point where the tree was too small to mill, I cut the top off completely, to be turned into firewood later.

I was surprised to see a trail running just past the severed top. It looked like it had once been well used, but was now overgrown. My curiosity got the better of me, and wanting a break after cutting off all the branches, I took a little walk to see where this trail went.

I must have followed it for at least half a mile, having to work my way around several naturally fallen trees in the process. There was a big nest in one of them. It was strongly built of small branches all woven together, and I thought it might be an eagle's nest. Several large, jet-black feathers stuck in the bowl of the nest told me I was right. There were plenty of bald eagles around. Sticking one of the feathers into my baseball cap, I kept walking.

About one hundred yards past the tree with the nest, I came out of the forest after pushing through some willows, and there I stood at the main trail, about three hundred yards up from my cabin. I had seen no evidence of human activity, except for the trail itself. If I cleared several sections from the two fallen trees, I could use this trail to get to my new woodcutting site more easily. It was too bad I hadn't known about this earlier, but it wasn't visible from the main trail, being hidden by the willows. I wanted to do more exploring of the general area. Who knew what I might discover that would be to my advantage?

After clearing this newfound trail the next day, I ran the wheeler to the two trees I had initially found for milling, but the path continued farther down the ridge past the new milling site. Curious to see where it led, I kept going. I had to clear several more fallen trees, later using one for milling, but finally came to the place where this track ended. It was an open lot about one hundred feet on a side, completely cleared, and still mostly bare except for some new willows and a few young spruce. I would have expected it to be more overgrown, considering how long it seemed to have been abandoned. I knew it had been a long while, because on one side of the clearing was a major stack of milled boards, all of them now weathered and split. It had taken a large number of trees to create so much lumber. A short distance from the stack was a torn up, rotten tent, flattened and half-covered by forest debris. Lifting a piece of the tent, I saw a mess of plastic dishes and cups, an old aluminum coffee pot, some ruined clothing, and a moldy old sleeping bag.

I assumed this was someone's attempt at homesteading, obviously never finished. This was a sad scene. It took a lot of sweat to create that massive stack of ruined boards. Someone must have had the idea that it would be better to cut all the lumber before starting to build, but then, never followed through. I wondered why there were all those now-useless things in the rotten old tent that could easily have been salvaged, but instead were left behind to rot away. Perhaps it was a sign of defeat, and that whoever had done so wanted nothing to remind them of their failure. Maybe after leaving the forest to go to town, they had decided to forget the whole thing and just never returned. Deciding there was no value in spending time pondering someone else's past decisions, I just shook my head and rode away, having my own work to do.

Episode

6

SINCE I WAS NOW LIVING FULL TIME ON THE HOMESTEAD, taking wild game for meat was a given. My only source of refrigeration was the outdoor air, when the ambient temperature was low enough to keep fresh meat from spoiling. I would probably can any meat remaining when winter was over and temperatures rose again, but for now I could enjoy the fresh meat.

My first few months at the cabin having been in the summer, I initially stocked up on canned meat from town. I had never been all that enthusiastic about eating Spam, corned beef, canned chicken, or fish. But until summer passed into fall, that's the way it would have to be. I could have brought in some steaks or pork chops, but I wanted to wait until I took my first moose to have fresh meat.

There were supposed to be squirrels, spruce hens, and rabbits in the area, but there didn't seem to be a large population of these smaller animals. So taking small game for food was not guaranteed. Besides, I didn't initially have a lot of free time to hunt, so canned meats came in handy. Mixed with potatoes, onions, eggs, or beans, they would make for some hearty meals until I could take a moose or black bear for a real source of protein.

To have a safe place to keep any harvested meat, I'd have to build a cache, a traditional way of keeping goods safe from predatory animals. It was supposed to be at least fifteen feet off the ground so a big bear couldn't reach it. To save time, I found three little spruce trees growing close together near the cabin to use for natural stilts to build the cache on, instead of cutting three poles and digging holes to set them in. The problem was I didn't have a ladder, so I found two small-diameter spruce trees to cut down and trim, then notched them to attach smaller branches as rungs. My rustic ladder actually worked out well, and sure looked like it belonged on a homestead.

The cache itself was a simple box with a small door in front and an angled roof, the whole structure covered with tar paper for waterproofing. It wasn't traditional as some of the old-time caches that looked like miniature cabins with little sod roofs, but it took less time to build and would work just as well.

September had soon slipped past, and temperatures had dropped below forty degrees. Except for a few clear, sunny days, cloudy skies and chill, scattered showers were the usual conditions. It was time to take a moose for meat. I had decided that moose hunting was just like deer hunting, which I'd already done, so I should do okay. Having seen moose in various parts of the forest, I would just point myself in a direction, and go on a stalk. There was lots of work to do before winter, but I knew it was the right time for a hunt.

I woke up early one morning in the middle of October to a hard frost. Daytime temps had been in the mid-thirties, but below freezing at night for several weeks. Conditions were now perfect for what I was going to do.

I dressed warmly, put on my waterproof, insulated boots, took the Winchester from its wall pegs and checked the magazine for cartridges, put a couple extra in my pocket, and walked out into the cold morning air. Everything felt right. It's kind of hard to explain that to someone who doesn't hunt. There was just something in the air that spoke to me, the same thing I had felt when deer hunting in the high desert of Nevada.

Working a cartridge into the gun's chamber and putting the safety on, I walked from the cabin and across the tundra to the woods on the other side. Slipping into the trees, I stood looking and listening, waiting for something to direct my next footsteps. After a few still moments, I moved deeper into the trees. There was a narrow, well-worn path that didn't appear to have been created by human feet. The dimensions were wrong and it meandered through the woods rather than going in a definite direction. Following it, and staying alert, I stopped at a scattering of moose droppings. Crushing one in my fingers, I could tell they were relatively fresh, though cold. There were also recent hoof prints visible on the frosty ground.

It is amazing to me how such a very large animal like a moose can be so perfectly concealed, until a slight movement of their head and outgrown antlers, or a shift of their body, finally gives them away. I had traveled about a quarter mile, still keeping to the animal trail, and was standing still listening, when something moving up ahead on the left revealed a moose within the trees. When the head and small rack of the young bull moose became clearly defined, it was like that vital piece of a puzzle which brings the whole picture into focus. Watching in silence, I was able to make out the shapes of several cow moose just beyond the bull, both of them larger than the young male, which might have been two or three years old, small compared to mature bulls I had seen.

Taking short, slow steps, needing to get into a better position for a clear shot while hoping the breeze wouldn't give me away, I moved forward. One of the cow moose turned in my direction and stood looking right at me. I froze in place, hoping to avoid detection. The cow moved out onto the trail ahead and I was sure she saw me, even though I wasn't moving. I was looking directly into her eyes, and that was why she knew I was there. Spinning away, she slipped off into the trees again and disappeared, the other cow following her. But the young bull, for whatever reason, came across the trail heading away from the cows. Lifting my rifle, I yelled, "HEY!" as loud as I could. The bull stopped dead in his tracks, turning his head toward me. When he did that, I fired. With all my focus on making a good shot, I didn't feel the recoil and barely heard the sound of the shot in the dense forest.

I had read that moose, being so large, can be mortally hit but still take a while to go down. But this one, not fully grown and very close to me when I shot, just crumpled onto its side in the trail, kicked several times, and lay still. The cartridge was loaded with a heavier bullet than I would have used for deer, and it had apparently done the trick. I stood for a while watching, making sure the moose was finished. I went up, poked him with my gun's muzzle, and got no reaction. I had taken my first moose.

In Nevada I had always hunted alone, preferring it that way. But at this time I wished someone was with me to share the moment, someone who would understand. I would have to be content to appreciate this on my own. Kneeling down, I put my hand on its body, feeling the warmth and smelling the unique scent of the animal, the same kind of scent as a deer, only stronger. I didn't enjoy killing him, but it was a necessity. His life for mine.

Setting the rifle against a nearby tree, I went to work dressing out the moose. Opening up the abdomen with my hunting knife, I cleaned out all the organs and viscera from its body. The mass of internals by themselves were almost as heavy as several of the deer I had taken in the past. I was careful to not get any dirt or hair on the meat, which would have spoiled the flavor.

After finding a stick to prop open the body cavity spreading the ribs, I put the heart and kidneys into a gallon plastic bag I had brought, and the liver into another, before I hiked back to the cabin to stash the meat. I returned on the wheeler to where the moose lay and quartered it, putting the pieces on the front and rear racks, then hauled them to the cabin. In two round trips, the job was done. It would have taken much more work to get the meat back to the cabin by hand, carrying a quarter at a time on a pack frame. Old Mr. Harmon might not appreciate the mechanical assist, but I sure did.

Back home with the butchered moose hanging on a cross pole I had attached between two spruce trees next to the cabin, I sprayed vinegar all over the bare meat, and then rubbed black pepper onto it. I had read that the vinegar would form a crust over the meat which helped preserve it, and the black pepper kept any lingering flies away. Putting all of it up into the cache, I had my meat for the winter and perhaps into spring. But as I had expected, I had developed a very healthy appetite living and working out in the trees, so it was possible the meat wouldn't last that long. I went into the cabin to wash up, then took a pan of water outside to wash down the wheeler's racks. Finished with the whole process, I sat in the cozy little cabin with a cup of Labrador tea, feeling good and hoping future hunting would go as easily.

Hearing the noisy jays outside, I looked out the door and saw them standing expectantly on the feeder. I had brought some little slices of meat in to fry and eat for lunch. Cutting one up into little squares, I took it out. I was surprised the two jays didn't flap away when I approached. They just stood waiting, making their seemingly never-ending raucous noises. When I put the meat bits on the feeder, they jumped right on it, one of them landing with a foot on one of my fingers, and didn't move it away. I stood very still as the birds continued eating. I was a little overwhelmed by the feelings I had about this tiny, spontaneous contact. The bird didn't break away until the meat scraps were all gone, after which they both flew into the closest tree to preen on a low branch barely above my head. It was satisfying to see how trusting they had become.

That night I had moose heart and onions for dinner, putting the rest of the organ meat in a lidded five-gallon plastic bucket in the spring box to keep it cold. The moose heart was rich but not gamey, and I knew it was good for me. The statement a fellow in town had made about the meat being special because it was from a wild, free animal, sounded right as I sat eating from my first harvested moose. I also discovered that eating such rich meat made me fart like an old horse, another reason it was good to be alone out here, I figured.

I'd had to defend myself to a few people at work in Nevada after deer hunting. I gave up trying to explain hunting and its importance to people who just didn't get it. I could understand their point of view, though they refused to accept mine. But here, taking a moose for my own sustenance, actually living on the same land as the animal, I was completely clear about it, knowing it was a righteous act.

I was grateful for being able to harvest my own food. Before eating, I gave a prayer of thanks, something I hadn't done since my childhood. I had never been very spiritual, but out here it felt right.

Episode

7

FOR THE NEXT SEVERAL MONTHS, I KEPT SEARCHING FOR AND milling trees I located along trails I had found or cut. I had a dozen stacks of fresh boards waiting to be hauled by time the first snow came in early December. By the beginning of January, I had them all up at the new cabin site, but temperatures had really dropped, going well below zero a number of times. I found I could comfortably work in temperatures down to about ten degrees, but I would build up a good sweat working in my insulated clothing even at that temperature, and then get chilled. When the temperatures dropped even lower, I would mostly keep to the cabin, reading and planning.

Whenever I went to town, I would get books from the library, mostly about Alaska, but also about the Yukon Territory of Canada. It seemed a great place, like the best of Alaska country, with lots of game and beautiful forests. The books kept me occupied when I was cabin bound. I really enjoyed sitting at my little table, wood crackling in the stove, with a good book in hand. The forest was quieter in the winter, sound muffled by the blanket of snow covering everything. This made it easier to lose myself in the words, a nice change from dealing with daily chores.

Building in the winter went well in spite of the shorter amount of daylight. But a heavy snowfall would slow things way down. In fact, during that first winter, from the end of January until the beginning of spring break up in early May, the snow got really deep making work difficult. Several times, it took a couple of hours to get all the snow off the new structure, leaving me with little work time. I learned to concentrate on a specific section of the cabin, and only took the time to clean off that chosen area. I looked forward to getting the roof up, but that wouldn't be for a while. It wasn't something that could really be done in winter. The lack of sufficient daylight hours to get some real building done was frustrating at times, even though I had learned to go with the rhythm of the season.

Sitting in the old cabin one January afternoon keeping warm, I came to the conclusion that if I still felt compelled to get things done quickly as if there was a deadline, coming here to live hadn't accomplished much for me after all. I already had this fine little cabin to live in. If the long winter darkness was inconvenient, so be it.

I wanted my new place to be sturdy and able to handle whatever extreme conditions Alaska could dish out, and keep me warm and dry. I needed to take my time and build it right. Besides, I figured the heavy snows were another test Alaska was throwing at me, and I'd just have to go with it.

One cold, but clear-skied February afternoon, Monty and his wife Bev, who I'd met once before, came riding up on their snow machines. Bev worked in town as a clerk part-time in the local motel in the winter, and as a crew boss on the fish processing boat moored offshore from town in summer. She would stay there for weeks at a time, living on the boat in the summer, rooming at the motel in winter.

Bev was no more than five feet tall, but the attitude she displayed made it obvious she was a feisty lady who wouldn't take guff from anyone. I picked up on that the first time I met her. There was something in the tone of her voice, even when she was being nice, that suggested a streak of toughness in her. It probably stood her in good stead when she did come home, living at the top of that crazy ridge trail. She had been born and raised right there in Hazel and had never gone farther than Anchorage.

After the three of us nodded in greeting, they walked around what there was of the new cabin, talking to each other. When they got back to me again, Monty, with a serious face, remarked that "it would probably last a couple of years if the weather stayed good."

Keeping a straight face too, I thanked him for his confidence in my building abilities.

Bev smiled at our interaction, but said nothing. After a brief silence, we were all smiling at the jest.

Not wanting to appear inhospitable, I offered them a cup of coffee down at the old cabin, but they politely refused. Monty said, "We've got trail to ride."

After Monty shook my hand, they turned, got on their snow machines, and headed to wherever it was they were going. He had mentioned once that they liked to go riding in the winter just for fun, sometimes into the hills above Ptarmigan Lake. I planned on exploring up there myself, but for now, I had nails to pound.

Episode

8

MY FIRST WINTER FINALLY STARTED FADING AWAY. THE DEEP cold of January and February was relenting by March, with just a few light snowfalls during that time, as winter tried unsuccessfully to maintain its dominance over the land. The start of spring had come, and with it a melting of the accumulated snows, releasing vast quantities of freed water everywhere. Monty had told me not to try to get to town or anywhere else for that matter, until most of the melt water had drained away, which he said would take three or four weeks. I heeded his words. Since I was low on supplies, all I could do was use what I had, and continue working on the new cabin. During that time, I was able to complete most of the outside wall framing, using all the two by sixes I had milled the previous winter.

I learned over time that this far north spring was just a passing notion, a long pause between the end of winter and the beginning of summer. That first spring was no different. Soon enough it was the middle of June, and my first spring in the bush was turning into summer. The snow and ice were completely gone, and all the water had drained off downhill over the descending bench lands, ultimately flowing in numerous small streams and waterfalls over the bluffs and down to Long Bay far below. By the middle of summer, the waterways were dried up, leaving steep, eroded notches in their place.

The potential rains of late July and August, which could make life so soggy, were still to come. The moderate summer temperatures were a welcome change from the overwhelming freeze of winter, and the forest had awakened, evident by the increase in animal noise and movement. I was enjoying not having to wear my bulky cold weather gear.

The moose meat was almost gone, and it was the right time to take a black bear for food. A bear taken in late spring to early summer, according to everything I had learned, would have the best meat. During those first few weeks after they came out of hibernation, the bears would be eating sweet grasses, roots, and sedges to get their bodies up to speed. I hoped I might find a bear that still had some fat on it for rendering into cooking oil. I had read that it was mild and sweet, and great for frying.

In my wanderings before winter, I had found a great hunting spot a dozen yards off to the side of a real bear "highway," a hard-packed old path bears had walked on for many years, roaming through their territory. I could tell by the different sizes and spacing of the paw-shaped indentations that both black and grizzly bears used the trail.

So, early one June morning, I slipped out of the cabin on foot and headed south, ghosting through a stretch of woods leading to the end of a long narrow strip of tundra. I wandered along the edge of that tundra as it ran to the west for a long mile, before I turned left and headed into the forest beyond, as thick a place as I'd ever want to work my way through, and only for a good reason.

Moving quietly to my hiding place, the collapsed wall of a small, long deserted log cabin that had gone bad, I settled in. Sitting in as comfortable a position as possible, I waited, well hidden behind the jumble of wall logs, watching the open stretch of bear trail just yards away. The builders had done a thorough job of clearing the land around the site to keep the cabin safe from falling trees and to let some light in.

The forest was taking the cleared area back, but the new growth was not yet as dense as the older forest, affording me a clear shot. The thick wall of trees surrounding this open circle of land lent an air of eeriness to the place.

I was beginning to think the hunt would end up a bust, after sitting there for about four hours without even so much as a squirrel or spruce hen making itself known. The forest was very quiet, and I tried to remain so myself. Just as I was considering calling it quits for the day, I froze where I sat, unable to move a muscle. My mouth went dry and my grip on the stock of George's rifle tightened until my knuckles popped.

A deep intake of breath had been drawn right behind my bare neck from something with great lung capacity. Immediately after that, a big whoosh of warm air blew against the back of my head, and the stench that accompanied it could only have come from one animal, and a huge one by my sense of it. Just as in the adventure stories I had read, time stood still as I waited for a bite from massive canines or a swat from a huge, clawed paw that would end my travels for good. But it never came. Managing to turn my head to the right very, very slowly so as not to provoke a reaction, all I saw was a glimpse of dark brown fur. Facing forward again, I sat still for long minutes, without another sound or feeling from what was behind me.

The physical tension no longer bearable, and unable to sit still any longer, I flung myself forward, twisting around as I did, coming up against the collapsed log wall. There was nothing in front of me but forest.

The sun filtering through the trees scattered a soft light around me that felt oddly out of place at that moment. I slumped against the old grayed logs, the rifle sliding from my hands, all energy drained out of me.

Finally, rising to study my surroundings, I saw in the soft ground visibly disturbed patches, as if some great weight had pressed down and twisted as it moved away. I searched for and found several very large, clear prints confirming that a giant grizzly, a brown bear, had caught me unawares. I got goose bumps in places where I never knew they could occur.

Grateful to be alive and whole, I cautiously hiked back to my cabin. I didn't expect another run-in with this forest giant since it hadn't finished me when it could have. Still, all my senses were on alert. Nothing I had studied about bears had prepared me for this. I would have expected loud roaring as it came crashing through the brush at me, eyes red and foam around its mouth.

Home again, I contemplated what had occurred. Maybe the bear was just curious and wanted to file my scent away in its memory, or maybe it had played a joke on me. Brown bears were pretty smart, so anything was possible. It might have been aware of why I was sitting there, another predator waiting for food to come by, but I would never know for sure. I decided to wait a few more days before hunting for bear at another spot.

As it turned out, that was just the first meeting I would have with that big brownie.

Episode

9

IT WAS THE MIDDLE OF SUMMER ON THE HOMESTEAD, AND BUG time was in full flight. It really was remarkable, if for no other reason than the enormous numbers of insects. I couldn't open the cabin door without paying for it by spending several minutes afterwards whacking all the mosquitoes and no-see-ums that had zipped in during a few seconds of access.

During my first summer at the cabin, the mosquitoes had been much fewer in numbers. The lack of snow the winter before and higher than normal summer temperatures had created a dry environment. This caused the mosquitoes' breeding grounds, the still pools and water logged muskeg, to evaporate quickly. But this second summer was very different, with loads of surface water everywhere, and plenty of bugs. I spent time chinking every little opening between the wall logs and any other gaps in the old cabin which I had missed when I first made repairs. I wanted the cabin as bug free as possible. Still, they found a way in. There is something really maddening about being asleep, only to have a high-pitched buzzing right in your ear wake you up!

I had bought some of those strange green coils that emitted a bug repelling smoke when you lit them. You're supposed to keep a window open to let fresh air in when using them. A lot of good that would do to keep the bugs away! I finally built a new window that would open in, and tacked some screening on the outside window framing.

I tried using a head net while working outside, but it really annoyed me, rubbing against my beard and face, catching on branches, and sliding around on my head.

The first time I went out to work at the new cabin site that second summer after the bugs became active, seemingly overnight, I had on a soft cloth shirt. I was only out a few minutes with my head net on when my shoulders and upper back started hurting with a burning sensation. I slapped my hand against my left shoulder and it came away covered in bloody bug mess. Yanking my head net off, I twisted my head both ways to see I don't know how many mosquitoes, all over my shoulders. I thought they only went after veins, but these things were everywhere! I know I let out a yell and took off running for the cabin, pulling the shirt off just as I got to the door, throwing it to one side. I sat in the cabin trying to think of a way to keep the bugs from zapping me any more than they already had. I didn't feel like sharing any more of my blood supply with them.

That's when I hit upon the idea of wearing a hard woven cotton shirt, thinking it might prevent them from getting to me. I also decided that what I really needed was some good bug repellent to use outdoors. I'd have to wear that irritating head net until I went to town. So, I bought some super bug "dope" in Hazel made from one hundred percent D.E.E.T., whatever that is. It was an incredibly efficient repellent, though I was told that regular use would probably leave me glowing in the dark. To keep the darned mosquitoes and flies off, I figured it was worth it. I still had to put up with the constant hum and buzz though, from the cloud of bugs all around me.

The next time I went out to work at the new cabin site, I built a little fire right where I would be working, throwing green branches on it to make smoke, which helped to keep the bugs away. Running the chain saw also seemed to help hold them at bay.

By August, I had been steadily milling boards for weeks and I needed a break. There was enough wood milled and stacked to get a lot of work done come winter. I had already made a couple of runs with boards up to the site to do a little building for a change of pace from the milling. But, I felt the need for a ride to town.

I loved the forest, and never lost any of my enthusiasm and enjoyment of the life. But, a quick run into town to blow the stink off was sometimes necessary. The ride itself was often more enjoyable than being in town. Once, I rode all the way to the graded dirt road, only to turn around and head back to the cabin, satisfied with just being on the trail. The times when I did go all the way to town, I would head right to the Log Cabin Cafe for a burger and coffee, and some good conversation with Cafe acquaintances. Afterward, having picked up a few incidental supplies, I'd head back to the homestead.

I usually stopped a few times on the trail just to enjoy the scenery or to watch some animal passing by. But in bug time, I tended to keep rolling just like the caribou, to keep them off and find some relief from the buzzing in my ears. I was lucky my wheeler never broke down. I could see how farther north, where the insects are in their greatest numbers, they might drive someone nuts if they were in a bad way, maybe hurt and alone out on the tundra. That would be a person's downfall, because the bugs would rise like a dark cloud off the muskeg and engulf anyone there.

But, I did that first casual run to town without any trouble, not stopping except once to answer the call of nature, which would have had to be done quickly, one hand swinging madly back and forth to chase the little buggers away. There are some places where bites are never acceptable.

Episode

10

Apart from the basics of life necessary for survival: food, water, and shelter, the major focus in my forest life was trees, finding the right ones, bringing them down, and using them for making boards and firewood. Firewood was easy enough. I'd take down any dry, small to medium sized tree that wouldn't produce a worthwhile amount of dimensional lumber, cut it into short lengths, then haul them to my little woodlot behind the old cabin.

The forest I lived in was full of dead trees, killed by bark beetles that burrowed into a tree by the thousands, eventually killing it, sap dripping from all the little boreholes they created. The trees died standing up, the moisture in them dispersing over time. It took years for them to dry out, but once they did, they were excellent for building. Just about all the trees I brought down were beetle killed, except the few live ones I had to clear from around my new building site.

I'd had no experience using a chainsaw before coming to Alaska, but I quickly learned how to handle one and keep from cutting off anything vital. To tell the truth, at first a chainsaw was a barely controllable wood chewing machine to me, a mechanical tiger shark happy to gnaw on anything its teeth could snag. I didn't like using them, but it was either that or haul lumber in from town. I never did get comfortable with them, which probably kept me safe, but I got pretty good at using them. I had to learn the right method to cut trees so they'd fall cleanly where I wanted them to, something I had trouble with at first.

The process was simple enough, just two cuts to remove a wedge of wood in front and one cut in back in the right place, but it took me a number of attempts to keep the cuts properly aligned. The result of not doing it right, was having the one I was felling not dropping where I wanted and possibly hanging up on several others. If it was a full-sized tree, as they usually were for milling, that meant spending lots of extra time working to get them all the way down. Usually, I'd have to take down the offending trees as well as the one I wanted. That could be scary, and I had to move quickly to avoid becoming a mashed thing on the forest floor, a good incentive for learning quickly. It made for exciting times.

There was one tree, though, that really got to me. It was a tall spruce of large diameter, standing dead, with few lower limbs and a nice straight trunk. It looked like it would be great for milling boards. The area around it was open, and I could get to it without having to cut a trail. So, I cranked up my felling saw and set to work. The two front cuts to remove the wedge went fine, but when I was making the back cut, instead of tipping forward it set straight down on the stump and stood there, unmoving, my chainsaw bar caught between the stump and the trunk. A chill ran through me. I didn't know what this tree was going to do. It could fall in any direction, or split and twist around. I just didn't know.

After standing there for several long minutes nervously waiting for something to happen, I backed away until I was at a safe distance, and sat down to consider my options. Even if my saw weren't stuck, I couldn't leave the tree like that. Chances were nobody would ever come by just as the tree decided to give it up if a strong wind or winter snows conspired to bring it down, but I just couldn't take that chance. I returned to my wheeler and rode back to the cabin. Gathering up my hand winch, rope, and a couple of plastic spreading wedges, I headed back to the spruce, hoping to find it already down, but it was still standing there waiting for me. Fastening the come along to another tree, I carefully tied the rope attached to the end of the winch's short cable around the cut tree as high as I could reach. After that, the fun really started.

I went back to the come along and started cranking up tension on the cable, putting pressure on the trunk in hopes of convincing it to topple, which meant it would come down in my direction. The tree was massively heavy, of course, and I was pretty sure I couldn't make it move at all. But once there was a lot of tension on the rope, I went back to the tree. There was a slight opening on the back cut now, so I was able to work my saw out of the cut, and I could now drive the wedges in. I did just that, and the tree started to fall just the way I wanted it to, so I stepped away to the side. But, with a loud "groaning" sound, it twisted, at the same time sliding backward on its cut end, coming toward me on the way down.

I jumped back, tripping as the shattered lower end barely missed me. I just lay there, adrenaline pumping, until my breathing slowed down.

I was safe, the tree was down, and it could be cut into milling length logs. But, when I walked to the cut end, I could see that it was rotten right through the middle, which explained why it had acted so strangely. Cranking up my saw again, I cut a five foot length off the base, but it was still too rotten. Another five foot length, but the rot was enough to reduce the milling to a much smaller number of boards. Another five feet and the rot was finally gone. All I could get was one twelve foot length, because of the tree tapering quickly toward the top. It was pretty much a total loss. The rotten wood wasn't even good for fires, so I just rolled the useless lengths out of the way to eventually decompose. I milled up the one twelve foot length so as not to feel the whole process was wasted, and the episode was over, another interesting day in the Alaska bush.

The only time I got dumb cutting a tree down was with one of the first I worked on. I could have walked to it, since it was just past the back edge of my land. But, I rode the big wheeler instead, more by reflex than out of laziness. I parked it at what seemed a safe distance and started on the tree. I carefully made my cuts, and the spruce started falling very nicely, right at the wheeler. Seeing what was happening, I smiled, knowing it was out of range. Wrong. When the tree fell, the very tip of it smacked right against the instrument cluster mounted in the middle of the handlebars. The plastic it was made out of was probably very tough stuff for normal use, but didn't hold up against a falling tree top. The housing literally blew apart, leaving the several instruments dangling from their wires, including the ignition switch.

Feeling like a real idiot, I took some of that priceless, universal fix-all, silver duct tape, and put everything together in a thick, weird looking bundle, attached to the bars again. The next time I went to town, I trailered the wheeler from Mary and Walt's place to the ATV shop to make sure I got everything I needed to make repairs. Of course, the parts I needed had to be ordered, but my own repairs would do until they came in. The duct tape would hold until my next run to town.

When I took the owner of the ATV shop out to see the wheeler, after a few chuckles he just had to take a photograph, enlarge the image, and put it up on the wall next to the counter with the caption, "Custom Homesteader ATV."

Episode

....

11

IT WAS A COOL LATE AUGUST MORNING, AND THE AIR WAS alive with the busy energy of the forest. It made itself known with the innumerable sounds which were absent in winter, but abounded in the warmer season, chattering squirrels, calling birds, and other, less tangible noises.

As always, when leaving the cabin for the first time in the morning, I took a moment to tune in to the forest, to listen and look around. There was always an intensity to the atmosphere, a tautness that came from the serious business of living, a constant concern for every living thing in the bush. I had become fully aware of that fact, and staying vigilant had become instinctive.

After breakfast, I had felt the urge to explore a patch of forest I hadn't hiked through before to help satisfy my desire to become familiar with as much of the surrounding country as possible. Cruising through the forest on foot was an enjoyable activity. There would be plenty of time later in the day to do the daily chores. Walking down the short slope behind the cabin beyond the spring box, I followed the way of least resistance through the trees and bushes. A little draw running below the cabin felt like the right way to go this time.

Alders growing thickly on both sides and overhead formed a natural tunnel down the little vale, as I quietly slipped along. It looked like I was following a well-traveled animal trail, so I needed to be extra alert. Moving at a deliberate pace, I noticed an almost circular opening in the alders, the start of a trail leading away to the right up the side of the draw. Without thinking, I started up this path. I just gave in to the impulse, a primordial urge moving me up that unknown, overgrown trail.

Because of the dense undergrowth I couldn't stand upright. So, bent over and feeling vulnerable, I moved slowly and carefully along, like an ancient being hoping to avoid some long-extinct predator.

After creeping in this awkward position for fifty yards or so, I stopped, seeing a small natural spring just off the side of the trail. Something had been drinking there. The surface of the small pool was still, and I didn't see or hear anything. But there was a strong scent lingering in the air. That, and the one clearly visible, oversized paw print on the edge of the pool was a sharp reminder that I wasn't the biggest animal in the woods. Adrenaline pumping, I moved only my eyes, an inner voice telling me, "This is not good."

Pulling my pistol out of its holster, I cautiously continued on, not wanting to go back down the way I had come in case whatever had been drinking at the spring had backtracked and was waiting below.

A short distance farther on, the trail opened out into a large meadow, filled with head-high grass, and continued to the right through the concealing growth. I stood still a moment, the bright sunlight failing to warm me, the strong scent and paw print by the spring still strong in my mind.

Taking a dozen or so tentative steps, I froze in my tracks, held by what lay ahead on the path. It was a very large mound of bear scat still steaming in the chill air. The heavy revolver in my hand suddenly felt irrelevant, because what had left the droppings behind was standing just ahead on the path.

The brown bear, big even for its enormous species, had stopped on the trail facing away from me. But its great furred head was turned in my direction, the look in its small intelligent eyes hard to read. A long jagged scar running diagonally across its muzzle added to the bear's somber demeanor. There was something else too, a feeling of familiarity, and I suddenly knew in my gut that this was the bear that had taken me by surprise a few weeks before, as I hunted by the old cabin ruins. I hadn't really seen the bear that time, but I somehow knew it was one and the same. Something made me slowly put my .44 back in its holster, a move not lost on the great animal in front of me.

The bear continued to stare at me, with a steady but neutral look in its eyes, so that I didn't know what to expect. I knew I shouldn't stare back at him, but I couldn't break away. Finally, he turned his head away and slowly moved off, one heavy step after another, fading into the tall grass.

After waiting several minutes to allow the bear ample time to leave, I turned and walked away in the other direction, still tense, but relieved about the way things had ended. Twice now that bear had scared the crap out of me, but hadn't hurt me. Still, I figured being afraid was the correct way to feel.

As I took the long way around to my cabin, it occurred to me that if there wasn't a good reason for going somewhere, perhaps I just shouldn't go. Unfortunately, there was a lot of territory I hadn't seen yet, so I'd just have to be careful in my random wonderings.

I was amazed that after two close confrontations the bear had not reacted aggressively. I was pretty sure he must be the big bruin in these woods. He was truly huge, but apparently not of a vengeful nature, not that I wanted to test my assumption. I considered it best to leave things the way they were so as not to change the nature of our connection.

Episode

12

MONTY DROPPED BY ONE SUMMER DAY TO SEE HOW I WAS doing. I mentioned how bad the trail had been that past spring.

He smiled, and said that at times of heavy break up I should take the "other trail," but not if I was going to bring back a heavy load from town. When I asked him what trail he meant, he told me how to get there from my place and said, "You should check out the trail and see what you think." After he left, I wrote down the directions he had given me.

Early that August, I decided to check out this other trail. I took my pistol and canteen, fueled up the wheeler, strapped my little chainsaw on the back rack, and headed out to find the beginning of Monty's trail. I had no idea what it would be like, but assumed it would probably be no worse than the other established trails we all took. Right… .

According to Monty, the upper end of the trail began behind a small log cabin, south of Waters' land. Riding down to the fifty-five-gallon drums below his homestead, I continued straight past them instead of turning right toward Bucky's place, almost immediately dropping down a short, steep slope that was rough and overgrown. Coming out to a very narrow bit of tundra, I went straight across on a boardwalk of wooden slabs nailed to spruce poles, then headed directly into a large alder patch. The denseness of the alders made for difficult maneuvering, and I had to do a lot of leaning and ducking to avoid them. Beyond the alders, it ran through a meadow of tall bear grass, which I usually tried to avoid, not liking unpleasant surprises. But, after the high grass, there was a stretch of very open forest, a cinch to travel through.

I had to traverse another narrow strip of tundra, and ride again into dense undergrowth which completely obscured the trail in places, branches smacking me in the face as I worked my way through. The variety of vegetation I might encounter passing through a small area of the bush always surprised me, but this was getting extreme. At this point I wondered if finding this other trail was worth the hassle, but already committed, I kept rolling. A hundred yards further on, I made a sharp left turn just past a large spruce with one straight branch running right over the trail, as described by Leer, and a small cabin came into view, behind which the trail I was seeking actually started. From there it ran all the way down to the head of the bay and the well-established lower trail.

Experiencing this trail made me consider the differences in human perceptions. Obviously Monty had a much higher threshold as to what constituted extreme conditions than I did, as evidenced by the incredible ridge trail I found so difficult, and now this.

The trail was a truly wild ride, a crude switchback route, running steeply downhill with constant tight twists and turns, low hanging branches and lots of devil's club. There were many roots sticking out into the path, often hidden by the lush grasses. I had been on difficult trails before, but the sharp angle of this one made for very strenuous going. There were places so steep and rough, that I had to lean way back to keep from pitching forward over the bars. For anyone to intentionally use this trail after having run it even once was just plain nuts. I considered turning around, but there was no place wide or level enough. This was a track where, once you started down it, there was no turning back.

There were a couple of "widow makers" hanging out over the trail. These were trees that had started to fall, but had stopped before coming completely down to earth. Leaning overhead, they were unpredictable and dangerous. Eventually, though it could take months or even years, they would drop all the way down, blocking the trail. I'd removed any that were hanging over the regularly used trails whenever I could. I did have my little chainsaw along, but the trail was so treacherous that I didn't even consider stopping the wheeler to remove the widow makers.

One small spruce had dropped so low that, coming on it just past a sharp turn, it knocked me almost completely off the wheeler, which kept on moving. I managed to hang onto one handlebar grip, getting to my feet and back onto the seat just in time to avoid a large stump jutting into the side of the trail. My forehead had gotten a pretty good thump, and my hat had been knocked off but I sure wasn't going back for it.

I must have covered a full mile of this miserable route, though it seemed like ten, before I got to the bottom. It emerged at the edge of Long Bay's headlands, well past the deserted shacks below Monty's ridge trail.

A short, narrow, wooden slab bridge spanned a small ditch where the trail came out. It looked all right, but when I rode over it, the slab on the left side tilted sharply, sending me sliding over sideways into the muddy trough beneath it. I wasn't hurt much, but had to spend a lot of time and energy getting the wheeler upright and out again, turning the air blue with my grumbled opinions of miserable trails and the people who cut them.

The rest of the run turned out to be relatively easy. After leaving the end of that evil trail, I rode along a clear track through some open country and over mud flats with numerous shallow sloughs running through them. I was really glad to have my larger, more powerful wheeler so I could make it through with little difficulty. I finally reached the deserted shacks. By the time I got there, I had vowed to never ride on that nasty other trail again, no matter how bad spring break up might be. I had a bunch of little cuts here and there, a roughed-up forehead, several devil's club spines in my cheek and neck, and was nursing a sore elbow and a bad knuckle from falling off the wooden slab bridge. The wheeler was okay, but one front plastic fender was badly scratched and the taillight had been broken. Oh, yeah, and my new canteen, which had been bungeed to the rear rack was gone, again.

It took me until early evening to get home. I rode all the way down the bay, but had to wait for the tide to go out to be able to get to the steep switchbacks to the Sandals' place. From there, I ran the wheeler to the overland trailhead and all the way back out to my cabin. It was running on fumes by the time I arrived. It was really great to be home. The day had been long, and I was beat up and muddy.

There might be a lesson in this somewhere, but I'll be darned if I can settle on the right one. I do know the word dumb is in there somewhere. I hoped Monty and I might have a good laugh over this, but that wouldn't be for a while.

Episode

13

OVER TIME, MY SENSES HAD BECOME CLEARER AND MORE acute. Being away from all the excessive noises, smells, and bright lights of the city, living with only the natural sounds and atmosphere of unspoiled nature, had given my body and mind a chance to heal. I knew that running my gasoline-powered tools and vehicles was the exact opposite of what was healthy out here, but it was a trade-off, and necessary to accomplish what I had set out to do.

My vision had always been good, but my ability to use that sight increased too. Contrast and colors became more distinct, and I seemed able to see more clearly at greater distances, though that could partly have been because of the wonderful clean air.

My sense of smell and hearing improved too, and I had become more observant of minor details in the natural world around me. Even on a calm, windless day, I was more aware of the scents of various animals and plants. I could hear a branch cracking under the weight of a large animal, moose or bear. Hearing squirrels was never a problem. They were the noisiest guys in the woods, always annoying, happy to give away my presence. They could put the jays to shame.

There was something else. That other ability, which some call the sixth sense, seemed to have surfaced more strongly. I had previously thought it existed only in wild animals as instinct. I would stop while walking through the trees or when hanging around the cabin and just know that something was around, some animal, without actually hearing or seeing it. A number of times, I "sensed" a wheeler or snow machine just before I actually heard it. I jokingly told myself I had tapped into the Force, just like a *Star Wars* Jedi knight could.

I came to fully comprehend that the main purpose of my senses was that of survival. I knew this must be true living in a city too, but existing in the bush made it more obvious. There was less danger in the woods than in a city, because the things that made it harder to know what was going on around me in an urban setting, the things that "clogged" my senses, were absent here.

I was stalking through the forest north of my land one fall day, hoping to come across a moose for winter meat. The woods were very quiet, not even a raucous squirrel to announce my presence. The intense stillness around me seemed to amplify every tiny scuff and bump my feet made, so I was taking extra care, moving slowly.

Coming to a large patch of alders, I worked my way past it hoping to catch a moose or even a black bear off guard, not an easy thing. As I slipped around the alders, staying close to them to remain undetected, I froze in place. The only part of me that moved was the thumb of my right hand as it pushed the safety of my rifle to off. Something was there, hidden deep in that dense alder thicket, thick enough to conceal a big, furry body. I didn't hear, see, or smell anything, but I knew that something was in there and aware of me.

I stood still for maybe 30 seconds, waiting for something to react to my presence there. When nothing exciting happened, I very carefully backed away, trying to keep my feet clear of roots on the uneven ground. Stopping when I had gained a comfortable distance from the alders, I waited again. Nothing happened. I stood very still, knowing that more time was needed to be sure it was clear. It was a tense situation, just like when that big bear snuck up behind me. I hoped for a similar outcome this time.

A branch snapped some distance behind the mass of intertwined alder branches. My tight gut relaxed, because I knew the potential danger had withdrawn. A blind standoff in the woods had turned out all right. Passing the edge of the thicket I saw nothing behind it, which was fine by me. I went back to ghosting along, fresh meat still my immediate goal, but this time I went home empty-handed.

My increased sensitivities made it difficult to be in town, especially my sense of smell. The odors my dulled senses had become oblivious to in the past were now very hard for me to deal with. The smell of diesel fuel was particularly irritating.

After the first time I experienced their stench, I avoided going near the giant dumpsters located near the docks where fishermen came in off the water and threw the remains of the halibut, salmon, and cod they caught. These dumpsters weren't emptied until they were almost full. Talk about stink.

Going into the supermarket could be really bad. The mixture of different fruits and vegetables combined with the smells of the deli and salad bar and the cosmetics section could be very unpleasant. The scents that women and men wore, the aftershaves, deodorants, and perfumes, were the worst. If I were close to a woman wearing a strong fragrance, I would sometimes get a slight headache. This was the reason I tried to shop quickly, pay, and leave. If the floors were being cleaned in the store, I'd have to leave and come back later because of the cleaning fluids they used.

On one particular trip, I was walking down a food aisle when a woman passed by me. She was wearing very heavy perfume, and the moment it assailed my nose I had an instant reaction. I developed a headache that didn't pass until I was on the road heading back to the trail. I had never anticipated such a side effect from being out in the woods full-time, but it showed what changes living remote had made on me. I considered it an acceptable trade-off, all things considered.

The one scent that immediately got my full attention out in the forest came from bears. Their powerful odor left no doubt what they were. Moose had an almost sweet smell from the plants they ate, but bears would eat just about anything, including rotten meat, which they often liked to roll around on, and so their scent could be really foul. On a rainy day, the smell of a wet bear was like a big, wet smelly dog stuck right up under my nose. Once I was familiar with that smell, it would always make me pause long enough to look all around me to see if my eyes could connect with what my nose had already detected. Riding or hiking downwind of a fresh pile of bear dung would do the same, especially if the creator of the poop had been feeding on salmon.

Something else changed as I continued homesteading: my sense of time. It had become less regimented. I had lost the need to know what day it was. Dates on a calendar just weren't significant anymore. Time became a more random thing. Before leaving my city life, I was always on a schedule, controlled by specific days, hours, and minutes. It's the way most people lead their life, or are led by it. After a few months homesteading, realizing I no longer needed the watch I'd worn for years, I took it off, placed it on a shelf, and never put it on again.

Living in the forest, I went to bed when I was tired, and got up when I opened my eyes after a night's sleep, awakening to bright summer sunlight, or a cold winter morning. In summer, I worked whenever I felt like it, and in winter, whenever there was available light or when weather permitted. When I was hungry I ate, and gathered food when it ran low. Out in the bush, what did numbers have to do with time? Not a thing.

What was required was knowing when important things needed to get done. I had to have firewood set for winter. I had to gather food at the right time, game meat when temperatures were cool enough to keep it from going bad, in the crispness of fall. In spring and summer, I harvested edible greens for salads, and I also collected mushrooms to put in soups and stews.

At the beginning of winter, and again just before spring break up, I hauled in supplies of flour, beans, sugar, powdered milk, coffee, and salt, enough to last for months. Before the winter snows came, the tundras, lakes, and creeks were usually already frozen hard enough to allow easier wheeler travel, but I preferred waiting, if possible, until the snows were deep enough to use the Skidoo and freighting sled for bringing in supplies. Perishables like eggs, butter, and produce I simply purchased whenever I was running low.

To think of time as consisting of light, temperature, hunger, and fatigue instead of linear mathematical calculations would have seemed so strange before, but living in the bush, reality had a very different nature.

One benefit from the more acute visual perceptions I had developed was the ability to easily spot unnatural things lying half buried in the soil amongst the trees, or lying out on the tundra. People traveling on the trail, moose hunting, going to their cabin, or just exploring often lost things off their wheelers or snow machines. Over time I found a hunting knife, sunglasses, a small bag of cheap silverware, and a box of rifle ammunition.

I also accumulated quite a collection of bungee cords. Not everyone who used them did so in such a way that they remained secure, firmly holding gear and supplies on racks, sleds, and little trailers. The rough country put people and gear to the test in many ways. On several occasions, I found small packs and boxes of personal gear just lying on the tundra. I took the first one home, and found the owner's ID inside. They lived in Hazel, so on my next trip to town, I took it to them. They were relieved to get it back, but they told me they had backtracked their trail and not been able to find it themselves. After that, I carried some red surveyors tape to tie on a found pack or parcel to make it more visible, and left it right where I found it. Hopefully, the person who lost it would come back and retrieve it.

I found all kinds of things as I wandered in the woods, too. There were several old chainsaws, corroded and useless, lying in the undergrowth. They had probably refused to start one time too many and were tossed aside. It was sad to see all the hand tools left to rot away, all the hammers, saws, and shovels. I even found a rusted-out wheelbarrow near an unfinished cabin. It was still upright, and full of organic debris, as if that had been its cargo on the day it was deserted. I checked back several times over the years to see if it was still there, and it was.

One thing I found wasn't particularly exciting or unique, but it still remains a reminder to me of the difficulties of trying to live the homestead life, and of the unknown outcomes of peoples' plans and dreams.

I found it while walking on a ridge north of my cabin. There wasn't really a trail, but for some reason the stretch of woods I was exploring had little of the dense undergrowth so common to most of the wooded areas in this part of the Alaska bush, so it was relatively easy and enjoyable to hike through. As I roamed, observing everything around me, I spied a funny little white "ring" sticking up out of the forest floor. Bending down, I slipped my finger into the little circle of hard material and gave it a tug, freeing a ceramic mug from where it must have lain for years. It was one of those very thick old coffee mugs, the kind that might have been used in a diner a long time ago. I wondered how it had gotten out there. There were no cabins or ruins visible in the area that might explain the cup's presence, but there were several old cut stumps very close to where I found it.

I sat on one of the stumps and mulled this over. I decided that whoever had cut down these spruce for firewood or building material had taken the mug full of coffee or tea to drink on a walk to the cutting site and hadn't taken it back with them afterwards, forgetting it in the details of their life. I imagined that this dirty old mug had been left in the middle of the Alaska bush just for me to find. It reminded me of something George Whiting had told me on the day we finalized our land transfer. He told me that there were secret, hidden places behind every tree if a person had the eyes to see them. I had come to fully understand what he'd meant.

I continued walking around, searching for the mug's former home, and finally discovered it, next to the post foundation, gray weathered floor platform, and two collapsed frame walls of an incomplete cabin.

The builder had erected what looked like a canvas tepee to live in while building his new home. The canvas lay in rotten tatters, the poles knocked down by repeated winter snows. Pulling the canvas aside, the remains of a fire ring that had probably provided the only warmth inside the minimal shelter was still visible. I had a feeling that construction might have ended during the first winter. Whatever the reason, the project was abandoned.

Surely, this was the mug's previous home. Scuffing around, I found several enameled plates, cruddy silverware, and a bent and dented old-fashioned coffee percolator. It was a sad scene, another dream gone belly up. I wondered if whoever had started this homestead still thought about it and regretted leaving.

I was getting hungry, so leaving the old cabin site, I walked home with my new treasure. After scrubbing it clean in hot soapy water, I brewed a pot of coffee, and enjoyed my first cupful in the fine old mug. Though it only held about three-quarters of a cup, the thickness of the mug would retain heat well, a definite plus.

Episode

14

NO MATTER WHAT YOU ARE DOING, WHERE YOU ARE GOING, or how, trails are all-important. In dense bush country, it is difficult to travel in a specific direction for very long, having to avoid tangled masses of undergrowth, blown-down trees, quagmires, and other natural pitfalls. Cleared trails are essential.

When traveling by wheeler, a small chainsaw, fueled, oiled, and sharpened goes along. It is part of the ritual of trail riding to spend some time working on it, trimming, widening, and clearing.

The vegetation covering the land is in constant flux, with changes in growth and mass being perpetual, too slow to see. But eventually, fallen trees will block a section of trail that was open the last time you came through, breaking the rhythm of the ride. Forward progress stops. You shut down your machine, climb off, and unstrap the saw from the carry rack. You crank it up and set to cutting away the branches and the section of trunk lying directly across the trail, making sure to leave enough clearance on either side for easy passage.

This isn't always properly done. Sometimes, someone in a hurry, irritated from having to stop for the second or third time to clear another fallen tree, might barely leave enough space to get through. It's easy enough to get tired of sawing away just to able to get down the trail; that's understandable, but when someone else comes scooting by and catches a front tire or bumper against the cut edge of a tree trunk or heavy root, it could be painful for the rider and damaging to the wheeler.

There are times when unexpected situations on a trail arise in sudden and surprising ways. On one journey, heading back to the cabin from town, I was riding along a part of the trail which ran along the far side of Wolf Creek Canyon, a stretch I had nicknamed the "Bear Poop Run" because of the bear scat always in evidence there, when something caught me totally off guard. I was cruising along a relatively smooth section and had just maneuvered around a familiar sharp right turn when I felt the ATV's steering go funny, coupled with a loud hissing sound from the right side. Stopping, I saw that both the front and rear right side tires were flat, with one very visible puncture in each sidewall.

Backtracking on foot down the trail, I found the reason for my dilemma. Sticking out of the low covering of small plants and eternal sphagnum moss on the edge of the trail were two points of a very old moose antler that had long ago been shed there, before a trail had ever been cut. I just happened to be the one to pass by on the correct trajectory for the exposed tines to puncture the tires. I had been bitten by the trail. Yanking the old antler from its resting place, I tossed it well off the trail.

I tried to continue on my way, but having both tires flat on the same side made it almost impossible to maintain control. Pulling up under a big old spruce, I considered the situation. Taking out the little wrench in the wheeler's tool kit that fit the lug nuts, I struggled and finally removed the front tires, swapping the two around so the flat tires were on opposing sides. I was able to make it back to the cabin that way, though not without a struggle.

Next morning, I repaired the two tires with the plug kit that had been sitting with the little tire pump in the cabin, instead of in the ATV's toolbox when I was on the trail. Pumping up the tires, I was ready to roll again. The next time I went into town, I would replace the damaged tires.

There were times when I felt that walking the overland trail would have been an easier proposition than riding, though much slower. I tried it once, walking the fifteen or so miles out to the road through the swamps and over the ridges. It got old very quickly, my feet catching on rocks and roots or getting mired down in knee-deep muck.

That was when the romance of it all quickly vanished, with the heavy pack on the return trip making a balancing act of forward movement over such terrain, leaving only the hard reality of hauling supplies by my own muscle power. Certainly the old timers did it because they had no choice, except to employ pack animals to do the job, horses or mules in summer, and dogs in winter. But then they had to add the extra chores of keeping their animals alive and healthy in the tough life they were already living in rough, dangerous territory.

But, walking the trails just for enjoyment could be an exciting and wonderful experience. I became aware of small details and new discoveries that riding on an ATV, and having to constantly watch for obstacles, didn't allow. Sometimes I didn't need an actual cut trail to follow. I often trod on land I knew no human had walked on before, but still I considered it a trail in progress if it took me someplace I might revisit.

The area I was living in wasn't like the vast tundra lands farther north I had read about, mile after mile of open land. This was a loosely interlocking jigsaw puzzle of muskeg and tree-covered ridges. I was becoming more and more familiar with the surrounding country, making mental notes of the shapes of the tundra I crossed and landmarks on the ridges such as certain large, exposed rocks and oddly shaped spruce, bent and twisted or half-fallen and jammed together.

One summer day when I was first out on the land, I decided to explore a little ridge that started just across from my five acres. After taking a big drink of spring water from the cooler in the old cabin, I walked through the trees and past the new building site, trying to visualize how it would look when my cabin was done. I crossed the main trail and continued on in the direction of the unexplored ridge. Stepping into the willow bushes, I started working my way through.

The willows I had entered proved to be a natural hedge along that part of the ridge, and once I got through them, I found myself in open forest again.

As I drifted along, finding my way between the trees, I got that familiar "being watched" feeling I had experienced so often since coming to this wild place. I had already concluded it was because this land had its own consciousness, and was aware of whatever went on. I came to believe the animals living here sensed everything too, and used that awareness in their own struggle for survival.

After traveling along the ridge for about half a mile I stopped, hearing the sound of running water. Zeroing in on it, I came to a large natural spring coming out from under the massive upturned base of a fallen spruce, a real giant. The area just beneath the great roots looming above me was a bed of very clean sand over which the spring flowed. Kneeling down and scooping a handful of the icy cold water, I drank. It tasted sweet and perfect as it chilled my mouth and throat. It was even better than the spring water at my cabin. I took handful after handful, unable to get my fill. Finally quenching my desire for this wonderful liquid, I carefully scooped out enough sand so I could fill my gallon container.

I remained crouched by the little pool, savoring the special feeling the place seemed to exude. Squatting there, the sound of the water and a slight breeze whispering through the tree tops made me feel transported to some parallel reality. It might have been what George really meant when he remarked upon secret hidden places in the trees.

I was hesitant to leave this place almost wishing that it was my land, but I realized that any changes would spoil its natural perfection. I had seen no obvious trail leading to it until I looked at the ground along the side of the fallen spruce's trunk. Animals walked right next to it, probably using the trunk for concealment to reach the spring. There was a small flattened surface across from me on the other side where they stood to drink, but I saw no clearly discernible tracks at this watering hole.

Ready to head back down the ridge, I caught a whiff of familiar animal scent on the air. Then I saw it, in that all-of-a-sudden way you sometimes see animals in the woods, instantly locking in on their position. It was a cow moose, standing only a few yards away, partially concealed in some willows. I didn't know how long she had been there, but I knew why she stood quietly waiting. Backing up slowly, I turned and walked away until I thought it was all right to stop and look back. Sure enough, she had walked up to the spring and was drinking her fill. It was nice of her to wait her turn, and I felt a strong kinship with her at that moment. Maybe if I had been carrying my pistol, which I normally did, it might have been different, the smell of the metal changing the animal's reaction. I really don't know.

Back at the cabin, I sat on the stump next to the front door and digested the whole episode, along with several large gulps of that blessed spring water. I had an overwhelming sense of well-being. My mind felt relaxed, but at the same time alert, in a way I couldn't remember experiencing before. I felt tuned into my natural wavelength. If being in these woods for such a relatively short time could do that for me, what would it be like later on down the line? I was more than willing to find out.

Episode

15

A THIN LAYER OF DUST COVERED ME, MY ATV, AND THE SUPPLIES it carried, from riding on the dirt road leading to the trail that would ultimately take me to my homestead. Once I left the road, there would be no more smooth surfaces to ride on, just tundra and wooded ridges.

It was typical weather for early June in central Alaska: chill temperatures and overcast skies. The sun, when it showed, was a muted sphere of light bearing no heat to warm the day.

As soon as I hit the trail, a cold, steady drizzle started falling. Spring break up, which had begun about a month prior, left behind plenty of water soaked into and lying on top of the muskeg tundra. My wheeler's knobby tires were flinging a mixture of water and small plants all over, changing my dusty covering to a coating of muddy streaks and bits of vegetation. By the time I reached my cabin, the ATV and I would look like a rolling swamp garden, organic matter and mud packed into and hanging from its undercarriage and my raingear.

The physical exertion of riding the ATV through this country raised a sweat even with the low temperature. The tough, rubberized material of the rain suit I was wearing held moisture in as well as keeping it out. By the time I got home, I would be soaked anyway.

This was prime moose hunting territory, and over the years hunters us-ing off-road vehicles had torn up the muskeg and done nothing to preserve it, moving instead to an unused portion to avoid the areas that had been turned to mire. The trail Ed had shown me had been discovered by others and now, it too was ruined. So, to travel unhampered through this country, there was nothing to do but learn the ins and outs to survive the journey, just as old-time riverboat pilots had learned to avoid the snags and sandbars waiting around the next bend.

After traversing miles of open muskeg and cutting across some low ridges, I rode across a wide tundra meadow until I reached Dankin Creek. A little bridge of hand-milled wooden slabs crossing the narrow, rocky stream. Riding over it this time on the heavily loaded wheeler, the boards didn't hold, two of them breaking, tipping the wheeler sideways into the creek. I ended up lying submerged in the cold flowing water, my right foot hung up under the foot peg and frame. I was able to pull it free, but not without leaving a big tear in my rubber boot and a nice gouge in my ankle.

Standing knee deep in the icy water, looking at my transportation lying in the creek like some disabled pack animal, I could feel the cold rapidly invading my body.

I did what I had done a half dozen times before in similar situations, I unhooked the bungee cords holding the wet cardboard boxes to the machine, and stacked the parcels on the far side of the creek to lighten the vehicle's weight. Clearing some stones from beneath the two wheels lying under water, and removing the broken wooden slabs from the bridge to make things easier, using all the strength I had, I tipped the wheeler back into an upright position. When I pushed the starter button, it growled to life just as I knew it would.

Climbing aboard and slipping into gear, I bounced and bumped up into the low willow bushes covering the creek bank. Leaving the engine running, I fastened the soaked boxes on the cargo racks and rode back onto the trail.

I needed to replace the broken bridge slabs, but I was too cold, and needed to get home and into some dry clothes. I would return the next day with my chainsaw to cut several rough boards and spike them into place.

After crossing the creek, I had only three or four miles of trail left before I got home. Much of that was on soggy, but passable flat ground. But I was worried that the wet cardboard boxes might come apart on the rougher, bumpy, dry ridge sections of the trail.

Taking it slow and easy, I managed to avoid shaking the boxes apart, and finally came to the short bit of trail that entered the trees surrounding my cabin. As was my way, despite being thoroughly chilled, I shut the engine off and sat in blessed silence for a minute, grateful to be home once again.

Glad to be off the trail, I soon forgot the roughness of the ride as I changed into dry clothes, bandaged my ankle, and unloaded the supplies from the barely intact boxes. Out of the three dozen eggs I had brought in wrapped in a heavy wool sweater, there were only two casualties from the harsh treatment they had received at Dankin Creek. I'd eat them in the morning.

Sitting by a freshly made fire, dry and clean, a mug of hot tea in hand, I felt renewed. There were no big chores to attend to, only to bring in some wood for the fire and a bucket of water from the spring box. Except for having to make a simple dinner, the rest of my evening was free. Tomorrow I would get to the things that needed doing, but not now.

The sound of a dry branch snapping nearby put my senses on alert. I quietly arose from my chair and slowly opened the front door a few inches just in time to see a large black bear moving through the trees. I toyed with the idea of taking it for food, but I had plenty of provisions, including some jars of canned moose meat. Besides, that bear would provide too much meat for me to preserve by canning, so much of it would spoil. I watched as it traveled deeper into the forest and disappeared.

Back in my chair at the table again, I picked up the book I had checked out from the library on my trip to town, written by a mother and daughter who had settled on the flatlands at the head of the bay more than fifty years before I had arrived. Taking time to visit with Mr. Harmon at his storage yard, I had mentioned the book. He smiled and told me he had known them, and how self-reliant and capable they were, especially for two women alone. Except for the lack of motorized equipment, they lived much the same as I was. I smiled as I read passages that I fully understood about life in this part of Alaska, though most of the people they referred to were probably long gone. I hoped I would do as well as they had.

Episode

16

LIVING OUT IN THE BUSH HAD CLEARED AWAY MY OLD WAYS OF thinking about life. I used to feel that one day rolled into the next with nothing exciting or interesting to differentiate one from another. Now, every day seemed new and unique, even if I had a continuing project to complete, or a chore to do that required daily attention. It didn't matter. Every time I stepped out of the cabin in the morning, everything seemed fresh and full of potential, a confirmation of being fully alive.

On one particular morning during my third July in the bush, I was more eager than usual to start my day. Silver salmon were running in Cold Water Slough and I was going to catch some there for the first time. The slough was located on the far side of the head of Long Bay. It was known to those who lived out this way, as well as a few longtime locals in Hazel. Monty Leer had told me about it, but not until he was sure I would "stick" in the country.

Hoisting my waterproof pack, canteen, knife, pistol, some moose jerky I had cured, and the small net I had made, I headed out the trail running between my cabin and the Waters' place.

I loved taking a walk down this path. Everything felt so right whenever I did, the feel of the air, the smells, and the quality of the light filtering through the spruce and birch trees. I even liked the way the trail felt beneath my boots. I never got that glancing over my shoulder feeling either.

Berries were in season, and they were unusually abundant this summer. I could slide some blueberries off into my hand as I walked along without breaking stride. There were also rose hips growing on scattered wild rose bushes and a few raspberry patches, if I wanted to stray off the trail a bit to pick some. It was paradise for me. Probably Waters wouldn't have liked me eating berries on what he seemed to considered his territory, but he wasn't around.

Crossing the trail at the fifty-five-gallon barrels leading to Bucky's homestead, instead of turning right toward Waters' place, I walked straight across in the direction of the bluffs, turning right on the next ridge over. Along the way, I could see several more incomplete homestead sites where others had given up, for one reason or another. Near the far end of the ridge I was walking along was a cabin platform that had never seen walls. The spruce floorboards were grayed out from numerous seasons sitting under rain, sun, and snow, but were still solid enough to stand on. From there I could see the glaciers and snowy, jagged peaks of the mountains across Long Bay. What a view it would have been through a south-facing window.

Descending the end of the ridge, the soil was worn away above and below the numerous roots extending across the trail forming natural rungs to step on or over on the way down to the narrow muskeg draw at the bottom.

Walking across that narrow tundra and over the tiny footbridge across the narrow creek in its center, I continued up the next ridge, the one that brought me to the final slopes that descended to the head of the bay. This was not such a fun part of the journey. When he had told me about the slough, Monty had sketched me a vague map of the way to go, but I had been in the area long enough to understand what he was describing. He warned me that the trail was not wide enough for a wheeler, so I'd have to walk.

I had to slip and slide beneath, through, and around thick patches of willow, alder, and devil's club. The slopes were steep, very steep, but at least the path was not on a narrow ridge like that trail up to the Leer's place, or as dangerous to run as that "other" wheeler trail. So, with numerous little bumps and scratches, about an hour later I reached the bottom of the bluff and could hike across the flats above the head of the bay to the first of two shallow creeks that needed to be crossed.

Sometimes I actually preferred going through the thick stuff, staying concealed and feeling almost protected by the foliage. It made me feel like a natural denizen of the woods. But, once out on the flats I was visible to whatever was there.

About half-way across the flats, I came across the ruins of a small cabin. It had a strange buried look to it, as if it had either grown into or out of the land. I suddenly realized I might have come across Mr. Harmon's old homestead, the one destroyed by the 1964 "Good Friday" earthquake that had done so much damage to Alaska. Supposedly, the head of the bay had settled six feet lower than it had been before the quake. That might account for the sunken appearance of the structure.

Hiking another half mile or so, I came to another cabin that looked similar to the first but this one was sunk all the way up to the window sills. The door was gone and it was weird looking inside, the soil being halfway up the walls just like on the outside. I wondered if this was the cabin the two women, the mother and daughter, had built and lived in until the mother became ill. Scrounging around for a few minutes, I dug out of the clay soil a little rusted-out, metal box, the kind a person might use to store recipes. In fact, there were a few recipes on little cards left in the box, mostly illegible and tattered. On one of them I could barely read the title "Mother Verna's Rose Hip relish." Seeing that, I knew this was their old home. I carefully slipped the old recipe into a small pocket on my little pack. I couldn't read the recipe, but it was a very real piece of homesteading history from this area. I was kind of surprised the box had been left there.

Coming to the first creek, I took off my boots and socks and waded across. Half an hour later, I reached the second stream and repeated the process. By now, I had become adept at crossing streams.

Various scents came to me on the steady light breeze coming up the bay, from different flowering plants and occasionally some animal. Once I smelled a moose nearby, and at one point I was pretty sure a bear was close. I wondered if it was my big bear, but didn't plan on finding out.

A short way past the second creek, I came to what I decided must be Cold Water Slough from the way Monty had described it. I walked out onto a smooth, almost round patch, devoid of any grasses or other vegetation. The slough curved partway around this spot on its way to the bay. Looking into the slough, I could see fish swimming upstream.

Setting my pack down, I unrolled my little net, put the loop at the end of the cord, attached to it around my wrist, and dropped it into the water. Almost instantly there was a heavy pull on it and a jerking sensation as a fine silver salmon became entangled in the netting. Pulling it out, I freed the salmon from the net, dropped it on the ground, and tossed the net back in again. A moment later, I pulled out two silvers. I continued until I had enough salmon to can for winter and a couple for fresh feasting. I had tossed back several females bulging with eggs to let them repopulate. Monty was right, this place was special and needed to be kept secret to protect the run.

I stood for a moment looking at the beautiful fish lying on the earth, sparkling silver, removed from their natural world. I felt grateful for the harvest provided by this incredible place, and being able to do what was needed to thrive. It was a privilege to be here and allowed to share in all of this, the land providing me with what I needed.

Just after cleaning the last fish, removing the head and internal bits to keep the meat fresh and to lighten my load on the way back, I heard a woofing sound across the slough in the thick brush on the other side. Someone was getting impatient and it was time to go. Speaking in a steady flat voice I made it known I was leaving and that there was still plenty for everyone. I suddenly realized what had made the ground so flat and free of plants, and quickly left the fishing grounds to the bears. Far be it for me to come between a bear and its needed protein, once I had enough for my own use.

The journey back across the creeks, the flats, and up the slopes felt very different than the way down. This time, I was carrying many pounds of freshly caught and sweet smelling fish in a pack on my back. The way back up the bluffs took well over an hour, and I felt vulnerable, knowing there were others in the woods that would find the scent of the fish very tempting. The thick underbrush didn't feel as protective as it had on the way down. The possibility of being ambushed came to mind, but I shook it off. Getting over to, and walking back up the trail to my place, my eyes and ears were working overtime. I was feeling pretty spooky by the time I reached my home, and was happy to finally get back into the cabin, latch the door, and take that pack off. It had been a great day, and I planned to fish at the slough every year.

Though I wanted to rest, I needed to start canning right away while the salmon was fresh. I would have fish for the winter, for chowder and salmon patties.

Cooking some fresh salmon steaks that night along with homemade skillet bread and canned string beans, I was totally blissed out, and ate until I couldn't eat anymore.

After dinner, I went outside to sit on my favorite stump with a cup of tea. I felt comfortable there, and more content than I had ever been. I couldn't conceive of being anywhere else at that moment or living any other kind of life. Alaska had captured me, heart and soul.

Episode

....

17

I WAS PARTWAY BACK TO MY CABIN ON THE OVERLAND TRAIL returning from an uneventful ride to town with a light load of perishables, things I never purchased in large amounts.

It was a beautiful summer day in late June. The sky was clear, and deep, deep blue, with the sun shining brightly. It had been a very dry winter and the rains of July and August were yet to come, so all the tundra was dry, which made carrying loads on the wheeler a lot easier. Instead of having to be careful where to ride to avoid the muckiest spots, I could observe more of what was going on around me.

There was a low, bare hill off to my right, about thirty feet high. For some reason, it didn't have the usual covering of trees and smaller vegetation. I had seen this mound many times, but never could come up with a reason why it was bald. On this ride, I saw something that caused me to jam on the brakes. Staring in disbelief, I sat and watched as something weird moved slowly along the top of the hill. It was a small, but brightly glowing ball of golden light!

I sat there trying to comprehend this bizarre vision, unable to figure out what it could be. But, living out in the woods had taught me one thing: you don't hesitate to deal with whatever comes along, because it could mean the difference between survival and destruction, or, in this case, solving a mystery. I pressed on the wheeler's thumb throttle and moved forward toward the hill and its strange ball of light.

Shutting down the wheeler, I got off and hiked up the slope. As I got to the top, the ball of light was still moving off to the left. Walking slowly up to it with my .44 out just in case, what I saw made me smile and shake my head. There, right in front of me was a porcupine, its quills all raised. The translucent golden brown quills had been absorbing and amplifying the sun's light, causing them to glow brightly, but now that I was right next to the slow, waddling thing, it was once again just a poor old porky. It turned its rodent head in my direction, peering at me with its squinty little eyes, not having a clue that it had been momentarily changed into a strange and mysterious object.

Something must have spooked it, maybe the noise of my machine coming along, so that it defensively raised its quills. But whatever the reason, this ordinarily innocuous little animal had been amazingly transformed.

I had come to expect unique experiences in bush Alaska, but this really topped anything I'd seen so far. As with other surprising moments, I had experienced this one by myself. But, if I'd been riding with someone else at a different speed or slightly off the trail, I might never have seen it at all. As I watched the porcupine continue on its way, its quills slowly lowered, and everything returned to normal, but what a strange vision it had been for a while.

Episode

....

18

MY SECOND WINTER IN THE BUSH STARTED SLOWLY. EVEN though it had already been very cold in late fall, there had been very little snowfall. I was still using the wheeler in early December. Riding had become rough, what little snow we'd had accentuating the now-frozen, uneven surface of the tundra and the rough ridge portions of the trail. This was very hard on the track system and skis of the snow machine, so I had to continue using the ATV.

Finally, one night near the end of December, there was a perfect snowfall, two feet of dry snow. I awoke in the morning to a sweet blanket of white covering everything. It felt like a reward for all my hard work. I actually yelled out "YEAH! YEAH!" as if my favorite team had declared a home run or touchdown. It was sometimes amusing to me how my priorities had changed out here.

The first thing I needed to do was go to town and bring back a load of bulk foods and a supply of fuel. I could carry three or four times the weight on a snow machine and sled than I could on a wheeler, so I had waited for a good snow, making do with what I had on hand. I waited until the next morning to let the snow settle down. After eating a big bowl of oatmeal with the last of my butter and a few raisins, I prepared for the journey.

Filling the snow machine fuel tank was necessary, as it had been drained for summer storage. I put the empty five-gallon fuel can in the sled, along with three others, to fill with gasoline in town. Putting my trail pack into the Skidoo's rear carrier, strapping my snowshoes on top, and hooking up the freight sled, I was ready to head out the winter trail, but this time, I had a companion.

It was a young dog I had found at the little pound in Hazel the previous September. I had named her Lucy. She appeared to be a husky/Afghan mix, with the deep chest and long legs of an Afghan and the coat and full tail of a husky.

Lucy was about four months old. The woman at the pound said that if I had come a day later, the pup would have been gone, the time limit for holding her having run out.

Lucy was sweet natured, and loved to run right from the start, which helped her fit into my way of life. She stuck close to me, even when I worked on the trees. The first few times I took her with me when I went milling, as soon as the chainsaw started up she made a beeline back to the cabin, where she hid in the outhouse. I tried tying her near the worksite, but she got all tangled up in the rope, whining and yipping until I let her loose, and back to the cabin she ran. But, wanting to be with me, she eventually summoned the courage to deal with the snarling saw and stayed around, but at a safe distance.

Lucy was with me for the first real snow of the year. I let her out into it and she happily ran, rolled, and generally fooled around, delighted with the new experience.

Now as we headed out the trail to town, I took it slow for a while, letting the young dog trot behind on the snow packed down by the snow machine and sled. But after a couple of miles, she began lagging behind, so I stopped. With a little coaxing and a hand up, Lucy overrode her mistrust of the noisy machine, and sat sideways on the seat behind me. Starting off slowly to let her get used to it, when I heard her happy little yips, I put on some speed, and together we cruised along the trail, my passenger barking as we zipped along.

Lucy didn't like being in town, though. She preferred lying low in the Cherokee while I ate my traditional breakfast at the Log Cabin Cafe and then took care of business. I'd come back to the Jeep from whatever I'd been doing to see a little round forehead and two big brown eyes watching as I returned. Her head would start jiggling, and I knew her tail was wagging at full speed

My purchases made, including some dried pig ears for Lucy to gnaw on, we headed home.

Back on the trail, sled loaded with basic provisions, cruising smoothly along, we had gotten as far as the tundra located about a mile behind my land. I had seen snow machine tracks there headed off to the left from the main trail I rode upon when I was headed to town. I had no idea whose they were, but had seen them twice last year too, one track at the beginning of winter and one toward the end.

This time, coming back in, to my right I saw a figure standing by a snow machine with the engine hood raised. Somebody was obviously having trouble, so I rode to see if I could help. I was about thirty yards away when a large dog arose from beside the stopped machine and came toward us. Lucy jumped off the back of the seat and before I could stop her, ran toward the other, larger dog. The moment she reached the animal, it lunged at her, and Lucy fell to the snow on her back, legs up in a submissive position, the other dog standing over her. I yelled out, not knowing what would happen next.

The man at the snow machine called out to his dog, "Luke, let up, let up!" and his dog backed away. I rode up on my snow machine to where Lucy was now standing quietly, watching the unknown pair.

The dog looked very wolflike to me. He had a thick silver gray coat and a long, heavy muzzle. His eyes held that eerie intelligence I had seen in films and photographs of wolves.

The man looked like something out of an old Alaska novel, except for the snow machine. He had on wool pants, a red plaid wool jacket and tall leather lace-up boots. He wore big fur mitts and a huge fur hat with ear flaps. His large wooden hauling sled carried a load of supplies, including a fifty-five-gallon drum of something, probably gasoline.

I asked if he needed some help. He told me the drive belt had broken and he needed to get to his cabin to retrieve the new one he had forgotten to stash in his snow machine's storage bin. He looked a little sheepish as he told me a mistake like this could have been a big problem if the weather was bad or he weren't so close to home.

Wanting to put him at ease, I quipped, "I'd forget my ass if it wasn't screwed on." He understood what I was doing.

He smiled, stuck out his bare hand and introduced himself. His name was Andrew Larsen. "Call me Andy."

I told him my name was Denny Caraway.

When I asked, he told me he'd been living out here for about fourteen years. When I mentioned buying George's homestead, he laughed and said he and George had been old cribbage buddies, but he hadn't seen him for years.

I wasn't familiar with cribbage, but figured it meant they knew each other well. I told him I had been living nearby for about a year and a half, adding that I was still a newcomer.

Andy said, "If you've lived out here more than a year, you're not new anymore, my friend. But just remember," he went on, "Like what I did, leaving that damned belt at the cabin, all it takes is one slip up and it could all be over. Be careful, out here, trouble's always just around the corner."

When I offered to take him to his cabin, Andy accepted, so I unhitched the sled from my snow machine to make riding easier. He got on behind, and we headed to his cabin to get the other belt. Andy's dog ran ahead and then waited for us to catch up. Lucy liked having another dog to run with, and had no trouble keeping up with Luke.

After a mile or so, Andy tapped my shoulder and pointed to a barely-noticeable gap in a heavily wooded area. As we rode closer, the dogs disappeared into the trees ahead of us. I rode into the forest on Andy's trail. It was a typical trail, quite narrow, with many twists and turns. It was a very tight path, but I managed not to bump into the many stumps and cut roots along the way. All of a sudden we were through, coming to a large cleared area, Larsen's homestead. What I saw there made my mouth drop open. I couldn't believe my eyes.

Andy's home was not a cabin, but a full-sized house, one that would not have been out of place in an upscale, suburban neighborhood. It was at least fifty feet long, and half of that length of it two stories high. There were two chimneys, one a round stovepipe and the other square, made of brick.

Andy said, "Hang on here, Denny, and I'll go get the belt."

I got off the snow machine and walked around the structure. I was just amazed to see such a building way out in the bush. It wasn't just that it was so large, it looked beautifully done, the outside walls, roof, and even the doors and windows having a crafted look to them, as if they had been custom built to a high degree.

Larsen called to me and we headed back to his machine, but I definitely wanted to return sometime to examine this incredible place thoroughly. I wondered how many trips it took him just to haul in all those chimney bricks.

As Andy worked to replace the belt, I told him his home was beautiful, and pretty damned big too.

He let out a laugh.

Yeah, the place drives me crazy. I didn't plan to keep building it like that. I just wanted a couple of rooms, but with a nice fireplace. I know a woodstove heats better, but I've always liked fireplaces, so now I have both. Once I started building, I couldn't stop. One thing led to another. I just kept adding rooms. Every time I figured I was done, I'd think of another project. I thought it was pretty much complete last year, but now I want to build a little room on top to sit in and enjoy the view. It's kind of crazy, but that's just me. Okay, the belt's on, let's crank her up.

His machine came right to life. We shook hands, and Andy promised to come visit me soon if he didn't get too busy with some project and forget. "I lose track of time pretty easily out here." I knew exactly what he meant.

What a place for a person to live in alone. I figured as long as he kept building, he wouldn't have to worry about getting bored. I wondered what it looked like inside.

As if reading my mind, he said, "Feel free to come by any time."

Ready to leave, I called to Lucy. She was reluctant to leave her new friend, but finally broke away after nuzzling Luke, and we headed back to the cabin. The idea of a hot meal and a mug of cocoa sounded really good. It had been quite a day.

Nearing our home, Lucy starting barking, knowing we were close. Racing past me, she tripped on something under the snow, rolling over several times before jumping up facing me, now totally covered with snow except for her two big brown eyes and a silly grin. I laughed so hard I nearly ran into a tree.

Episode

19

IT HAD BEEN ABOUT A MONTH SINCE I HELPED ANDY LARSEN fix his snow machine, and he hadn't come to visit me yet. I figured he was absorbed in his ongoing house-building project and had forgotten to come by, as he said he might, so I decided to take him up on his open invitation to visit. It would be good to chew the fat with him, but I also wanted to get a better look at that fancy structure he was continually enlarging.

I had recently taken a barren cow moose that was standing right out on the tundra next to my old cabin. I still needed some meat and had waited for the right moose, but it had never materialized. Since I was a full-time homesteader needing meat, I jumped at the opportunity, knowing there was no season for cow moose. I had learned this was accepted homesteader behavior unless somebody complained.

Lucy had been fascinated with the whole process. Though she ran off when I took my shot, she soon returned to watch me take care of the moose, sometimes a little too closely. It's kind of hard to dress out a moose when a furry head and busy nose keep poking right in the middle of everything.

The smells when I opened the animal really got her going. She seemed to get excited and nervous at the same time. Lucy seemed to know this was an important event.

After getting the meat processed, bagged, and in the cache, I decided to take Andy a hind quarter. It would be good to see him again. I knew Lucy would be happy to see Luke, too. They had become good friends. He had actually come visiting several times since he and Lucy had met. They would run and romp around together out on the tundra for a long hour or two before coming back to rest right outside the cabin, licking the snow off each other, and finally curling up for a nap. When I would call Lucy into the cabin for the night, Luke would stay outside for a while, probably hoping Lucy would come out again. I'd open the door and tell him, "Luke, Lucy is staying in now, so go home and come back another time." I swear I could see the disappointment on his face, as if he knew just what I was saying. He'd walk slowly away, tail hanging down, until, a short distance from the cabin, he'd start running for home.

A few days after I took the moose, Lucy and I went on a leisurely run to Andy's place to take him the hind quarter. The weather was crisp and clear, making for a pleasant run. Just before we entered Andy's trail, Lucy started running faster, dashing into the woods eager to see her friend.

I pulled up in front of Larsen's house, noticing that the small upper room Andy had mentioned was finished. Luke and Lucy were on the deck, nuzzling each other. Suddenly, They ran off through the trees, happily chasing each other.

I yelled, "Hello the cabin!" The muffled sawing noises I heard coming from inside the place stopped. A moment later, the big wooden front door opened. Andy came out and invited me in.

If the outside had piqued my interest, the interior really grabbed me. The place looked as if a master cabinet maker had built it. Andy had created everything from native spruce and birch, and it all seemed to fit together perfectly. The cabinets and interior doors were hung perfectly level and even. The wall, floor, and ceiling joints had nice handmade moldings. It was incredible. The doors were stained, and clear coated with some kind of matte finish. All the walls were made of tongue and groove boards he had made himself, and coated with a slightly amber finish. The wooden floors were painted a dark reddish brown. It was like being inside a complex wooden sculpture. I had the silly thought of asking Andy if he needed a butler, just so I could live in the place.

He proceeded to give me a tour of the whole structure. There was an interior outhouse built into one corner of the back storage room. It was outside vented and odorless. Andy told me the hole was about twelve feet deep, and probably wouldn't have to be filled in for many years with just him living there. "This way, I don't need to freeze my butt off going outside in the middle of the night in January."

He fixed us coffee and some buttered, homemade sourdough bread. I suddenly remembered the moose meat and went out to the snow machine. The two dogs were sniffing around it and I shooed them off, bringing the quarter into the little arctic entry way to keep it safe. Larsen really appreciated the meat. Spending all his time building didn't leave him much time to hunt.

He offered to cook some of it for dinner, so I stayed on, sharing the delicious, fresh wild meat, canned green beans, and more bread and butter. All the good food consumed, Andy suggested we play cribbage.

When I told him I didn't know how, he was more than happy to teach me.

Andy said he hadn't had anyone to play cribbage with since George had left, and I told him that once I learned, I hoped to give him some competition. The game came pretty easy to me, but once we began playing in earnest, Andy beat me every game we played. Still, I enjoyed myself.

Larsen showed me several plans for an outside sauna and laundry room, joined by a short connecting hallway. He'd already begun the foundation. I could think of a lot worse ways to keep busy.

By the time Lucy and I left for home, it was dark and had grown a lot colder. Just before we left the frozen tundra to enter the last stretch of trail through the woods to my cabin, I stopped to watch the aurora borealis, showing green and yellow in the winter sky. It was just amazing. Lucy sat leaning against my leg. Just as I was going to start the Skidoo to get home, I heard a wolf call in the distance, not loud, but very clear. I cupped my hands to my mouth, and tried to duplicate the sound, which seemed to be coming from the head of the bay, miles away and far below us. After several attempts at howling, there was what seemed like an answering call. We called back and forth half a dozen times, Lucy joining in, before they stopped. Either they figured out we weren't authentic wolves or they had been distracted. Either way, it made for a magical moment, though Lucy seemed to take it in stride. I cranked up the machine, and we headed for home.

Episode

20

WINTER HAD TURNED INTO SPRING AND SPRING TO SUMMER.
The cabin building was going well. During the winter, I had located a number of
beetle-killed trees that were good for milling, their wood dried out from standing dead for years. I marked them with bright surveyor's tape so I could locate
them when winter was over.

I'd been able to stay mostly to myself, keeping interactions with my neighbors to a minimum. I had fewer distractions that way, and could concentrate
more on what I had to do. I hadn't gone to town unless it was essential, but I
never felt lonely. I was healthy and fit, and my level of contentment was high. The
perfect moments I had hoped for living here had turned into perfect days. My
life was better than I could have hoped for.

Lucy was a good companion. She was almost a year old now, and had grown
quite a bit, but she was not quite through with her puppyhood, still enjoying a
good romp out on the tundra, just running around for the sheer joy of living.
She loved to run on the trail, too, and was able to keep up with me riding the
wheeler, all the way to the trailhead. She was a secure, healthy animal, and fun
to be with.

I woke up one morning in June to Lucy whining at the foot of my bed. I'd
slept later than usual, because I'd pushed my physical limits the day before, milling an impressive stack of boards.

I got out of bed, the bare floorboards unpleasantly cold under my bare feet even though it was summer. Putting my wool socks on, I gave Lucy a good scratch behind the ears and let her out to do her business and romp around a bit as she always did. I stood by the open door, admiring the scenery and breathing in the fresh morning air, a great way to wake up. The blue jays showed up just as I was going back inside and I brought a handful of dried crumbs from my home-made bread and poured them on the feeder. I watched the birds eating for a little while before I went back inside the cabin. I put food in Lucy's dish, then started making my own breakfast.

Lucy usually scratched at the door after being out for a few minutes in the morning, but not this time. I had cooked breakfast, including frying an extra egg for her food dish, eaten my meal, and still she hadn't come back. I opened the door and whistled, then loudly called her name, which usually brought her bounding back to the cabin, but not this time. I wondered if she had decided to roam a bit. As more time went by, I started to worry. Finally, putting on my boots, coat, and hat and taking the Winchester in hand, I set out to see what was up.

Walking out toward the middle of the tundra, I wasn't sure where to look, so I called out again, as loudly as I could, while looking in all directions. Nothing. I wondered if she had gone to Andy's place to see Luke, but she had never done that, not without me. Maybe she was changing her ways as she got older, but I didn't like this. She was going to get a real scolding when she showed up.

I began searching in earnest, walking down my side of the tundra to its lower reach, then back up the other side all the way to the upper end. I found nothing that could tell me where she had gone. But, at the upper end of the tundra was the beginning of a trail that meandered down to where it connected to a short trail leading to an old cabin on the edge of the bluffs. I decided to check it out. Right at the beginning of the shorter trail, in a muddy patch, were several fresh dog tracks. They looked like Lucy's. I called out, but heard no answering bark. I followed the trail to where it ran into a very narrow strip of tundra. Tracking the paw prints visible in the muddy parts of the trail, I saw that there were now several sets, overlapping each other. I didn't know of any other dogs living nearby except for Larsen's dog Luke. My stomach knotted up. A little farther down the path, the prints disappeared completely. Where to look now? I spotted some movement in the trees to my right and moved cautiously in that direction.

Taking a chance, I called out loudly to Lucy. When I did, two coyotes came dashing out of the trees where I had seen the movement, running along the edge of the tundra. They seemed bigger than the ones I used to see in the desert. One of them looked like it was favoring a leg as it ran. In a few seconds they were gone. Running to the place I had first seen them, I immediately regretted moving so quickly.

There on the ground was my poor pup. The coyotes had apparently ambushed her. She had been pretty badly torn up. Young as she was, she had not gone down easily. There were clumps of coyote fur lying around mixed with her own. She must have given one of them a good bite. I felt like firing a shot after them, but knew it would be a useless gesture. I just knelt down by Lucy's remains, a lump in my throat. I couldn't believe I hadn't heard anything while Lucy was fighting the coyotes.

Picking her up, I walked to the new cabin site. I'd be damned if I'd let those coyotes or some other predator make a meal of her. The ground around the new cabin was soft enough so I could dig easily. I dug a hole about fifty feet behind the unfinished structure, placed Lucy in the ground, stood for a quiet moment, and covered her over. I took a big rock I had uncovered digging a foundation hole and placed it at one end of her resting place. After saying a little prayer over my friend, I walked back to the old cabin, vowing never to have another dog.

When Monty had come by last fall right after I'd gotten Lucy, he'd told me I shouldn't expect to have a dog for very long out here. Monty said, "There's just too many things waiting to happen."

At the time, I'd told him I'd keep an eye on her and she'd be fine. I guess he knew what he was talking about, and that's why he didn't have a dog. Larsen's dog Luke was capable of taking care of himself, especially with his wolf blood, or maybe he had just been lucky, but I decided that for me, having a dog was not a good idea.

My heart heavy, I took a break from work, keeping to the cabin. Tomorrow, I would begin another day of building. I had a lot to do.

Episode

21

I LIKED SPRING BLACK BEAR AS A SOURCE OF FOOD, THOUGH the temperatures at that time of year, late May to mid-June, required me to jar up all the meat I could to keep it from spoiling. I hand ground meat and cut chunks for stews from my first bear and canned it using a pressure cooker and Ball jars. But I also saved several steaks and the ribs, putting them in a covered bucket in the spring box to keep them fresh.

I had found a good spot to sit and wait for a black bear. There was a small hillock, a large mound really, with willows growing all over it and one birch at its top. Sitting at the base of the birch tree, I had a clear view of a well-defined bear trail twenty-five yards away. The sphagnum moss gave me a comfortable seat while waiting for a bruin to come by, and I'd have plenty of time to make a clean shot. While there were still some soggy patches left here and there in low, shady places, the top of the mound was well drained and dry.

I was sitting comfortably with my back against the birch tree, and the warm sun in the clear sky lulled me into doing something I knew was just plain wrong. I dozed off, rifle resting across my lap.

It wasn't a sound or smell that woke me, but a strong sense of another presence that brought me around. Opening one eye a little, I immediately saw the source of that feeling. About 30 feet away, directly in front of me, was that big old brownie again. I knew it was him by a very clear diagonal scar across his snout.

He was standing on all fours, quietly observing me. I opened both eyes, careful not to look directly into his. I marveled at the enormous size of the old bruiser. Big nose wiggling, his head moving slightly, he sniffed a scent which was being carried to him by the slight breeze. I'd brought a nice piece of homemade moose jerky and a small apple with me in case I had to wait there for very long. I figured that's what he was smelling.

At that moment, I did something on pure impulse. If I hadn't already had several episodes with the big guy showing no aggression, I would never have taken the risk.

Moving as slowly as possible, I reached with my left hand into my jacket pocket. The bear's appearance changed immediately. He tensed up, crouching very slightly, the look in his eyes intensifying. I saw that his attention was focused on my moving left arm. Still he kept his position. Hoping I hadn't made a big mistake, I continued with my little plan.

Once I had the apple out, I just sat there with it cupped in my hand. His nose was working overtime as I sat there with the bit of food showing. Taking a slow intake of breath, I flipped the apple forward, where it landed about six feet from the bear. As soon as the apple left my hand, he froze in place, all his focus on the little red delicious lying on the moss. He stayed that way for a long minute before moving carefully forward, just like a dog in an uncertain situation. It was almost comical, watching this huge, powerful animal acting so cautious over a little apple. I saw his nose twitching just above the piece of fruit, then he hooked it with one long front claw, taking it into his mouth and consuming it in quick little bites, his attention on me as he did so. When he was done, he moved his ponderous head up and down as if hoping for another goody. Remembering the jerky, I repeated the process. The old bear was still cautious, but when I tossed the rest of my snack to him, he went right for the dried moose meat. When that was gone, the bear standing watching expectantly, I quietly spoke, telling him that was it, no more munchies. I slowly lifted both hands up, palms toward him to show they were empty, not really expecting him to understand such a human gesture, but he seemed to get the message.

My hands back on the old Winchester with the safety off and one in the chamber, I sat still and waited. As close as he was, if the bear decided to make me the rest of his meal I wouldn't have had time to do anything about it. Though he had never acted aggressively toward me, I wasn't feeling very skookum, falling asleep carrying food again, just like on my first trip into this country. But, as before, the big Brownie showed no bad intentions. With a little snort, probably to show his dissatisfaction at such a paltry offering, the bear turned away slowly and drifted out of sight beyond the willows. I relaxed my grip on the Winchester.

What the heck was the connection this bear had with me? He obviously considered the area I lived in part of his territory, but had decided to accept my presence here, and had never, to my knowledge, come close to the cabin. I hoped it would stay that way, and wondered how far I could go in dealing with this bear. This, to my mind, wasn't proper behavior for a wild animal. I would just have to wait and see how this played out. If he came to my cabin to spend the winter, I was in trouble.

That day's bear hunt was over. But as it turned out, I didn't have to wait very much longer to get a spring bear, though not in the usual way.

Several days later a bad bear knocked on my cabin door. I was sitting at the little wooden table early that morning, sharpening the saw chain in preparation for the day's milling. My little battery-powered radio was playing Bob Seeger's "Old Time Rock and Roll," and the volume was up pretty high.

I stopped filing, and turned the radio off. Something was up, I just wasn't sure what. Several loud thumping noises sounded on the front door, followed by some heavy scratching sounds which were definitely not human.

I stood up, moved to the back corner, picked up the Winchester, loaded a round, and waited for whatever was to come next. The cabin was so small that I felt the thumping on the door as much as heard it. Then here was some scraping on the door, like claws being dragged down the wood. I yelled as loudly as I could to scare the animal off. Everything went quiet. I stood a while, just waiting.

Cautiously, I moved toward the front door, my rifle ready. I lifted the latch with the gun's muzzle and pushed it outward. Nothing. Stepping out onto the little porch and looking to my left, I saw the source of the noises. Scarcely fifty feet away was a big black bear, maybe three hundred pounds. It was walking away very slowly, softly moaning. I had the feeling it didn't want to leave without something tasty in its belly.

I yelled hoping to run it off, but that didn't happen. The bear stopped moving, but then I saw it start to lean in my direction. I knew it was going to turn toward me, and I had to react. I swung the gun up to my shoulder, drew a quick bead behind his front leg, and snapped off a shot. That did it!

The bear spun around, biting at where the bullet had struck. I jacked another round into the chamber, took aim at the exposed chest and fired again. The bear bawled very loudly and just lay down flat on its back. I heard a whoosh of air as it released its final breath. The moment was over. George's old Winchester had done its job again.

I remained standing on the porch step a few minutes, to be sure it was over. I knew the bear was done for, but I still waited. A slight shiver run down my back. When that stopped, I went to the bear. Its fur was badly rubbed and thin, but that didn't matter. Accidently or not, I had my spring bear meat. There were going to be a lot of quart jars to fill.

Going back into the cabin, I got my knives and sharpener, and set to work field dressing, skinning, and butchering the downed animal. I took the meat into the cabin and began cutting and grinding it all up to fit into the jars for canning, with the exception of one nice roast for cooking that night in my Dutch oven, and the heart and kidneys to stash in the spring box. Getting it all done took well into the evening.

Whatever couldn't be used, guts, hide, and bones, I took far off into the trees on my wheeler and dumped for other forest animals to make use of. Two days later, there was nothing left where I had dumped the remains, except for some torn up moss and dirt.

I took several quart jars of meat to Monty, which actually made him smile.

After I told him how it had gone with the bear, he asked me if, by any chance, it had a hole in one ear.

Surprised at his question, I told him yes, it had a big hole in its right ear. I figured it had been from another bear's tooth in a fight.

Monty smiled at that, and told me there had been a black bear messing around his and Waters' homesteads for a couple of years, getting into the gardens and tearing things up in general. The bear had usually come at night, but on one daytime occasion he had gotten a shot off and knew he had hit the bear in the ear by the way the bruin had pawed at it after he had fired. The bear took off after that, and Monty figured it would stay away. But it had come by his place about a week ago, tearing up a shed to get at the compost stored inside, taking off before Monty could take a shot.

Monty said, "I think you did us all a favor, putting that bear down. I hope he cooks up tasty."

Episode

22

AND THEN THERE WERE THE BERRIES. I KNEW THERE WOULD BE berries in Alaska. George had stated that for him, they were one of the benefits of living remote, and almost made up for the bugs. He loved berries, and knew how good they were put up in jars, baked in pies or cobblers, or simply picked and eaten straight off the bush. He told me that after my first berry season, I would look forward to it every year. As usual, George was right.

My first summer, I collected a bunch of blueberries in an old saucepan. They were wonderfully fresh and sweet, and I understood what George meant. I regretted not gathering more that first year, but made up for it in the following years. They were so tasty, I could never get enough. There were many different kinds, too: blueberries, low bush cranberries, salmon berries, raspberries, and currants. They were all wonderful and were all around me.

The only ones that weren't good fresh picked were high bush cranberries, as they were called. Right off the bush they were incredibly tart, kind of like raw rhubarb, and made my mouth pucker. But made into jelly, or baked in a cobbler in my Dutch oven, they were really, really good.

In my general area, there was always a small amount of currants in season, but no major crop, so I just didn't bother harvesting them. To me, they were the aristocrats of berries, with very distinctive, subtle flavor. It was unfortunate that they didn't grow in larger numbers.

One summer, however, the currants went wild and so did I. The first time I crammed a whole handful of currants into my mouth so that the juice ran down my chin, I was hooked. They were wonderful. For as long as they were on the vine, I'd go out for a while every day during that special summer. I would think to myself, "I ought to get some milling done." But instead, I'd grab my small metal bucket and go currant picking until it was full. When the sunlight hit currants growing on the vine, they looked like little glowing rubies. I just had to pick them. That summer currants were not just a natural fruit, they were an obsession.

Of course, there were others that wanted and needed berries too. Birds and bears ate them, and I even saw squirrels eating them. It was funny to see spruce hens picking and swallowing blueberries and crow berries. I usually watched for bears, not wanting a confrontation. But when my currant fever was running, I didn't care.

Searching near the edge of the bluffs overlooking the head of the bay, I saw a huge mass of them actually hanging a few feet over the top edge of the cliff, but they were there in such a great amount, I had to try for them. As I walked toward them, off to my left I saw a full-grown black bear headed in their direction too, or so I thought. I wasn't sure if he'd seen me and ignored my presence, intent on the currants, probably just as taken as I was with the bunches of them hanging there.

My craving got the better of my common sense. I had my .44 on my hip as usual. Pulling it out, I started running at the bear, banging the pistol butt against my bucket and loudly yelling something unintelligible. I saw the bear's little eyes pop open and its jaw drop. It spun around and took off, disappearing into the willows. I didn't stop to consider what a foolish thing I had just done. The bear's reaction could have been the opposite of what he did. But at the time, it didn't matter to me. Those currants were mine. It took some care to gather them all, hanging over the bluff as they were, without slipping over the edge, but I did it. If that bear had returned, I wouldn't have noticed until he bit me on the butt.

Eventually, my currant fever subsided. I had a good supply stashed at the cabin and made good use of them, making jelly with the pressure cooker, using pint jars. I even made a jar of currant syrup.

I often made oatmeal for breakfast, just so I could add currants. I made a stew from one of my last jars of moose meat and even tossed in a handful. Heck, I even made some currant tea, which didn't turn out so well. After all that, there was just enough to make a small pastry. It wasn't a pie, but I made some dough, pouring mixed blueberries and currants on it along with some butter and sugar. Folding and pinching the edges together, I put it in my Dutch oven and baked it on the wood stove. It turned out to be so good that by evening's end it was all gone.

That was the only summer when currants grew in such abundance. Maybe that was a good thing. I might not have survived another.

I took a jar of the jelly to George on one of the visits I always tried to make when I went to town, but the rest stayed in my cabin.

Episode

23

THE CABIN FRAMING WAS COMPLETE AND WRAPPED IN TAR paper. The roof was up and covered with good asbestos shingles. There was still a lot of milling to do, even though there was already a sizeable stack of boards at the cabin site. Enough one-inch thick boards had to be made to cover all the exterior walls and the interior, once the insulation was put in. I felt satisfied with what I had already accomplished. I had mastered the process of milling, increasing the number of boards I could cut in one session.

I had just come up from the old cabin to get some work done. It was another relatively bug-free day, always a blessing out there. The winter had not provided a lot of snowfall, and the land had thoroughly dried up by July, the rainy season yet to come.

I was getting ready to start up the generator, when I heard some barking a short distance away. Standing still, I heard more barking, closer this time. I whistled, to see what would happen. A minute later, Andy Larsen's dog Luke came trotting up to me. We knew each other well. After Lucy had been taken by the coyotes, Luke came a number of times to visit her. I couldn't convey to him that she was gone, or maybe he didn't want to accept that fact. He'd hang around for a while waiting for her to show, before going home. After a half-dozen times, he accepted that she was no longer here, but he still made a few house calls for an ear scratch, a little light conversation, and a snack. This time he came right up to me and put his head against my leg. I said hello to him, patting his big furry head. He sat down and stared at me. He had a worried look in his eyes, at least that's how it appeared to me.

The thing that made Luke's visit strange was that Andy should have already gone up to Anchorage to work before break up, as he always did. I decided a visit to his place might be a good idea. Luke walked to the old cabin with me, where I fed him a big slice of bread with butter. He sucked it down like he was really hungry. I gave him another and he did the same.

I wheeled to Andy's homestead with Luke leading the way. When we got there it was quiet, no saw noise or radio playing. I knocked on the front door, and a minute later Andy opened it. He walked back inside without a word and sat on the worn old couch in the front room. I walked in and sat in a chair facing him. He still hadn't spoken to me and I was starting to feel a little edgy. Finally, I asked Andy what was going on, why he was still here.

He just said, "Why, you writing a book?"

Ignoring his cranky remark, I asked him again why he hadn't left.

He kept giving me a hard look, but then his face softened, and he told me that after he'd finished up the little third-story room, he'd begun work on the sauna and laundry. This was a lot of work, and winter had finally turned to spring, but Andy hadn't done enough to satisfy his building compulsion. The sauna was finished, but the laundry room was still incomplete, and he had just kept on sawing and hammering. By the end of spring, the laundry room was done too, but now he felt compelled to add onto his storage shed, so ....

Observing Andy while he explained how his obsession had taken control of him, I saw how scruffy and gaunt he looked, with long face stubble and unkempt hair. He was wearing rumpled, dirty clothes smelling of sweat and sawdust. I realized he had gone "bushy," which I'd heard can happen when someone has stayed too long in the woods without any human contact. I hadn't seen him for months, and I was sure no one else had either.

When Larsen told me he was almost out of fuel for the saw and wanted to borrow some from me just to finish up a few small things, I told him I thought he really needed to get to Anchorage and go to work so he could afford to stay out here next winter.

Andy paused and seemed to struggle with the idea of leaving, even though it was the rational thing to do. Finally, after letting out a heavy sigh he nodded in agreement, mentioning his food was running a little low, too. It turned out he had a little oatmeal left, and that was it. He only had Labrador and spruce needle tea to drink. The dog food had run out a couple of days ago, which explained why Luke had gulped down the bread and butter I had given him. Larsen didn't hunt, so he had no fresh meat.

Standing up, I said, "Come on, let's go to my place and get something to eat."

Without hesitation, he put on his coat and boots, and the two of us rode to my little cabin.

As we cruised down the trail, I thought about how my plans to live off by myself had not quite come around the way I'd hoped for. True, Andy was a good guy whose company I enjoyed, but that wasn't the point. Seeing how Andy had gone sour from being alone for too long a time, I decided a little human contact might not be a bad thing. My trips to Hazel hadn't done me any harm. Still, I was alone a heck of a lot more than I used to be, and that was just fine.

When we got to my cabin, I sat Andy down and started heating up the Dutch oven. I had cooked up a big pot of "goop," which was shredded meat, beans, bacon, onion, corn, and elbow macaroni all mixed together. I'd concocted the recipe when I was a young guy in college, and it made for a hearty meal. Using bear meat made it even better.

When I served it up and handed Andy a big bowlful, he started spooning it into his mouth almost nonstop. It took him just a few minutes to finish. I dished him up another bowl with a slice of buttered bread, and the same thing happened. This was getting interesting. The third bowl went a little slower, and by the time he had finished it he seemed satisfied, but he had yet another slice of buttered bread.

I gave Luke half a quart jar of bear meat, and he had followed Andy's example, finishing the rest of the jar off after giving me a pleading look I couldn't resist. Right after eating that last bowl, Andy fell asleep. I guess his full stomach had put him into hibernation mode. I had never seen anybody eat like that. I left him snoring contentedly, and went up to the new cabin site to work. Luke stayed by Andy's side.

A couple of hours later, Andy showed up and thanked me for the food. He seemed to be in a better mood and more lucid. I told him he should get up to Anchorage right away and make some winter money. That was when he mentioned his little wheeler had a bad bearing in its rear end, and he couldn't get out without the parts he needed. He had planned to get a new wheeler after he'd earned enough money. So, I said I would take him to his van early the next morning on my wheeler. He said he would walk back home and meet me there around seven a.m. the next morning. I gave him some bread, eggs, a potato, and ground coffee to have for breakfast.

The next day, I took him out to the trailhead where his old van was parked. Shaking hands, he said he'd see me next winter. I told him that was a definite, but before the next summer arrived, I'd make sure he left on time. Andy laughed and drove off with Luke, the dog's big wolfish head sticking out of the window as he barked happily.

A few weeks later when I was at the post office, there was a package notice in my post office box. It turned out to be something from Andy. Opening it in the Jeep, I was surprised to find a really nice Randall hunting knife. It had a finely made leather hilt, and a long, beautifully crafted blade. It would be a great all-around woods knife.

An enclosed note simply said: "Thanks, neighbor, see you in the winter."

Episode

24

AS I CONTINUED TO EXPLORE THE FOREST, I FOUND MORE evidence that others had tried to settle here and failed to stick. Though the actual reasons for their leaving were unknown to me, I was certain the forest itself was the major cause of their going.

I knew the bugs and bears, the isolation, and hard work were probably enough to send some packing in the direction of civilization. Perhaps some of them were physically able to cope, but they weren't mentally suited to the life. I could understand that. I'd had some moments of my own, but always managed to keep going.

I came across remnants of homesteads in various states of development. I found places only flagged for surveying, and others that'd had some woodworking on the site, some cut logs, and partial or complete foundations. There were tools left behind, shovels and axes, and mattocks for breaking ground, and on one site a couple miles from George's place, I actually found a huge old chainsaw, cruddy and ruined by years out in the weather.

Several sites still held personal possessions: clothes, books, even personal letters, all ruined by years of dampness, cold, and marauding bears. Some things were still sound though, in watertight containers and heavy plastic bags, stashed away as if their owners would be back soon. I even found a full-size, lidded metal trash can suspended under a high tree branch on a rusty, braided metal cable, out of the reach of bears, but the lid had come off and the bottom of it had rusted out. A scattered pile of almost unrecognizable debris lay underneath.

It was sad to come upon a weathered floor platform, and know that a home, with lantern lit, and woodstove crackling warm would never exist there. Someone's dreams went unfulfilled, their romantic illusions of living in the forest shattered by bug bites, constant physical labor, or who knows what. I guess sometimes the mind and body can't follow where the heart wants to lead.

I loved all the challenges living the homestead life presented and felt they made me a stronger, more competent person. It was mainly my love of the country that kept me there. That early dunking in the slough was the only time I'd had any real doubts about being able to make it. Once my initial lack of confidence and experience was replaced by the realization that I could deal with whatever came, failing never crossed my mind again.

Episode

25

ABOUT A MILE WEST OF MY HOMESTEAD, THERE WAS A VERY narrow, short strip of tundra hemmed in by heavy forest. The tundra wasn't visible unless you were right at its mouth. Walking the short distance to its end one morning, I saw the start of an overgrown footpath going into the trees. Peering up that old path as far as I could, and seeing that it hadn't been walked on for a long time, I just had to find out where it led. It wound through dense woods for at least half a mile, changing direction several times, and running along the rim of Wolf Creek Canyon for a short distance. I had no idea where it was going, and was considering letting it go and heading back to do some building, when I pushed through some willows and there before me was a small, derelict cabin. Behind it at the bottom of a short slope was a well, its thick wooden cover warped and split but still in place.

The cabin looked as if it had been deserted for many years. The walls and roof had all collapsed, heavy snow loads and one fallen spruce doing their worst. I could see that when it was new it had been a nice little structure, a snug home for whoever had built it. What was left of the windows showed them to have been handmade, and the door too, out of native spruce. It looked as if everything had been left behind. I could see what was left of the kitchen counter and sink with dishes and pots scattered about. I usually rummaged around a deserted place out of curiosity, but for some reason I felt I should just let it be. As with all the ruins I had seen, the place might still belong to someone, and it would be proper to leave it alone.

I started back toward the trail, but a few yards from the ruined cabin I spotted something, a small structure off to the right that I had missed coming in. It turned out to be a little gazebo, located right near the edge of the canyon. I could tell that at one time the brush had been trimmed to give an incredible view of the canyon and beyond. It was really huge there, wide and deep, and the canyon walls were completely vertical at that point.

The roof of the gazebo was still intact and solid, so I sat inside on the split-log bench for several minutes, enjoying the view and the sense of tranquility there. But, things to do were waiting for me, so reluctantly I left and headed back toward my own home. Still, I was curious to know more about this place.

I made a basic supply run to town three weeks later, purchased some much-needed goods, had lunch at the Cafe, and headed home again. On the way out of town, I stopped in to visit George Whiting. I often brought coffee with me, as I did this time, because we always drank some when I was there. Whenever I visited, George always met me at the door with a mug, often laced with a shot of Bailey's Irish Cream, his favorite toddy. As we talked, I asked George about the homestead I had discovered, and his face lost its normally peaceful, happy appearance. He said:

"What you found is the old homestead of my very dear friend, Larry Cole. He had settled his place the same time I did mine. I had known Larry from our fishing days, both of us having owned fishing boats for catching salmon and herring. We used to bring them right into Long Bay for processing, until we tired of the work. After that, we decided to homestead up the head of the bay. Truth is, Larry was a better, more experienced builder and he helped me get my place together."

He had a wife, Margaret, who was the apple of his eye. They were best friends and great partners. If it were possible, she loved being out in the bush even more than he did. They had, well, a sensitive way about them, being out there. They used to haul in everything they could in the winter on their snowmobile, only using it so they could haul larger loads. They hiked into town only once or twice in the summer months. Carrying heavily loaded packs back in was pretty rough work. They were true homesteaders, all right. The two of them built the sweetest little cabin I ever saw, a tribute to their capabilities and their love of the life.

The trail to their place was never wide open, just clear enough to walk on. They even left their snow machine just off the start of the trail. Somebody stole it shortly after Larry left the place, about fifteen years ago.

A year or so before Larry left the homestead, Margaret had been diagnosed with cancer. She went for several treatments up in Anchorage but they seemed to make her feel worse, so Larry honored Margaret's wishes and took her back to the homestead to live out her time on the land she loved so much. I would go over once a week or so to visit toward the end, bringing supplies from town when Larry needed to stay with her all the time.

One summer afternoon, he walked to my cabin. The life was all drained out of his face and his eyes. He told me Margaret had passed in the night, and asked if I might help put her to rest. We went to his place, Larry and I, and took Margaret from their cabin, wrapped in her favorite quilt, and buried her in the special spot they had already picked out. When she was laid to rest, Larry asked me for one more bit of help. When we were through doing what needed to be done, he walked into the cabin, hefted the big pack he had filled, shook my hand, and left. I went into town just a few days later, but Larry was gone. I never saw him again or ever went back to their place. Margaret had named it Raven's Wing.

Giving me a look, George told me that hardly anyone knew about the place, and that it would be nice if it stayed that way.

I nodded my agreement to keep quiet. As I was leaving, I said I hoped Margaret had a nice spot to rest in.

That's when George told me the last favor Larry had asked him for was help in putting up a small structure over her grave. They used to sit at that spot together on a little homemade bench and enjoy the view of the canyon. A little chill ran up my spine.

Driving back out the road, I vowed to keep my promise to George and let Raven's Wing be at peace, after one more visit.

Picking some nice wild flowers along the way, I went back to Raven's Wing one last time, and left the natural bouquet on the log bench in the gazebo after standing in respectful silence for a minute. There was no reason now for me to visit there again.

Episode

26

ONCE AGAIN, I HAD TO TAKE THE OVERLAND TRAIL TO TOWN. Preparations had become second nature. I'd take one change of socks and a T-shirt, a canteen of water, my rain suit, and the small chainsaw. I always brought along basic emergency gear, including a half roll of toilet paper, useful for a number of reasons. These went into my pack along with the extra clothes. The emergency gear consisted of fire-making materials, a space blanket, a knife, and a small folding wood saw. Not much to carry, but this would all come in very handy if I got stranded or hurt on the trail.

Of course my .44 Magnum came along, a constant companion on the trail. By day's end, it might weigh heavily on my hip, but I figured it was there to be comforting, not comfortable. It was so much easier to carry than the Winchester.

My sturdy wheeler sat outside, always ready to head out on the trail. I topped up the gas tank, checked the oil, then bungeed my gear securely on the rear rack so it wouldn't fall off somewhere on the trail. Bungee cords are indispensable. Tough but elastic, they work for all shapes and sizes of goods. I could get down-right creative at times, fastening various parcels on the racks.

I put a nail-riddled bear board over the window and one lying face up in front of the door. It sounds mean, but a bear can wreak havoc on an undefended cabin and everything inside.

I always got what I called "trail jitters" just before a journey, a mixture of excitement and nervousness. But, as soon as I started my ride, they'd fade away.

Warming up my ATV, I headed out. From the time I left the cabin to when I actually got to town was a four- to five-hour trip on an average summer's day. In winter, it was much quicker on a snow machine if snow conditions were good and the trail nicely packed.

The trails appeared slightly different every time I rode them. They were always changing, usually in minute ways, young trees growing taller, old trees falling, and various debris on the path. Sometimes there was evidence of people, often some piece of trash, paper or plastic, or some small bit off a wheeler or snow machine. Ride the trails often enough, and something is bound to break off.

If I didn't pay constant attention to the trail I was riding on, no matter what season it was, it could reach up and grab me. It might catch a front wheel or ski, spin me around, jam me up or roll me over, making me hurt and occasionally bleed for my lack of concentration.

Riding on the open tundra I could relax a bit, knowing there'd be no problem just rolling along. On higher ground, running the tree-covered ridges, I'd have to stay alert all the time. Often too narrow, strewn with rocks and knotted roots, the trails could be unforgiving to the careless traveler. No matter how many times I rode them, keeping them clear, my dues were never paid up. I never got a free ride.

Older trails, sometimes unused for years, would become overgrown with vegetation, concealing roots, snags, and rocks, silently waiting for anyone foolish enough to go that way.

As I continued my run, I came to the stretch of trail running along the rim of Wolf Creek Canyon. It always seemed an active area, with lots of animal and human sign. I was just a short distance from the new crossing over Wolf Creek. Monty and I had constructed a wood plank bridge over the creek, at a narrow place where the creek began dropping and widening into a canyon.

The main bridge poles were about sixteen feet long, and large enough in diameter to give plenty of support over the seven- or eight-foot wide creek. It was about four feet down to the normal water level. During spring break up, the water would often flood over the banks, so the heavy poles helped prevent the water from moving the bridge out of position. We did well together, Monty and I, but it was hard work getting the bridge into place.

Before we built this bridge, a quarter mile of rough, boggy ground had to be negotiated to reach the old crossing. The new bridge eliminated all that. Monty and I nailed slabs to the poles with double-headed nails. He told me it was because if a slab broke, we could easily pull the nail and replace the slab from a stack we had stashed just up trail under a big spruce.

There is a short downhill section just before the bridge. This time when I came to the top of the little slope, I was stunned to see that the bridge was gone, completely gone. I just couldn't figure who or what had done this, or why. It made no sense, but it just wasn't there. Riding down to the edge of the creek, I checked things out and saw several of the bridge slabs jammed into rocks just downstream, but nothing else. For all I knew, the rest of it was far down the canyon. On the bank where the bridge had been, I found a bunch of bent nails lying around. So somebody had done this on purpose. I was pissed. There was nothing I could do but yell, so I did. It didn't make me feel much better, though.

I still needed to get to town, so there was nothing else to do but take the rough old way around. After tossing all the bent nails I could find into the creek to prevent flat tires, I continued my ride.

About halfway to the old crossing, the left front wheel dropped down hard into a bog hole about two feet deep, concealed by matted grasses. I almost fell off, but managed to pull myself up onto the edge of the seat.

Working to get out of the hole, I gave a hard yank on the handlebar, and it broke off at the steering column, the sharp movement throwing me onto the ground. That was it, this ride was over. There was absolutely no way I could ride the ATV in its present condition. I figured the abuse the machine had taken for years on the rugged trails had finally taken its toll.

It's funny how, when a mechanical device breaks, it's worse than if you had never had it to use at all. It becomes instantly useless, a dead lump to be dealt with. I was glad Mr. Harmon wasn't there to see it. I was sure he'd have something very negative to say about modern conveniences.

Sitting next to my crippled machine, I sipped from my canteen and considered my situation. Unfortunately, all my tools were at the homestead. I'd have to go to town for the needed parts, head back to my cabin for tools, and hike out to the wheeler again. My original ATV, stashed below Monty's ridge trail in some alders near the deserted shacks, would carry me down along the bay to get to Hazel, but I'd have to hike down the ridge trail to get to it.

First though, I'd have to stash my broken wheeler in the nearby trees. I really wasn't worried about somebody coming along and doing something rude to it, but it just seemed like the right thing to do.

A short while later, I had the wheeler out of the hole and pushed into the trees enough to be well concealed. I'd had to keep correcting the front wheels by hand to keep the ATV going in the right direction. After covering it with some spruce branches and tying the little chainsaw to a high tree limb, I started on foot over and down to the shacks at the head of the bay. This was going to be a full day. I would figure out the bridge disappearance later.

It was a long stretch to get down to the shacks, but I was in pretty good shape, and covered the distance without much effort. Being on foot, I could cut across country instead of going around areas my wheeler couldn't get through.

Descending the ridge, I found the little ATV waiting for me where I'd left it, stashed in some alders under a little tarp. Even though it was pretty useless for running over swampy terrain, the ride along the bay was a piece of cake for the little rig. I had been lucky enough to hit it at low tide. When I arrived at the slough where I had taken that miserable dunking, I rode about fifty feet to the right of the trail, where there was a low-lying metal grating bridge so covered with mud that if you weren't already aware of it, you'd never know it was there. Ed had told me about it on the ride when he showed me the way out to George's place. I'd mentioned wading across the slough on that first hike to the cabin. I hadn't told him about the dunking, though.

In early afternoon, I pulled the wheeler into Walt and Mary's place where my jeep was parked. Mary was out feeding their horses and walked to say hello. I told her what had happened, and she nodded and smiled. She and Walt had probably gone through just about everything a person could, living in this country. She patted me on the shoulder and went back to the horses. She hadn't asked me if I needed any help, and that was fine. As nice a person as she was, I figured it just meant she knew I could take care of things myself, so I actually took it as a compliment. After warming up the Cherokee, I headed into town.

At the ATV shop, I learned they didn't have the parts and it would take three days to get them. So, I would just have to hang around town until they arrived. I figured it would be a drag, but it turned out okay. I rented a motel room, roamed the beaches on the seaward side of town, and hung out at the Cafe. I also spent time at the library, looking for Alaska books I hadn't read yet.

Driving to Harry's beach shanties the next afternoon, I bought a small batch of steamed clams from him. He had just come back from his "secret" clamming place across the Inlet and was busy steaming some that were left over after he had sold most of his catch in town. I walked to the beach, found a big driftwood log to lean against, opened up the newspaper-wrapped bunch of clams and took my time enjoying the tasty morsels.

A big black dog came trotting by and, smelling the clams, came and sat directly in front of me, staring intently at my food. It obviously wanted me to share, so, holding out a shelled clam to him, I was amazed when he sniffed it, gave me a disappointed look and left without eating it. No accounting for taste, I guess.

Several days later, the parts came in. With them stashed in my pack, I drove into town to gather up a few needed perishable goods, drove back up the road, parked my jeep once again at Walt and Mary's, then rode the little wheeler down the twisty trail to the beach and up the bay, until I got to the old shacks. Parking and covering the wheeler in the alders again, I hiked up that damned ridge trail carrying the full pack. In a way, it was good the ATV shop didn't have the parts right away, because I probably would have felt compelled to make the run back on the same day, which would have been a rough go.

Bypassing Waters' homestead, I hiked to my place, stopping along the way to pick some rose hips for making tea. Finally back at the cabin, I opened a jar of bear meat and made a simple little stew with an onion, a carrot, and a potato. While it was cooking, I sat half dozing on the chair. It had been a long day and I was beat. I hadn't slept well while in town. By the time I finished eating, all I wanted to do was hit the sack. Before I had a chance to do that, I was roused by the raucous jays crying out for food. I actually put the little bit of stew that was left, now cold, on their feeding place, and they did not hesitate to finish it off.

I had no idea what time it was. It could have been six thirty or eleven, but it didn't matter. I was tired, so I slept.

The next morning early, I hoofed it to the busted wheeler with the new parts, my pack jammed with the tools I figured I needed. Back at Wolf Creek, the wheeler was sitting undisturbed. It was kind of strange, repairing the ATV way out in the woods like that, but it sure was sweet when I started it up and headed home.

Back at my cabin, I unloaded the wheeler, put away the tools, and tossed the broken parts behind the cabin. Everything done, I heated some water, made a mug of tea, and plopped myself down on the stump outside the front door.

I smiled, realizing that before coming to Alaska and living this life, if I had read a story about someone in a remote place like this having to do what I'd just done to get their ATV fixed, I would have thought it a crazy thing. It would have seemed unreal, repairing a machine out in the wilderness, the way it had actually happened. Now I just accepted whatever came along, and moved on to the next situation. In the bush, anything was possible.

Episode

....

27

LIVING IN THE FOREST, I CAME TO BELIEVE THAT DAYTIME WAS for people, and nighttime belonged to the moose, bear, and other creatures. During the day I'd get my chores done, but come evening it felt right to be back in my cabin. In those months when there was no full darkness, I still felt better staying around my own place at night.

When darkness returned, riding or walking a trail at night was just plain eerie, and I tried to avoid it as much as possible. My perceptions of a route I knew by heart in the daylight were totally altered at night. Peering into the limited light of my ATV or snow machine's narrow headlight beam, gave an unnatural aspect to a journey. Even extra bright bulbs in the headlights seemed unable to break through the denser atmosphere of nighttime in the woods. The light just seemed to be absorbed beyond a limited point, so everything to the sides and behind me was pitch black.

In daylight, I'd have a better chance of spotting a situation before I was in the middle of it. At night, I wouldn't know what lay ahead until I got there. The darkness all around seemed to slide against me as I rode along, like some palpable substance instead of just air without light.

On nighttime runs, I would sometimes catch flashes of light reflected from some animal's eyes, little glowing orbs floating in the darkness. I'd never stop out of curiosity, especially if these orbs were well above ground level.

Maybe some primitive streak in me came out on this wild land at night. I would feel out of place, as if I were breaking some natural taboo by traveling in the dark. But whatever it was, it always made me edgy, and the sight of my cabin finally coming into view was always welcome indeed, though even the cabin took on an unnatural aspect in the headlights. As usual, I'd shut off the engine and sit for a brief moment of relief and satisfaction before unloading and going inside.

Settled in my cabin with the front door latched and the lamp lit, I could still feel the living energy of the forest just outside. After a nighttime journey, I sometimes felt as if I'd been followed back to the cabin by the spirit of the woods. It would linger a while, until it either no longer found me to be of any interest or knew I wasn't coming out again. At least that's the way it felt. That might sound strange, but you have to be living out there to understand that it's a very different world.

One late fall afternoon, the minimal light mostly blocked by the dense forest around me, I was on that part of the main trail which ran on my side of Wolf Creek Canyon, heading back in to the cabin. I came to a spot where the trail went across an easy little dip in the land. In my headlights, I saw something odd in the trail ahead of me. Stopping to inspect whatever it was, I quickly realized that it was a truly massive mound of bear plops. Lord knows I had seen plenty of scat before, which wasn't interesting enough to make me stop, but this pile was really impressive. I figured a truly large brown bear, crossing the trail after working its way up the steep side of the canyon on its way to higher country, had paused long enough to leave this behind. Thinking about where this scat had come from, I considered the probable size of the body that surrounded the orifice through which this huge pile of poop had exited, and that was when I asked myself why I was standing there, illuminated by the lights, night coming on, the wheeler engine rumbling in the background. I climbed back on my machine and continued the ride, marveling at the wonders of nature.

On one run in early winter, I overstayed my time in town, visiting with a retired homesteader I had met. I should already have been on the trail home, but whenever I'd make the acquaintance of an old-timer, a long hour was spent comparing experiences. By the time I got to the trailhead, it was already dark on a moonless night. I had no intention of spending the night in town, so there was nothing to do but ride the trail. I was still using the wheeler because of the lack of snow.

Everything went fine until I was about three miles or so from the cabin. I was on an alternate trail I had recently cleared on an easier piece of land to travel, when the wheeler just stopped. The headlights shut down too. I took the flashlight out of my pack and looked for the problem.

I tried, but I couldn't find the source of the problem. I finally decided to let it be until daylight came. I wanted to stay with the supplies, because the smell that even packaged food gives off might attract some interested animal. But the idea of hanging around until daylight, hungry and tired, didn't appeal. I decided to hike to the cabin and come back in the morning. The supplies would be on their own.

I felt jittery as I carefully walked down the newly finished trail. The flashlight was just adequate and no more, but the fresh cuts from trail clearing were very visible and helped me find my way. But then the flashlight started flickering and suddenly died out completely. I was in total darkness, not even a sliver of moon to show the way.

It was cold, but I was wearing insulated coveralls and bunny boots. I stood pondering what to do. I tried to walk down the trail. After stumbling around for a while, I knew I had to wait until morning, when there would be enough light to be able to make my way to the cabin. I found my way to a nice big spruce with long, low-lying branches I could lie under. Clearing a smooth place to lie on, I settled in for a long evening. It was too damned dark to search for firewood, so I had to do without. I dozed off and on, lying there listening for noises in the forest. But, everything was still, and it turned out to be a cold, boring wait.

When morning light finally came, I headed to the cabin to get warm and eat something. I immediately stoked up a good fire to get some heat going. After changing into fresh clothing and eating, I gathered up a few basic tools, and hiked back to the wheeler. I was happy to see the supplies hadn't been touched. It only took a few minutes to discover that a main wire had popped apart at a connector. All I had to do was reconnect them, and the wheeler was fine.

Episode

28

WINTER CAME EARLY ONE YEAR. THOUGH IT WAS STILL November, there was already a good layer of snow covering the frozen land.

I had decided to take Monty Leer's ridge trail down to the old shacks and retrieve my little wheeler. I wanted to bring the little beastie back to my cabin before the snow got deeper, to keep it safe and dry over the winter. I'd have to bring it in on the overland trail. Though I kept it covered with a tarp in the alders near the shacks, it would be safer tucked under the new cabin platform.

The hike out wasn't bad until I got onto the ridge trail. I made it down about a third of the way with little trouble, but the trail became very slick at that point, a coating of ice having formed beneath the thin layer of snow. I didn't know why the trail had frozen that way, but the why of it didn't matter. This was a trail that was sketchy at best, even in summer. I was well into the icy part and couldn't conceive of trying to go back up the steep trail, so it was down or nothing.

I managed to keep from sliding over the edge, hanging on to anything available on the inside of the trail, until I was almost all the way down. I was about fifty feet up from the bottom when I lost it. I had been half sitting and sliding down on my gloved hands and boot heels, when my feet went out from under me and just like a car sliding out of control, I couldn't stop myself from slipping over the edge. I slid, tumbled and bounced the last fifty feet to the bottom of the slope, landing flat on my back.

I lay there, the breath knocked out of me, waiting for some kind of pain to start somewhere in my body. But, it never did. I was basically unharmed except for a burning sensation on my cheek where I apparently had contacted some devil's club during the fall. Still lying there, with a glove off I could feel the little tips, and pulled out the ones I could grasp. Getting to my feet, I shook and brushed off all the loose snow. I was okay, and damned lucky at that.

Continuing on my way, I quickly reached the shacks and the alders where the wheeler was stashed. I immediately saw that the little tarp had been pulled off, and things didn't look right. There were big chunks bitten out of the seat, and one of the handlebar grips had been chewed up too. But I didn't see any punctures like a bear's teeth would make. There was a clear bite mark showing who had been snacking on my machine. It had been one of those free-roaming cattle living out on the grass flats and in the bushes along its edges. Well, what was chewed was chewed, and there wasn't a thing I could do. I had nothing with me in my pack to fix it.

After finally getting the cold little wheeler engine to start and warm up, I sat on the messed-up seat with the folded tarp over it, and rode out the trail that way. I'd make repairs after I got it home.

The trip out along the bay and up the switchback trail to the Sandals' compound was pretty uneventful, but there was a long stretch of ugly drift ice mixed with frozen mud scattered all over the beach, running from the corral down to the base of the trail leading up to the Sandal's parking lot, and I had to pick my way carefully to get through. It reminded me why I had gotten the larger ATV. The lack of suspension and ground clearance and the ruined seat made for a very unpleasant ride. But, I made it to the bottom of the switchback trail and took a five-minute breather. I just stood and looked around me at the bay and the glaciered mountains across the water, a gorgeous scene I never tired of. But, I had miles to go. The wheeler restarted easily, and I headed up the trail. Its surface had -some slick spots, but I rode in low gear VERY slowly and managed to make it to the top.

When I got up to the parking lot, there was an older fellow standing there, wearing an army parka and some dirty, white rubber boots. He also wore a knitted hat displaying all the colors of the rainbow. I pulled up to him and stepped off the machine, glad to be off that miserable seat. The man gave the seat a studied look, smiled and shook my extended hand. His name was Jeremy. He turned out to be one of the original Sandals. I told him what had happened to the seat. Jeremy gave it a close inspection, then told me to ride on over to a big outbuilding next to the largest house in the compound, to see if he had the means to fix it.

The place was crammed full of, well, anything and everything that might come in handy some day, like today. Jeremy rummaged around the shed and came up with a couple of pieces of dense foam. Taking a box knife from the workbench, he set about cutting a big square out of the middle of the seat, and fitted the new foam to it. When he had it all nicely trimmed, to hold it in place he took a roll of silver-gray duct tape and started covering the whole seat with it. Jeremy had added an extra layer of foam on the back half of the seat so that it appeared to be "stepped up" midway down its length. It was quite a sight when he got done, strange looking, but really cushy to sit on.

Grateful to Jeremy for fixing the wheeler's seat and thereby saving my own, I asked him if there was anything I could do for him, perhaps bring him some moose meat when next I took one.

He declined, being a total vegetarian. Putting on a serious face, and assuming a voice like Marlon Brando in *The Godfather*, he said that someday he might call on me to do something for him.

Laughing, I thanked him, and went on my way.

I rode along the dirt road, and quickly reached the trailhead, turning off the road to head out on the main trail, made easier to ride by the winter freeze. I was reasonably warm in my hooded, insulated coveralls and thick, wool gloves. The trip would be an easy go.

Things went fine along the overland trail. I went slowly to keep the wind chill down, making it easier on myself and the little ATV. The light snow cover was easy to ride through, and the few little drifts were not a problem. I loved riding over the boggy areas in their present frozen condition.

Arriving at the winter crossing over Wolf Creek, I saw the old pole bridge was in good shape, but decided to ride straight across the frozen pool instead. I don't know why I made that decision. The bridge was right there, just to my left, but the wide pool looked like it was frozen hard. I couldn't see any movement of water under the ice. So, I started across.

As soon as all four wheels on the ice and I had traveled a few feet, the ice collapsed, sending me and the wheeler into four feet of freezing, quickly flowing water.

I tried to stand up and push away from the wheeler, but slipped and went completely under, the frigid water sucking the breath out of me. The current was surprisingly strong, but I managed to grab the broken edge of the ice, stand up, and get to the side of the pool. Luckily, the water by the edge of the pool was shallow enough that I could crawl up onto the unbroken ice. I stood there, already beginning to shiver. I immediately thought of getting into the trees and starting a fire, but realized that my pack and the fire-starting supplies in it were bungeed on the back of the little wheeler, which was completely under the ice, and probably moving downstream. I also remembered that my .44 in its holster was strapped onto the front rack. The man who sold me the little wheeler had said that in a pinch it would float, the oversized tires making it buoyant. I guess he meant unless there was a sheet of ice over it.

I had to think fast. I was really starting to feel the effects of the cold water chilling me down. As quickly as I could, I stripped out of my soaked coveralls, which were already stiffening up, removed my waterlogged gloves, and stood there in my thermal underwear and bunny boots. The deep cold was affecting my thinking, but I had to decide what to do and where to go.

At first I was going to head north, to Ptarmigan Lake Lodge, but realized it was more than three miles away. But then, I remembered the cabin about a mile and a half further south down the winter trail. I had passed it many times on my snow machine. Trying to reach it was the best choice. I forced myself to start jogging, hoping the physical effort would keep me from freezing. I had never been much of a runner, but I'd never had to run to save my life before.

Walking across the pole bridge, I ran down the open winter trail, grateful the snow on its surface was hard-packed. Having to plow through thigh-deep snow or worse would have meant my end. The bunny boots were pretty clumsy to run in, but I just kept going. I had gone about half a mile, when I saw a cow moose standing right across the trail ahead of me. I didn't want to stop or have to work my way through the brush and trees on either side to go around her, so, screaming at the top of my lungs and waving my arms, I charged straight at her. I could see her eyes get big and her ears go back. Just as I about to run into her, she turned away and bolted into the trees. It could have gone either way. You just never know with moose. I kept on running.

It was getting harder to keep moving, the cold sinking deeper into me. Just when I thought I might not be able to get there, the cabin showed in the trees on the edge of a little meadow. Running across and up onto the front porch, I banged loudly on the door, but there was no answer. I had seen no smoke coming from the stove pipe. There was no lock on the door, but the wooden latch handle was missing. I felt along the top of the thick front door frame. There it was! Shivering so hard that I could barely slip the handle into its slot, I finally managed to do it, and was able to open the door. The cabin interior felt even colder than the outside temperature.

Inside with the door shut, I went to the wood stove and opened its door. Whoever owned the cabin knew how to do things right. There was a perfect little stack of paper, kindling, and small sticks in the stove. I picked up the box of wooden matches where it lay by the hearth, and took one out to strike. The first one flew out of my numb fingers, but the next one took, and I stuck it into the fire starter which caught almost immediately.

Pulling off my bunny boots, wet socks, and half-frozen long johns, I took a wool blanket off the bed and wrapped it around me. Pulling a chair over to the stove, I waited for the fire to build up, adding larger wood from the stack next to the stove as soon as it was ready. Now I could feel the heat emanating from the open door, and held the blanket out to trap the heat around me, with its bottom edge tucked under my bare feet.

By the time I had added the second batch of full-sized firewood, I was not shivering as much. The ice caked on my mustache and beard had melted away. It was a nice cabin, though I wished it was smaller so it would heat up faster.

Looking around, I saw some clothing folded on a chair and checked it out. While the canvas pants were a little tight, they would do, and the thick flannel shirt was just the right size. There were no socks that I could see, but there was a pair of worn-out slippers by the bed. They that were too small, but I managed to get my feet in, providing some protection from the cold wooden floor. There was a nice furry hat and wool coat hanging on wooden pegs. I regretted not bringing my frozen coveralls from the creek, but they would have been too awkward and heavy to carry, and would have slowed me down. I hoped I could retrieve them later.

Feeling better, I inspected the kitchen area to see what I could find. There wasn't much, but I was very hungry. Taking a small saucepan from a shelf, I went outside and packed it full of snow, heating it on the woodstove to make a cup of coffee from the jar of instant I found. There was a can of Spam, which, at that moment, might as well have been prime rib. Opening the can, I set it on the stove to thaw. When it was soft enough, I just broke off pieces from the block of homogenized meat with my fingers and ate it. By the time I had finished, exhaustion had overtaken me. Loading a couple more pieces of wood into the stove and damping it down for the night, I fell down on the bed and pulled the wool blanket over my head.

As I lay there drifting off, I said a little prayer of thanks for the cabin and my survival just before everything faded out.

The next morning I stoked up the fire, as I had done several times during the night. I made another cup of instant coffee, and ate a few pilot bread crackers with chunks of half-frozen peanut butter on them. I wrote a note to the owners of the cabin telling them what had happened, saying I would soon return the clothes, restock the wood, and replace what I had eaten. I jotted down directions to my cabin, and signed it. Putting on the coat and hat, and my dried socks and bunny boots, I headed out the door leaving the latch handle back on top of the door frame then started hiking to my cabin, still three miles away.

I kept up a steady pace, the night's sleep having refreshed me, the big hard crackers and peanut butter fueling me enough to keep going until my cabin came into view. Pausing for a moment, I stood and stared at George's sweet old place that had done so well for me. I got a lump in my throat when I realized that I had arrived in more ways than one. I had survived the challenges Alaska had confronted me with thus far, and come out okay.

For a moment I wished someone was there to share this with me, but that wasn't what this life was all about. I nodded, went into the cabin, and shut the door. Firing up the stove and warming the place took very little time. I ate some leftover moose stew and biscuits washed down with a mug full of hot tea. How good could it get? Another perfect moment.

As I sat contentedly with a second mug of tea, I made plans for the next day. Tomorrow I would use my big wheeler to take the borrowed clothes back to the cabin, cut and split up some wood, and leave a nice chunk of moose meat and a pint jar of real coffee to make up for what I ate and drank. Afterwards, I'd go check out the creek crossing for my coveralls and the little wheeler.

The cabin was still unoccupied, so I left the clothes neatly folded, and put the moose meat wrapped in foil and the coffee on the kitchen counter with a note of thanks and an invitation to visit some time. There was firewood stacked outside, so I split more than I had used, and built a new fire starter in the stove. Satisfied, I rode back to the creek.

My coveralls were still lying where I had left them, hard as wood. But walking along the creek bank for a ways, I saw no sign of the wheeler. In fact, I never did find it. It must have worked its way somewhere down the canyon and would probably never be found. I had never heard of anyone hiking in the canyon. The creek running through it and the dense undergrowth would make hiking extremely difficult, and it was supposedly full of bears, a bad combination. As soon as possible, I had to replace my lost .44 Magnum and holster, which I've always regretted losing.

With my coveralls bungeed on the back rack, I headed home. As I rode, I began feeling a little feverish and got a bad headache. By the time I got back to my cabin I felt better, though a little cough had started. Not having much of an appetite, I made a little pot of soup and had it with bread and butter, took two aspirin, and went to bed.

The next morning I awoke with a definite cold, my head all clogged, and feeling feverish again. The cough had gotten stronger. So, I took it easy for the majority of the day. That afternoon, feeling better again I made the mistake of going out into the cold weather to do some work on the new cabin. I hadn't been busy for more than an hour, but had worked up a sweat, and all of a sudden felt really dizzy and hot. Dropping my tools in the bin, I headed straight back to the old cabin, drank some hot tea, and went to bed. I tossed and turned all night, the coughing keeping me awake, and I was still up at dawn, soaked in sweat and feeling really bad. When I stood up to go relieve myself, I was so dizzy, I almost fell, so I peed in an empty jar, drank more tea and returned to bed after taking a bunch of aspirin, the only medicine I had. I awoke several times to drink some water and drop right back onto my wet sheets. I seemed to have lost all my energy, and had no appetite. The cough was deeper and just wouldn't stop.

Knowing I needed help, I managed to dress, and went out to the snow machine to go to town to see the doctor. A couple of half-hearted pulls on the starter cord made me so dizzy that I actually fell on my butt. Giving up, I made it back into the cabin. Cramming more wood into the stove, I collapsed onto my bed still in my insulated coveralls and boots, too tired to take them off. I must have just passed out.

I don't know how long I slept, but when I came around I was in a really bad way, feeling very weak, coughing loudly as I woke up. The stove had died out and the cabin was cold. Knowing I had no choice, I somehow managed to bring in a couple armfuls of wood, got the fire going, and forced myself to eat some oatmeal I cooked up. Loading up the woodstove to the max, I dropped off to sleep again after removing the old sheets, and replacing them with a heavy sleeping bag. I took off all my clothes and crawled in, falling into a restless sleep dotted with strange, eerie dreams. I managed to wake up a few times to load up the stove again. But the last time up, I came around close to peeing myself, my control slipping away. I knew I was in deep trouble, but was too far gone to go for help. Using my last resources, I took the Winchester, opened the cabin door and fired three shots, counted slowly to ten and fired three more. Making it back to my bed, I collapsed in a fit of coughing that brought up a little blood, just before blacking out.

I must have been a blessed man that day, because I woke to Monty Leer sitting me up and making me drink some hot tea. He told me I was really sick. "No duh," I think I said. Monty just grunted and dressed me in dry clothes to go to town. He got me out to his snow machine, put me on the back of its seat, and started it up. Just before taking off, he pulled my hood down tight and yelled at me to hold onto his gun belt and not let go, no matter what. I wrapped my fingers around the belt, somehow managing to hang on as Monty took off, racing at high speed when he could over the open parts of the trail, and zipping through the twisty parts.

The whole ride was a distorted blur to me. But it was finally over, and Leer got me into his truck and down to the little Hazel medical center, which had two rooms for people with serious problems who needed extended care. The next step would have been to get me up the road north to a real hospital, but I remember insisting, between hacking and sneezing, that I wanted to stay in Hazel.

Dr. Morton, the town G.P., ran a bunch of tests and x-rays. It turned out I had a major case of pneumonia, but the doc decided I could be treated adequately at the clinic. Putting me in the one open bed, he gave me a massive dose of antibiotics, and put me on intravenous fluids for hydration and nutrition and some kind of pain pills. He also put some heat packs on my chest. I was really out of it the first two days, but came around on the third, managing to down some oatmeal and Jello. I guess I was pretty healthy otherwise, and started recovering quickly, but I still had to spend a week in the clinic. By the time I was really feeling better, around the fifth day, all I could think of was getting the heck out of town and back home into the trees. I was really feeling out of my element. I guess I had gone a little feral and didn't like the situation at all. The clinic had some really obnoxious, medicinal smells that were hard to deal with.

Monty visited me several times, and I probably told him a dozen times how much I appreciated his help, which had probably saved my life. He finally said no more thanks was necessary and I should just get well and go back home. He told me to ask Dr. Morton for some medicine in case I got sick again. The doctor had no trouble giving me prescriptions for antibiotics and also some painkillers in case I got hurt out on the homestead. Being a remote homesteader had its perks.

Before I left the hospital to stay at the local motel for a few more days of rest and recovery, I had a surprise visit. Gwen O'Mara came to see me, and brought me some really wonderful chicken soup and a big slice of apple pie. It was delicious, especially after what they'd been feeding me at the clinic, and I had no trouble finishing all of it. Gwen seemed to enjoy watching me put it all away. She didn't smile, but I knew her ways. Lying back feeling satisfied, it was probably the best moment I had while recovering. The two of us carried on some small talk, Gwen sharing a little town gossip with me that was entertaining and welcome after the boring stay at the clinic. Gwen and I had become quite friendly when I was at the Cafe, though we had never socialized otherwise. But I didn't expect this visit, which, besides Monty coming by, was the only one I received. Bucky Waters certainly hadn't dropped in, which was fine by me.

Just before she left, Gwen told me she was very glad I was recovering. She hesitated a moment, then said that the town of Hazel would be the lesser if I weren't around. After she said that, we were both silent, giving each other a long deep look, until she broke away and left. I lay there thinking about what had just occurred, before falling asleep again.

A couple of days later after relaxing and keeping warm at the motel, I headed home with Monty on his snow machine, with a big load of supplies in his freight sled. I was wearing a warm, lined balaclava to keep the cold air away from my lungs. My cabin was waiting for me, and nothing had been disturbed. I spent another week mostly staying warm, but slowly getting back into working again. Soon everything was back to normal, which suited me just fine. There was always plenty to do on the homestead.

Episode

29

WHENEVER ONE SEASON CHANGED TO THE NEXT, THE AIR FELT different, the temperature dropping or rising. But there was something else I could never put my finger on that made me aware of the change.

In spring, the great melt would begin, and in summer all life was on the move, reviving itself from the stress of winter. At the start of fall, the tips of the grasses and trees would attain that first hoary edging of frost, and breath became visible. In winter, all that had been soft and loose became hard and unmoving. There was that intangible too, as if the specific essence or "spirit" of the season had come back.

Every living thing sensed when fall had returned, and their instincts prompted them to do what was necessary to survive another winter. The noisy squirrels would be filling their seed caches, and the bears would be fattening up to survive hibernation, if they were lucky. The moose just had to go through the struggle of finding enough food during the coldest months.

I had a good supply of dried and drying firewood, and would soon be harvesting a moose for winter meat, which, along with the fish I had canned, would see me through. The transformation from fall to winter would happen quickly. The river of life was moving all around me and I was a part of that flow. I had adapted to and absorbed the land's rhythms into my life, which enabled me to survive and be well.

But all the while I was in the forest, there was always the chance that my own species would remind me why I was out there by making things unpleasant, annoying, or worse. That was a year-round possibility, with no seasonal limits. Such situations served to remind me that nothing is always perfect, not even remotely.

On this particular first fall morning the air chill and clear, I had been up early, waking up filled with the need to start the search for my yearly moose. I had been completely out of game meat for almost two weeks. While I loved salmon, canned fish was only good for patties and chowder, while the taste of bean and potato soup became a boring proposition. I craved red meat, steaks, and roasts.

Game meat, at first, had tasted strong and heavy. But I soon came to appreciate its pure qualities, flavor, and richness. As one person in town said, "It's strong because it's from a wild animal with a free spirit."

So, taking a moose was in order. I would also take one black bear, but that would be in late spring or early summer. The year before I'd had no luck, missing a shot at the only bear that presented itself. There were usually a large number of black bears in my neck of the woods, but they had just not been around, at least not where I had hunted.

I ate, dressed, and geared up for the first stalk of the year. I checked the Winchester before loading it and stepping out the door. There were several areas where I could go to look for moose. One was relatively close to Bucky Waters' homestead. He had confronted me the previous fall about hunting "too close" to his place, ruining his own hunting attempts. I knew he hadn't hunted moose or bear since I'd been living there. It turned out he had gotten into trouble hunting out of season the year before I'd shown up, losing his rifle and his hunting privileges for several years, and getting a pretty stiff fine as well. If he had been discreet about it, being a homesteader it would have been okay. But the dummy had tried to sell some of the meat to an Alaska State Trooper's brother-in-law who didn't appreciate poaching, so Waters was caught. Anyway, I figured he was just taking his troubles out on me.

I spent that first fall morning observing the woods around me. I saw several moose, but they were both cows with calves. I wanted to take a young bull, or an old bull past his prime. But there weren't any that day, so I hiked the several miles back home to settle in for the rest of the day. It was just a little rustic cabin, but with my boots off, my feet up by the stove and a cup of something warm, I could just as well have been in a fancy mansion or castle, just relaxing, and feeling content.

I was still doing that, when, in mid-afternoon, I heard the sound of a small motor outside. It sounded like an ATV out on the tundra, being run pretty hard, but then it went silent. I was reluctant to leave my comfortable surroundings, but had to see what was going on.

Out on the tundra was a wheeler, its rider leaning over the gas tank, head resting on the middle of the handlebars. As I walked toward it, I heard the distinct sound of crying. I hesitated a moment, wondering what this was all about.

Moving closer, I called out to the rider, still unaware of my presence, who jerked upright with a startled look on her face. It was a woman in her early twenties, face all runny with tears, and eyes reddened. She had stopped crying momentarily when she saw me, but then she started again.

I calmed her down, telling her she was okay and not to cry, not knowing what else to say. Introducing myself and telling her my cabin was just inside the trees, I invited her in for a cup of tea. She gave me a distrustful look, so, smiling, I assured her I was pretty harmless and she was safe. She nodded her head in cautious acceptance, and restarted the wheeler. I walked back the short distance to my cabin with her following, the engine sounding strained because she kept it revved up in first gear the whole way.

Getting her settled in the cabin on George's old chair, I offered her a paper towel to dry her face. Sitting on the stump after fixing her a mug of Lipton tea and honey, I waited until she had calmed down, and asked why she was out on the tundra like that. As soon as she started talking, I regretted wanting to know.

I was staying with Bucky Waters at his place, and everything was going fine for a week or so. After that, he started acting negative about everything I said or did, so I finally started giving him back the attitude he was laying on me. It got really bad today.

She began to sob again, but finally collected herself and continued. I had the feeling there was more to this situation, but didn't want to push the poor girl.

"When I insisted he take me back to town, Bucky told me to get out. He told me to take his ATV and to leave it at the trailhead we had come in from."

The girl started crying again, but I had heard all I needed to hear. I knew Waters had brought women out to his place several times, but they had never stayed more than a week or two at the most, or so I was told. Now I understood and believed it. I figured he had brought them there to "experience the homestead life" and to bed them. When he was tired of them or they realized he was just using them, he'd take them back to town. That was bad enough, but sending this girl away alone like this was over the top. It seemed strange that he'd let her take his wheeler, but that was apparently what had happened.

Talking again, she told me she wasn't sure of the way out to the trailhead and she had nothing with her besides a few pieces of clothing in a small backpack, along with some light rain gear and a water bottle. She had nothing to protect herself with, though I doubted she would know what to do at any rate. I told her I would take her out to the trailhead the next day, and that she could relax and hang with me until morning. With no suspicious looks this time, she thanked me.

So, we spent a quiet evening together, talking and eating some salmon patties and beans for supper. Afterwards, I walked her up to the new cabin site, mainly as a distraction from her situation.

She seemed like a sweet girl, but was not much of an outdoors person from what I could tell. She had come up to Alaska for a summer adventure, and had stayed on longer. Waters had seduced her with his used car salesman charm to entice her out to his place, then dumped her when she wouldn't take any more of his crap.

We talked about life in the woods and what it took to live on a remote homestead. I taught her how to play cribbage, which we did until it grew very late. I let her have the bed, and I slept on the floor with several blankets and a sleeping bag. I woke once in the early hours to her quietly weeping. I was going to reach over and pat her on the arm, but thought the better of it. My animosity toward Waters deepened.

The next morning, I made us a hearty breakfast before getting ready to escort her out to the road. I checked the fuel tank on Waters' wheeler and had to add a couple of gallons of gas to fill it. She wouldn't have made it all the way out with the low fuel level in the machine.

It wasn't going to be an easy ride, because she really didn't know how to run the wheeler properly, so I explained the basics on operating the machine and she seemed to grasp the concepts. We got almost halfway to the trailhead, before she got stuck in a deep, mucky hole.

I looked at the machine sitting up to its engine in mire, and the girl hanging onto it. I had loaned her an old set of rubberized rain gear that was too large for her. She looked like a poor little waif sitting there waiting for rescue. She had such a helpless look on her face, I started laughing. Her face got red, but then she started laughing too.

I stood there thinking about leaving the wheeler for Bucky to retrieve, and having her ride behind me on my ATV. At that point, I really disliked the man, but wondered if I should lower myself to his level. I figured I ought to get his ATV to the trailhead. I wasn't usually a vengeful man, but I guess living out in the bush had taught me to follow my gut feelings.

Once I got the girl and her little pack on my wheeler, we continued our run to the road.

The rest of the ride was rough and bumpy, especially where the trail ran along the rim of Wolf Creek Canyon. It was dry, but full of hard places, rocks, and roots. Riding two up made things even more uncomfortable, but she was getting into the rhythm of it, the constant shifting and maneuvering, and she even walked through the roughest stretches, so things didn't go too badly and we made it to the trailhead several hours later. Before getting there though, something occurred making it a special ride in spite of the circumstances.

As we rode along the edge of a large muskeg meadow avoiding the deeper, wetter middle ground, we spotted a pair of sand hill cranes a short distance ahead of us. The tall, dun-colored birds with red heads appeared to be eating, rhythmically dipping with their long, sharp bills, and lifting their heads up to swallow. As we slowly drew near with our noisy vehicle, I expected them to take flight, but instead they walked at an angle toward us, and once they were only a few yards away, they walked alongside the wheeler, pacing us with stiff strides on their long, thin bird legs. I stopped and shut off the motor, hoping to prolong the opportunity to watch them.

After several minutes, the cranes peering at us with obvious curiosity, one of them came closer and gave the rear plastic fender a hard peck near the girl's leg. Startled, my passenger let out a little squeal. The two cranes reacted immediately. The one that had pecked the machine jumped back, stretched its neck up as high as it could, beak pointed skyward, extended its large wings and gave out a deep, loud warble, unlike anything I had ever heard from a bird. The second one followed suit, their voices joining in an unearthly duet. The two large birds made a short take-off run and winged away, both still making that strange warbling call. We watched them until they had flown out of sight.

Sitting there after their departure, we didn't speak, but exchanged a look, recognizing that we had shared a unique moment. I restarted the wheeler, and we continued on our way.

We soon arrived at the trailhead. Since she didn't have a car or truck, I offered to drive her to town, but she insisted on hitchhiking, not wanting to "cause me any more inconvenience," as she put it. I told her there wasn't much traffic, but she just smiled, then gave me a hug and a kiss on the cheek. Before she let me go, she whispered in my ear, "My name is Katie." Watching her walking down the road, I figured she needed time to be alone with her thoughts.

Climbing back on the wheeler to head home, I spotted Norm Flagler standing behind a light screen of willows next to his heavily loaded wheeler, obviously getting ready to head out to his place. Norm was a bulky man, more than six feet tall and heavily built. He had a long, wild beard on a wide face with a nose that had been broken once or twice. He was standing there staring at me, a scowl on his face, and had probably watched the whole goodbye scene.

I'd had virtually no interactions with Flagler while living in the woods. He'd first homesteaded his place the same time as Bucky and Monty Leer had started theirs, and he knew them very well, but he and Monty didn't get along. Leer said their politics were one hundred eighty degrees apart. He told me Norm didn't like people much, which was probably the main reason he lived in the bush. His twelve-by-twelve foot cabin was well below the end of the tundra near my place. I'd seen it once while exploring. It was surrounded by uncut forest, well hidden in the trees, only a chance following of his vague foot trail letting me find it at all. Monty told me Norm usually hid his wheeler in the woods, walking the last part of the way to his cabin to keep his place concealed. I never told Flagler I had been there.

My only other meeting with him was the previous winter while I was snow-shoeing on the winter trail just for fun. Norm came past my cabin riding his dilapidated old snow machine. With me standing in the trail, he was forced to stop. The snow machine engine stalled, which seemed to irritate him. Introducing myself, he responded by grumbling, "Yeah, Waters told me all about you." He cranked up his old Skidoo, I moved over, and Flagler rode around me without another word. I had wondered what Waters had told him. Now, seeing him at the trailhead, I just nodded at him and hit the trail, not waiting for a response.

I thought of heading down to see Waters and giving him a piece of my mind about the way he had treated the girl, but knew it wouldn't do any good. It wouldn't be forgotten though. Bucky had proven himself to be a real piece of work, and a number of people in town had verified my own thoughts about him when I had made a few casual inquiries. As I lay in my little bunk that night I wondered where this might lead, knowing myself well enough to realize that at some point I'd have to say something about the girl.

The next morning, I went to work on my new place. The cooling fall weather had taken care of the last remnant of insects, and I enjoyed working in cooler weather. The used wood stove I had bought and installed could be fired up when I needed to get warm. It was a good-sized stove and would easily keep my new, larger place warm in winter when the cabin was done.

I had finished putting the roof beams up, and was cutting and nailing the roof boards across them. Working on the cabin always mellowed me out. It was coming along well, and the roof would be fully covered before winter came. Though still unfinished, everything was coming out just the way I wanted it.

Laying up another roof board, I heard a wheeler coming from the direction of Waters' homestead. It stopped on the trail across from the new cabin site, and two people came walking up: Monty Leer and Bucky Waters. Seeing Waters, I could feel my neck heating up. Climbing down to be polite, I shook hands with Monty and disregarded Bucky.

Monty walked around the cabin. Still ignoring Waters, I watched Monty checking out the place. Coming back, he said to me, "Judging from the way you've built this place so far, we may be stuck with you for a while."

I smiled and said I hoped he was right. Bucky remained silent.

When I asked Monty where he was headed, he told me someone who had been visiting with Bucky had taken his wheeler without asking a couple of days ago, so they were going to see if it had been left at the trailhead.

When he said that, I turned, looked Waters right in the eyes, and said, "Oh, is that so?" His face reddened and he looked away without saying a word.

I hadn't heard Flagler's machine come past last night, but I had turned in pretty early and slept soundly. Norm hung out at Waters' place a lot, so he might have gone by and told him about seeing me and the girl at the trailhead. Turning back to Monty, I told him the machine was not at the trailhead, because I had escorted the young woman out. "I found her sitting on the wheeler near my place. She was in sad shape, lost and crying, so I let her stay at my place two nights ago and took her out to the trailhead." I could feel Waters' eyes on me as I talked. "Before we left, I put a couple of gallons of gas in the machine so she could make it all the way. It's a good thing I found her or she could have been in deep trouble."

Bucky blurted out, "If the wheeler isn't at the trailhead, then where is it?"

I told him where it was and why.

His face went beet red, with no sign of his usual smiley face. "Couldn't you get it out of the hole?"

"I probably could have, but I wanted to get the girl out to the road as quickly as I could. I figured it was the right thing to do."

Waters was really pissed now. He stood there fuming. I stood facing him, just hoping for something to happen.

But Monty broke the tension. Looking at Bucky, then back at me, he said, "Sounds like it was a good thing she came by your place. I'm sure she appreciated your help."

"Yeah," Bucky responded through gritted teeth, "Knowing her, I bet she was really grateful."

I turned and got right in his face. It was all I could do to keep from hitting him and I probably should have, but for some reason I held myself back. He had a startled look on his face as if he wasn't expecting this at all. I said, "We're done, Waters. I don't think you'll have any reason to be up here again."

Turning away, I nodded to Monty, who was obviously wondering what was going on.

Climbing up on the roof to continue building, I was glad to hear the wheeler start up and move away. A moment later, distracted by what had just happened and not having cooled down completely, I gave my thumb a good whack with the hammer. Waiting for the throbbing to start, I just sat there, listening to the wheeler sounds fading off into the distance. Not in the mood to build anymore, I climbed down, went to the old cabin, walked behind it to the rebuilt spring box and stuck my hurting thumb in the icy cold water. In spite of the pain, I was glad to be alone again.

Episode

....

30

SITTING ALONE IN THE OLD CABIN, ESPECIALLY EARLY IN THE morning, allowed me time to contemplate life. I considered the changes between my city life and living in this elemental garden. Being here allowed me greater clarity of mind, and I found myself wondering about things I hadn't considered before. I realized the excesses of the city had denied me the rhythm and balance the natural world contained, which now enhanced everything I did, no matter how basic or slight. My life here was more fulfilling on physical, emotional, and spiritual levels than it had ever been before.

I came to really enjoy and appreciate my first cup of coffee in the morning. Rather than being just a means of waking up and getting my inner wheels turning, it became a much-enjoyed ritual for me, boiling the water, scooping the grounds, and waiting while the percolator prepared the brew. The sweet, clear water from the spring box enhanced the flavor of the common, store-bought coffee. The early morning hours somehow added a feeling of contentment, while the muffled popping of firewood served to accentuate the peacefulness. Sitting there near the stove in the old wooden chair, I could feel the presence of the forest surrounding me. It was a comforting thing. All of this added to the pleasure of that early-morning cup.

I had just taken my first swallow, when there was the sound of heavy boot steps outside the cabin, and then a loud knock on the door. It was Norm Flagler.

I was surprised to see him standing there. This was the first time he had come to my place.

I invited Norm in but he declined, none too graciously. He said he and Bucky were going to do some trail work the next morning, near the Wolf Creek bridge. They had rebuilt the slab and pole bridge after it disappeared, staking the poles and spiking the slabs, so the bridge would be locked in place. It wasn't going anywhere. Norm gruffly told me I should come help with the trail work. I just nodded. Without another word, he turned and walked away.

I sat back down in my chair my mellow mood all gone, and considered the brief interaction with Norm. I knew something was up, I just didn't know what. I would go out the next day, but I planned to be on my guard around those two.

Dismissing the strange visit by Flagler, I focused on the work to be done. I walked up to the new cabin site to continue putting up the outer wall boards I had started working on the day before. It was really great, putting a "skin" on the cabin's frame. Despite all the work I had done already, putting the first few wall boards up somehow brought everything together, and made the cabin more of a reality.

When I got up to the cabin site, I discovered it had been visited by a bear. The plastic storage bin I kept my tools in had been dragged some distance from where I had placed it and had been chewed on. That was okay, but I discovered that the bruin had also messed around with the generator. It had punctured the plastic gas tank, efficiently draining it of all fuel. The plastic handle had been gnawed off the pull start cord too, allowing it to slip into the starter mechanism, rendering it useless. I could fix the problems by improvising a new pull start handle, and plugging the tooth holes in the gas tank. A little work time might be wasted, but I was okay with that. I knew I would get everything done. Going back to the old cabin, I made a mug of tea. It was an unusually warm day, so leaving the cabin door open I sat sipping my tea, enjoying the moment.

Returning to the worksite with what I needed to fix things, I made the repairs to the generator. It took several hours, and I decided to spend the rest of the day hanging out at the old cabin.

After breakfast early the next morning, I put on my old canvas work pants, worn flannel shirt, and boots expecting a full day's work. By now, all my clothes were in the same worn-out condition as the ones Monty wore: ripped, with smears of dried sap on them. I strapped on my revolver, took along my canteen and a couple of Spam sandwiches, and headed out to the bridge, my little trail saw bungeed to the wheeler's front rack.

The trail was surrounded with the thick, green foliage of summer. As always, I stayed alert as I passed through, anticipating somebody with thick fur and a cranky attitude being concealed there. But, as usual nothing occurred. I knew very well that if I became complacent, not giving the bush its due respect, that was when it could jump up and bite me.

When I arrived at the bridge, the guys weren't there yet. Half an hour later, while I was pondering what they might want to do to the trail, Flagler showed up on his decrepit-looking wheeler. He didn't take decent care of his equipment and it showed, but the wheels still kept turning. He sat there looking at me as if my presence was unexpected.

I walked to him, nodded, and asked if Bucky was coming along soon.

He just grunted and said he didn't think I would show.

I asked him why he thought that, a little heat building in my neck, not a good sign.

He told me in a loud, growly voice that Bucky had told him I refused to do any work on the trails, and that the two of them should make sure I did since I was using them regularly.

My anger was rising. Obviously Bucky was setting me up for a confrontation with Norm, knowing how he disliked new people coming into the area. I told Norm he shouldn't take everything he was told at face value, because it could put him in an awkward situation.

Norm's face turned a very deep red. He tried to say something, but just sputtered and snorted instead.

At that very moment Bucky showed up, coming down the short slope before the bridge a little too quickly. He had to stop suddenly to avoid hitting the back of Norm's wheeler.

Bucky shut off his machine and sat there, looking from Norm to me and back again. His eyes seemed to gleam with satisfaction. He probably figured his plan had worked.

As soon as Norm had told me what Bucky had insinuated to him about me, I knew what was happening. Over time, I had talked to a number of people in town after what the store clerk had told me about Waters early on. I wanted to make sure this wasn't just some grudge the clerk had against him. The general consensus from the folks I asked was that Bucky was an okay guy, but I really shouldn't get involved in his schemes or loan him any money. Someone must have tipped Waters off that I was asking around about him, and this was his way of getting even.

My suspicions were verified when, after some words were passed between Bucky and myself, he told me I'd be better off if I kept my ignorant mouth shut.

Norm was silent now, just glaring at me. Oh yeah, that was it. This wasn't about trail work. Waters had just wanted to get me out here, with Norm as backup. That was when I went all cold inside. I backed off a few steps, actually stepping onto the first slab of the little bridge, unsnapped the safety strap of the .44's holster and told the two of them if they wanted to settle this thing, they could step right up and get to it, all the while wondering where this was coming from inside me.

It's amazing how quickly the right thing being said can totally defuse a situation. They both clammed up, their faces going blank. I must have looked like I meant what I said, and truth to tell I did mean it. Here I was in the middle of the bush with two uncivilized characters who were obviously bent on making trouble for me. I wasn't sure what they were capable of, or what exactly they had in mind, but at that particular moment I really didn't care.

When it became obvious that neither of them was going to do anything, I walked up to within inches of big Norm's face and told him if he was feeling froggy, he could just start jumping.

With that expressionless look still on his face, he turned and walked away a few feet, practicing avoidance behavior I guess.

Bucky had moved closer to me. I had my back to him, but I turned to face him. He put his open hand on my chest and started to say something, but I told him in a very flat voice he'd better take his hand off my chest. He froze, his hand still in place. I repeated what I had said in the same flat voice, putting my hand on the grip of my pistol. He jerked his hand away as if it had been burnt. At that point, the whole scene just stopped as if time had ceased to flow. Norm had his back to me and Bucky was still facing me, his arms now hanging limply at his sides.

For a moment, it almost felt as if the whole forest was focused on this one tiny focal point of heavy energy. I couldn't remember ever having been this angry.

I looked back and forth between the two a few times. Speaking as calmly as I could, I told them that if and when I felt like working on the trail I would, but if they ever tried to tell me I had to do anything I would finish what had been started. I got on my wheeler and rode back up the trail toward home.

When I got back to my cabin, I was still all riled up. There was about a cord of wood next to the cabin waiting to be split, so I took my maul and went at it. When I'd done about half of it, I had settled down and my adrenaline flow subsided. I went inside to eat the Spam sandwiches.

Later that afternoon, I heard some wheelers going by, their engine noises fading out as they continued on their way. It was undoubtedly Bucky and Norm, but I didn't care. I thought about Norm Flagler. Though I didn't expect that he and I would ever do any close bonding, I decided that he had let Waters talk him into the bridge incident and that he was now aware he had been used. I would let things pass with him. But Waters, well, that was a very different situation. He was on my permanent black list and I just knew that sometime he and I would have to settle our differences. But for now, maybe I would have fewer hassles with Waters.

I had established myself out here in the bush, but I'd come to realize that even in this wilderness I still had to deal with other people's BS. Still, I had found more peace here than I had ever known before. I would have to be content with that.

I went back up to the new cabin site to continue putting up the wall covering. When I ran out of boards, I'd go into the woods and continue milling.

Episode

31

DURING THE SUMMER MONTHS, TOURISTS FROM THE LOWER 48 States would come to Hazel for the good fishing in the waters off her coastal side and in the nearby streams and rivers accessible by road and boat. Alaska fishing has always been a big draw for visitors.

But, there were also young people who came north for the adventure of working in Alaska for the summer. Many of them were suburban college kids. Most of them found the available seasonal work heavy and messy. They could take just so much fish processing work, with long hours of being hip deep in fish guts, canning the fish onboard the big processing ship moored off shore. So, they would quit, spending all their time either hiking around, casually exploring the country or sitting and drinking beers at the local pubs, acting as if they were now true Alaskans after a few days or weeks dealing with fish slime. The locals in Hazel found their behavior occasionally amusing, but always obnoxious.

I was glad to be living remote and away from the foolishness when this influx of cheechakos was in town. Occasionally, pairs or small groups of these naïve youngsters would find their way into our territory, usually by getting lost. Luckily, it wasn't a common occurrence, so I didn't have to waste too much of my time showing them the way back out, after feeding them and answering a load of wide-eyed questions.

When he had the chance, Bucky would bring some of these enthusiastic and gullible kids out to his place under the guise of learning what it was like to homestead. In truth, he was just getting free labor for things he didn't want to do himself, mostly cleaning up milling sites, clearing brush, digging holes, or working in the garden. Monty had done the same, though he would let these young people know what was involved. But, it always ended the same way it did with Waters' recruits.

Waters' little deception usually ended in a few days when the innocents had enough of broken blisters, splinters, sore backs and numerous bug bites, not to mention a lack of decent food. In other words, the reality of life in the bush was a poor replacement for what they had expected, though I'm not sure if they had a clear idea of what to expect. Waters would try to get as much work out of these kids as he could until they caught on and found their way back to town.

There was one young man who stayed way too long. His name was Dave. He managed to work for Waters a few days, but then he came wandering my way asking for a little food to fill his empty gut. I immediately noticed that young Dave was pretty ripe, even though Waters had a nice outside shower stall. Yeah, the boy was stinky. His clothes looked like they hadn't been cleaned in a while either.

I obliged Dave with some leftover stew and bread in a plastic container, mainly just to get his smell out of my cabin. Dave told me that Bucky mentioned I might need some help at my place, and had told him how to get here. I told Dave that Waters was mistaken and he didn't seem too upset by that. Once he had the food, Dave left right away without any sort of a thank you. I figured that was the end of it, but things don't always go as expected.

Instead of going back to town, Dave took a little time to explore the area around our homesteads. Discovering one of several nearby boarded-up cabins, he took up residence there. It was one of the places owned by people who rarely came out here, but it was still their property. The one Dave was squatting in had some canned and dry food, propane, and other supplies. He somehow decided he had the right to commandeer the place.

Andy Larsen visited me several weeks after Dave had come by my cabin. Andy had returned the winter after I had fed him. He seemed to have fully recovered from his case of "bushiness." But he was still working on his "mansion in the woods." He had purchased a new wheeler and brought out extra food, planning to spend most of the summer getting things done. Andy was his usual amiable self, but still preferred being alone, so this visit was unexpected.

We talked about things in general, weather, building, and such, but then he mentioned a "raggedy-assed, smelly young fella" he had met on the trail near his place. This guy had said that I'd told him he could move into the cabin he was squatting in, but he had run out of food and asked Andy if he could "borrow" some.

Andy, being the man that he was, took Dave back to his homestead. Larsen remarked on how smelly Dave really was at such close range.

I nodded knowingly. At that point he was tagged "Stinky Dave." As "Stinky" had done with me, he took the food offered by Andy and left without a word.

Andy smiled when he told me Luke had kept a distance from Dave, growling quietly every time Dave tried to pet him. We decided that Luke was an intelligent dog. After we agreed to keep each other posted on the situation, Andy headed home.

A few days later while I was out milling wood, someone walked into my cabin, took some food, my old work boots, and a pair of socks. It could only have been Dave. That was bad enough, but it was the last straw when I discovered he had taken one of my last two rolls of toilet paper before he departed.

Early the next morning, I rode around to everybody's cabins, Waters' included, suggesting a get-together to discuss the Stinky Dave situation. Luckily, everyone was home. We all met at my place that afternoon, except for Bucky. He later told Monty he was too busy to deal with this kind of petty stuff. That was funny, considering he was the one who had brought Dave out in the first place. During our palaver, we discovered that he had "borrowed" things from all of us.

The decision was unanimous, Dave had to leave, one way or another. We didn't know how far he was willing to go to remain in the woods, and we didn't want to wait to find out. That might sound overly dramatic, but living out here we were left to take care of our own business. That part of the Alaska way of life still existed.

It was decided that early the next morning Monty and I would go looking for Dave. That's when we found him sleeping in the "borrowed" cabin. The smell of wood smoke is unmistakable, and it led us right to him. Finding him there in someone else's place made it easier for us to deal with him. He had made a mess of the cabin. I guess we were serious enough in our demeanor that he took it to heart. He didn't resist. The .44s on our hips probably emphasized our mood.

We had Dave gather up the few belongings that were actually his, put him up behind Monty on the wheeler, (we had flipped a coin) and took him to the top of the ridge trail behind Monty's place. We walked him down to the bay and several miles further along the trail, to where he couldn't miss the rest of the way back to the road and town. Monty and I stood for a long moment glaring at him, before Monty strongly advised him not to come back into the area again. Stinky Dave didn't hesitate; he turned and walked away without a word. We never saw or smelled him again.

Episode

32

THERE WAS A PAIR OF YOUNG GUYS WHO CAME OUT TO MY PART of the bush. I didn't expect them to make it, considering the way they arrived. It was probably fortunate for them that the memory of Stinky Dave had faded out, as they were better received than they might have been.

Having milled boards and worked on the new cabin for several weeks straight, I decided, one July morning, to take a break and hike down a little-used trail close by my place. I walked south to where the old trail started. It ran down to edge of the bluffs. At its lower end was a cabin on a point of land that gave a breathtaking view of Long Bay and the mountains beyond. The cabin, a two-storied affair with heavy sliding glass doors on one end opening onto a little deck, was sturdily built by the owner, a Mr. Simmons, who had passed away several years before I bought my land.

He had been given the handle "Slow Poke Simmons" by the other homesteaders. Apparently, he would run the trail to his cabin at a very slow rate of speed, riding the same type of wheeler as the first one I'd tried to use. But, going at a relaxed pace, Mr. Simmons spared himself the abuse pushing the hard-tailed little wheeler would have created.

Trail conditions back then, years before I had arrived, were much better, most of the boggy places not having been created yet. Still, he just putt-putted over and around the rougher spots, stopping every few miles to have a can of beer, which was a beverage he supposedly enjoyed on a steady basis. It had taken him more than five years to complete his place. At least that's the way the story went, according to Monty.

They couldn't tell me how he had transported the large, heavy glass doors out there. He didn't have a trailer to lay them on and no one saw him bring them out, but there they were, solidly in place so he could sit inside or on his deck and look out upon that marvelous view in comfort, probably with a fresh brew in hand. I was sorry I never got to meet him. He sounded like an interesting fellow.

I occasionally walked down this trail to the Simmons place because I just liked the way it wandered easily through the trees. It was as natural a route through the forest as I had traveled on. It was on this hike that I discovered the boys.

I carried my rifle with me when I walked the Simmons trail as the country along the edge of the bluffs, for whatever reason, had lots of bears around. Maybe they liked the nice views too.

On this particular hike, as I neared the cabin I heard voices engaged in a subdued conversation. I quietly moved closer to see what was going on. Standing behind a large spruce tree across from the cabin, I saw two young guys on the front deck. It looked as though they were trying to find a way to open the locked sliding doors. They didn't seem to have any guns with them. One of them went around behind the place, and I took the opportunity to sneak up on the one still standing on the deck. I snapped at him in a loud rough voice, "What are you doing here?"

I had heard about people jumping off the ground when frightened, but this was the first time I had actually seen it happen. He jumped about a foot off the deck, landing on the ground next to it facing me, a startled look in his eyes. I was amused by his reaction, and it was difficult to keep from smiling. The guy called to his partner. When the other one came around the corner, the sight of me standing there, rifle in hand, had an effect on him too. My appearance must have added to their concern. My beard and hair were long and bushy, and my clothes ragged. I made them sit on the edge of the deck and demanded an explanation of why they were snooping around the place. Once I knew their situation, I could understand why they were there.

They were two brothers who had come out from Connecticut to enjoy a road trip to Alaska. They'd bought a camper van and had been traveling for more than a month through the Lower 48 before they made it through Canada, finally ending up in Hazel. It was the first time they had ever left Connecticut.

The brothers had fallen in love with Alaska, something I could certainly understand. As they described their reactions to the place, they were like echoes of my own feelings when I had first arrived.

The boys had decided they wanted to try and make a place for themselves. Like me, they had located someone who had remote land to sell. Unfortunately, their seller hadn't been as helpful, knowledgeable, or honest as George Whiting had been with me.

With the skimpy amount of information they had been given on how to find the land, and a definite lack of decent equipment and supplies, they had started out from town two days before I came across them. Unable to find a trail up the bluffs, they had wandered around aimlessly down at the head of the bay, sleeping at the old "ruins" in front of Monty's ridge trail.

Finally, they had just worked their way up the bluff through the thick under-growth and had ended up right below the Simmons cabin. They were scratched and bug bitten, almost out of food and water, and exhausted. It turned out to be a good thing that I had come upon them.

I took them to Simmons' spring box, and let them drink their fill. Afterwards, we sat on the deck and talked. When they handed me the map the landowner had given them showing the location of the land he was selling, I thought I might have been to the place once. It was way beyond my land, deep into heavy brush close to the rim of Wolf Creek Canyon, but farther down, below the trail to my place. I had only come across it by chance. It would be a hard go to settle there, nothing like my homestead site.

When I explained what the situation was, how hard it would be to bring in gear and supplies, and how, when spring break up came they would not be able to travel for weeks, they weren't discouraged at all. They seemed to think that this made it all the more exciting. I just let them be, figuring they would find out by themselves in time. I didn't think they would make it anyway.

After suggesting they stay in their tent on the deck for the night, I invited them to come to breakfast the next morning, and gave them simple directions to my place.

Walking home, I decided it might be nice to have a visit with someone other than my homestead neighbors. At least I hoped so. I had been pretty much alone for weeks. That night, I prepared the sourdough starter for pancakes.

The morning was starting to wear on, and the boys hadn't shown yet. The food was waiting, staying warm on the wood stove. I went outside, prepared to go find out what was going on, when I heard faint voices below my place. I called out and got a response. I continued to yell until they finally came into view. They apparently had gone left when they should have gone right at the lower tundra, and wandered around trying to figure things out.

They were just as rough-looking, scratched, bug-bitten and dirty as when I had last seen them, so I took them out back of the cabin with a pot of hot water, soap, and towels for washing. Cleaned up, they came into the cabin and sat down expectantly at the table. When I put the plates of flapjacks, eggs and sliced fried Spam in front of them, it was as if I had thrown raw meat into a pool full of alligators. They started stuffing everything they could into their mouths, looking like squirrels with a bunch of acorns in their cheeks. It really was amazing. I never even put a thing on my plate. There was a half-pint jar of my precious currant jelly. It was the last of the delicious stuff. These two characters actually ignored the syrup, and kept spreading the jelly on their cakes until it was all gone. They drank all the coffee, except for the one cup I sipped as I sat watching them consume everything on the table. I half expected them to eat the plates. They made Andy's eating of my goop seem a minor event.

All finished, and their bellies full, they started talking about all their plans for getting set up after buying the land. They hadn't even seen it yet! I just nodded and smiled, figuring they'd be gone in a few days. They planned on finding the land the next day and, thinking it might discourage them to see how remote and overgrown the place was, I offered to show them the way. The brothers were quick to accept my offer.

If ever there was a pair of cheechakos greener than I had been, it was these two. They asked if they could stay outside my cabin that night, and I said it would be all right, but silently wondered if I had enough food to feed them for another day. I was glad they wanted to spend the night outside, as the younger brother didn't mind releasing gas without warning whenever conditions demanded, which seemed to be on a regular basis.

I hadn't intended to ask them to do anything, but remembering how my last bit of currant jelly has been sucked down their gullets, I suggested that splitting some wood would be appreciated, while I went to work on my new cabin. When they heard I was building a cabin, they got all excited to see it, so my plan to get a chance to be alone had backfired. I was trapped, so reluctantly I took them with me to the new site. They were all gung-ho to help me, but I really didn't want them to do anything. I had no idea what they were capable of, and felt they might jinx the place if they did. It got awkward. Again, I suggested they split some wood, as that would help me a lot. They reluctantly agreed and went back to the old cabin.

I got a few hours of work done, before checking on the boys to see if they were doing okay. I needn't have worried. When I got to the cabin, they were laid out in their little tent on sleeping bags, snoozing away. There was a tiny pile of freshly split wood next to the cabin. I went in to make a pot of coffee and have a cup quietly by myself. The loaf of the bread I had made several days before was now almost gone. What was left was sitting on the table along with a partial stick of butter. I took the butter back to its bucket in the spring box, hid the bread on a shelf behind some books, and went out to rouse the boys. As I stood there watching them snoring away, considering whether or not to wake them, one of them farted loudly in his sleep. Zipping up their tent door quickly, I went back to the building site and got some more work done.

They showed up about an hour later, but basically ignoring them, I kept on working. They walked around talking to each other, then went back to the cabin. Knocking off building a little while later, I rejoined them, but not having any desire to engage in small talk, I took to splitting more firewood. They must have felt guilty watching me, and began stacking the wood.

Done for the day, I washed up, then went into the cabin to make dinner, the boys trailing behind. I made a pot of salmon chowder with some of my canned fish. That disappeared too, along with the rest of the bread. When they asked if there was any more bread. I curtly told them there wasn't.

The next morning, after a meager breakfast of oatmeal and coffee, we headed out. The homestead land they were looking for was about three miles from my place. I led the way until we came to a large, wet piece of tundra that had to be crossed. They hesitated. Earlier, I'd noticed that one of them was wearing tennis shoes and the other had on short boots. I knew they were not going to be happy with this hike. By the time we crossed the tundra, their feet were totally soaked and cold. But we soon hit drier ground.

The boys and I had to bushwhack through some heavy brush, with no actual trail to guide us. If I hadn't been there once before in my wanderings, we might never have found the place. Eventually, we came to a vague trail leading to a site that I thought was the parcel they were looking for. We located one of the corner markers, a state survey monument that had numbers corresponding with what the landowner had written down on the map.

The parcel was pretty typical for the area, covered with lots of middle-sized spruce mixed with birches and willows. We had to push our way through, and I knew the owner hadn't been there in years. The ground itself was pretty level and would have made a good building site, but there was no water source. This was a dry stretch near the rim of the canyon where there was no easy access to water, no streams or springs nearby.

The brothers wanted this to work so badly that they even considered hauling water in from somewhere else.

I urged them to understand that without nearby available water it wouldn't be feasible, which was probably why the owner had never done anything with the land himself.

Crestfallen, they finally admitted I was probably right.

Walking back to my cabin, I told them there were probably more pieces of land available, and that they should go into town, regroup, and find something better. They told me their money was getting low and they should probably get jobs. Asking them how they had planned on buying the land, one said they would sell the van to pay for it. When I questioned how they would get out to the trailhead with their stuff, they just looked at each other with blank faces.

The next morning after they devoured the last of my oatmeal and eggs, I walked with them out the lower trail that ran along the bay up to where their van was parked. Throwing the packs into their rig, they gave me a ride to Walt and Mary's place to get my Jeep. After their visit, I needed to go to town to replace my perishable supplies.

As I drove around town making my purchases, I saw the brothers' van outside the Log Cabin Cafe. Parking, I walked in and sat down at their table just as the food arrived. Smiling at Hazel, I ordered a full breakfast, then sat and watched the boys eat until my food was served. We all sat there afterwards, sipping our coffee and talking about Alaska. Finished, I got up, and wishing them luck I picked up my check from the table, placed it on top of theirs, and left.

Early that afternoon, I parked my jeep at Walt and Mary's once again. Luckily Walt was home, and when I told him what was up, he gave me a ride to the Sandals' parking lot, saving me a boring walk down the dusty dirt road. After he dropped me off, I hoisted my pack and started the hike back up along the bay. Even though I wasn't really looking forward to the hike, it was very pleasant to be doing it alone. The brothers had worn me out, as if I had been baby sitting some overactive little boys. In truth, that's what I had been doing. It was a reminder of how good it was to be living remote.

The weather was nice, there were ripe berries along the trail, and no troublesome animals around to bother me. Well, there was one small black bear, but I just walked by and it kept munching berries, ignoring me.

A few weeks later, I saw the boys again. I was working on my cabin, putting up outer boards on the back wall, when I was hailed by someone in front of my site. It was Bucky Waters and the two brothers. I couldn't believe he had the brass to come up to my land after the bridge incident. I could feel my anger start to rise, but managed to stay relatively calm.

Bucky walked up to me, the boys a few steps behind. Waters just nodded, and I'm not sure if I nodded back or not. The two innocents came forward and enthusiastically shook my hand. My own response was less animated, especially since they had showed up with Waters. They told me that he was nice enough to give them some work out in the woods. I stared at Bucky and nodded slowly.

The boys and I shared some small talk, then Bucky interrupted and asked me if I had cut down a spruce tree on the trail to his place. When I told him I had, he stated firmly that he was the one who had cut the trail, long before I had arrived, to haul milled boards to his place while he was building his cabin. He was still using it for his other building projects, and he didn't like me taking down a tree without asking.

The heat already warming my neck traveled up into my face, just like at the bridge. This bastard just wouldn't quit. But I now realized that he couldn't deal with anything by himself, always needing backup. I saw the boys looking from him to me, caught off guard by this unexpected turn of events. I knew what Waters was saying might have some merit, but there were plenty of trees in that area usable for milling, and the one I took was way up at my end of the trail. Giving myself a moment to calm down, I told him that if that was the way he felt, I would get my trees elsewhere after I had finished that one.

He took the advantage, and said I should leave that one alone.

I had felled the tree, limbed it, and cut it into three usable lengths, which was a lot of work. I looked straight at Bucky and repeated what I had just said. I told him I hadn't seen his name stamped on the tree.

He saw I was standing firm, paused for a moment, and cautioned me to see that it didn't happen again. With that, he turned and walked away, the boys trailing behind looking back several times.

It was obvious Waters wasn't going to leave me alone, ready to hassle me every chance he got. He apparently considered himself the king of these woods. As I watched him walking away, the two boys following obediently behind, it struck me that Waters was not only intent on making problems for me, but that he probably wanted to run me out.

I gave a little inward laugh. I thought I could get away from annoying, unpleasant, divisive people by moving to the deep woods in Alaska. Apparently I was wrong about that. But, I would rather have this life in the bush, than to give it all up and leave because of a piece of work like Bucky Waters. So here I would stay, and deal with whatever came.

The moment I finished thinking that, there was a crashing noise near the back of my land that sounded like a big tree falling, but I never did find one that had recently come done.

I only saw the two boys once more, in town a month or so later. I asked them how things were and they apparently had tired of Waters working them like mules, so they had come back to Hazel to find work, which hadn't gone too well. But, they had put together almost enough money to get back home. I still had plenty of money from my old life, so I took them to the bank with me and drew out three hundred dollars. They were stunned, but I told them I would ap-preciate it if they repaid me when they could and wrote down my full name and P.O. box number for them.

I guess they did make it home, because about three months later I received an envelope postmarked Connecticut, with a money order in it for three hun-dred and fifty dollars.

Episode

....

33

THIS WHEELER JOURNEY TO TOWN WAS A LITTLE ROUGHER than most. There was lots of water on the tundra from spring break up. The winter snow load had been heavier than usual, and the summer rains had come early. This made getting the wheeler out to the road a real hassle, even with the deep-lugged tires I had put on it to combat the mud of the trail. In several extra boggy places, I actually had to get off the big machine to lighten the load and walk alongside while working the throttle.

On a good, relatively dry day, it took about two and a half hours to reach the road. This time it took more than four, and when I finally got to my truck and headed into town, it was mid-afternoon. I was in a crappy mood, tired, and covered with muck.

I had really worked up an appetite making the run, and headed right to the Log Cabin Cafe. When I got there, I saw that Hazel had not come in to work and Gwen was handling things alone. Coming over, she took a long look at my muddy condition, and with a twinkle in her blue eyes said, "Should have brought you a mop, so you could clean up before you leave."

I looked back toward the door and saw a trail of muddy boot prints leading from the door to where I was sitting. I mumbled, "Sorry about that."

Gwen was a real sport though, and having been born and raised in Alaska, wasn't really that bothered about the dirt on the floor. "Don't worry," she said, "It comes with the job."

Ten minutes later she came back with my meal, which I polished off with no trouble, wiping the plate clean with a piece of bread. I never had a problem eating a good meal after running the trail to town.

I was sitting, peacefully digesting, and was in need of a second cup of coffee. There were no other customers left in the Cafe. Gwen came with a fresh pot, but instead of refilling my cup right away, she stood there giving me a different kind of look.

As if coming to some sort of decision, she finally filled my cup and asked me if I had any plans for the evening, "Or is this a quick round trip back to your cabin?" Gwen obviously had something on her mind, but I didn't want to get it wrong. I had never thought of her in that way. But she was attractive, with those piercing blue eyes and slim figure.

I asked her what she had in mind, and waited for her to respond.

"Well, Denny, I thought it might be nice to hang out together, that is, if you'd want to. Maybe you could go to my place and take a shower, instead of looking like a mud monster. I have to close the Cafe down, and I'll be heading home right after that."

Quiet for a moment and not wanting to seem too eager, I told her that sounded fine to me.

Going behind the counter, she came back with the key to her home, saying, "I'll be there in a while."

I knew where her place was, a couple of miles outside of town on the road I took to drive out to the trail. She still lived in the log cabin her folks had built way back when, but it had been enlarged to four rooms from two, and upgraded with electricity, running water, and indoor plumbing. The outhouse behind it was a reminder of its more basic beginnings. Her mom now lived in an apartment in town, so Gwen had the cabin all to herself.

When I walked into her home, careful to leave my boots, coat, and pack by the door, I was surprised to see that it not only held a lot of memorabilia from the old days, photos and such, but some nice furnishings, a good leather couch and arm chair, and a coffee table nicely made from an old hatch cover. There was a finely done painting of Long Bay, with those grand mountains in the background. I immediately felt comfortable being there, but knew I had to clean up before I could settle in and relax. I pulled pants and a T-shirt from my pack, and stripped down to get cleaned up.

The hot shower felt great, the first real wash off I'd had since my last trip to town weeks ago, when I cleaned up at the public showers in the Hazel Laundromat. Now, enjoying the moment, I considered what was going on. I hadn't even thought about being with a woman since before I had left Nevada. I liked women, but it just hadn't been part of my plans. I didn't know for sure what would happen, but going with the flow seemed the right trail to follow.

I had just stepped out of the shower and was toweling off, having opened the bathroom door to let the steam out. Looking up, I saw Gwen standing in the doorway. I had nowhere to hide, so I just stood there, everything out in the open. Gwen stood checking me out, one hand on her hip. "Well, this is a different view than I usually get when I come home." After several long seconds, she turned and walked away. I didn't say anything, just dressed, and sat on her couch in T-shirt and pants, barefoot, waiting for the next move. I figured I should let her make it. I had a feeling this wasn't something she did often.

Coming into the living room, Gwen stood looking at me with her usual poker face. "I normally have a drink to relax when I get home," she said. "Care to join me?"

I nodded, and she went to a cabinet and produced a half-empty bottle of Jack Daniels, and two crystal whiskey glasses. We both sat there, quietly sipping our drinks and sharing space. It wasn't an awkward kind of silence, especially from a man and woman on their first get-together. It was more like being familiar and comfortable with each other, without words getting in the way.

After pouring us both another shot, she excused herself and went to take a shower. I sat there looking at a family album that was on the coffee table, while the second dose of bourbon pleasantly warmed my innards and relaxed my mind. There were some great old photos of the land around Hazel before it had really developed, including some images of her folks fishing and clamming there and across the inlet on various remote beaches. I also saw one photo of George Whiting when he was a young man, holding up two big clams, with Hazel standing nearby smiling at him. He looked perfect in his old-fashioned outdoor clothing and torn up hat, a big grin on his face.

The bathroom door opened and Gwen stepped out, wrapped in a towel, her wet hair glistening. There was a softness in the way she looked that I'd never seen before. In the Cafe, she always spoke in a clear strong voice, but now she said quietly, "I'd just like to know if I need to put clothes on or if that would be a waste of time."

I knew she was asking for approval, not just for us being together, but for her intentional display. I realized that this moment could affect our connection forever. Besides, I found Gwen very appealing in just a towel. Getting up and going to her, I looked into her blue eyes, gave her a little kiss and said, "If you'll lead the way, you can forget about getting dressed."

Gwen gave me a sweet smile and took me by the hand. She said, "This cabin is pretty small, Mr. Caraway. If you can't find the way, it's a wonder you ever make it to town."

"Don't worry, Gwen, I can find my way from here." And I did.

For the next several days, my time was spent hanging out at Gwen's place or casually shopping for the supplies I needed, eating lunch at the Log Cabin Cafe, and enjoying the evenings with her.

On the third morning when I went into town, I bought a copy of the *Hazel Bugler*. There was a small article about a case of sexual assault that caught my attention. It seemed a young woman, a Katie McDonnell, had gone to a remote cabin outside Hazel with a man she knew slightly, a Mr. Waters. According to her allegations, he had sexually abused her before forcing her to leave. But, there had been insufficient evidence that the sex had not been consensual, and the charges had been dismissed at the court hearing. I got a chill all over, reading that.

This explained why she had been so distressed. The bastard was just too much. It was amazing that he hadn't already been brought down by someone he had wronged. The more I learned what he was capable of, the less I liked living near him in the woods. I wondered what he was going to do next.

Thinking about Waters, my mind drifted to a dark place, but I shook it off. I couldn't do anything about what had happened. If the girl had initially told me what had occurred, things would have gone differently.

It's funny how the mind works. Thinking about this reminded me once again that he had never returned the hundred bucks he had borrowed from me, before I was on to his ways. I had thought to ask him for its return several times, but I knew he'd just make excuses, thinking it some kind of victory to not return the money to me.

I went down to the Cafe for lunch. Smiling, Gwen took me to a table in the back of the room and fed me some very tasty ribs that were served on Fridays. She and I had been definitely enjoying our time together. She was good to be with, and she apparently felt the same about me. I figured that neither one of us were looking for anything permanent, just enjoying the way we made each other feel. Even so, things could always go sour. I hoped nothing would happen to spoil what was going on. When Gwen took a break and sat with me, I handed her the *Bugler* and pointed to the article I had read earlier. When she was done, she just shook her head.

Gwen must have seen something in my eyes as I sat thinking about Waters again.

She said, "I wonder if anyone will ever take any action against Bucky. He's scammed a lot of people over the years; that's why he's not welcome in the Cafe. But this is the worst." She gave me a pointed look and said, "I hope nobody I know ever gets in trouble over him."

I responded to her obvious concern, "Probably not, Gwennie, it wouldn't be worth the bother."

She said, "Well, that's good. By the way, if you want any dessert, calling me Gwennie won't get it."

I got her point. "Okay Gwen, I'll remember."

That afternoon, I headed back to my homestead after saying a warm good-bye to Gwen. For once, I was reluctant to leave town.

Episode

34

AT THE END OF MY THIRD SUMMER ON THE HOMESTEAD, George Whiting passed away. I heard the announcement on the little battery-powered radio I had at the cabin for listening to the local news and to receive Bushlines from the radio station in town, KHOM. Bushlines were personal messages broadcast to people living in remote areas.

Apparently, George was carrying an arm load of firewood into the house when he had a heart attack and died there on his front porch. The whole town went into mourning. George was one of the longest-lived residents of Hazel besides Hazel O'Mara herself and a couple of other old-timers, including Mr. Harmon. George would be sorely missed, I'd definitely miss his good company.

I was caught off guard, as I had seen George just two weeks before and he seemed fine. It was a sad day for me. I packed a few things, and traveled to town for the memorial service.

There must have been two hundred people at the cemetery on that overcast, drizzly day. George's daughter had come up from Seattle with her two fidgety little boys, who had unfortunately only met their grandpa a couple of times.

At the service, Mr. Falmouth, a minister in town, made a nice speech about the man he had known for many years, after which Hazel O'Mara said a few words about George. She cited his good qualities and his steadiness in any situation. The last thing she said was: "He was a good man, a match for anyone in this town, including my husband Benny, who was a peach. George was a sweetheart, even if he didn't give me much business at the Cafe. But I forgive him for that."

There were a few self-conscious chuckles in the crowd.

I went to the Cafe afterwards for the reception, as did a number of George's close friends. Hazel treated us all to her famous homemade berry pie. As she poured me a cup of coffee, I looked at her and she at me. She put the coffee pot down and I stood and gave her a hug. When I realized she was crying, it startled me. I just never thought of Hazel as the crying type. But as quickly as it had started, it stopped. She pulled away, and mumbled something about having to help the others. I nodded and sat back down. It wasn't until weeks later that Gwen, who had seen me give her mom a hug, confided in me that Hazel and George had become very close after Benny's death, "Closer than bark on a tree," was the way she put it. I stored that nugget of information away, keeping it to myself.

George's passing had taken the wind out of Hazel O'Mara's sails. She stopped working full-time at the Cafe, leaving it to Gwen to run the business. On my trips to town after George was gone, I almost never saw her there.

One afternoon at the Cafe, I asked Gwen how her mom was doing.

She stood there a minute without speaking. It seemed as if she was trying to find the best way to answer my question. Finally, Gwen told me she was sure her mom was on her way to being with Benny again, and that her time would be soon.

I never asked her how or why she felt this way; I just accepted that coming from her it was probably true.

For all of us who knew George, life went on as it is known to do, but it was missing an important element. George was an elder of the town, a piece of its history, and his passing was a real loss. His dying also made me realize how much I felt a part of Hazel, even though I lived well outside its physical boundaries.

The first time I visited Gwen after George had left us, we spent some time talking about him. She had known him her whole life, and had a lot of great stories to tell. It was at this time that she told me how close her mom and George had been.

Gwen and I had made a definite connection, not just a brief moment in the sack. After that first time together, we treated each other as close friends, but never looked for anything beyond that. I think we both felt it was safer that way, not wanting to make something out of our relationship that would greatly alter our lives. We were both middle-aged people and were comfortable with the way things were. Though we didn't get together at her place every time I came to town, our intimate moments enhanced the rest of our relationship, even my times at the Cafe. I don't think anyone knew the full extent of what we shared, and we kept it that way.

A year almost to the day after George had died, I had come into town, and after going to the post office I picked up a copy of the *Bugler* to read over breakfast. Getting back into the Cherokee, I saw a notice on the front page:

> The town of Hazel has lost its founder and respected friend. Hazel O'Mara, born February 8th, 1922, died August 29th, 1994, who came to this part of Alaska with her husband Benny … has left us … advice that always proved correct … survived by her daughter Gwen … . Her loving strength will be sorely missed. Memorial services will be next Sunday at the Chapel by the Bay at 9:30 a.m. Reception at Gwen O'Mara's home, following the services.

After sitting there coming to grips with this loss so soon after George's passing, I went to the Cafe, but it was closed as I had expected. I headed to Gwen's cabin, wondering, for some reason, if I was really close enough to her to arrive uninvited, but I needn't have worried. When I knocked on the door, Gwen opened it, and when she saw me she slipped outside the door, took me by the hand around to the back of the cabin, grabbed me around the middle, buried her face in my coat front and cried. She hung onto me so long that I knew she was letting it all out. All I could do was hold her and allow it to happen.

After she was all cried out, she looked up and thanked me for coming, and said she had hoped I would be there. We walked back to the front door and went in to join the folks who had come to offer their condolences.

I hadn't realized that Gwen's feelings for me were so strong that my being there would be that important to her. I stayed around until the others had left, just sitting on the couch, watching Gwen move around the place, fiddling with this and that. She put on a record of old Irish songs, then came and sat close to me. I put my arm around her and we just sat silently listening to the sweet old sentimental tunes. By the time it was over, Gwen had fallen asleep, exhausted from the circumstances. I just put my feet up on the coffee table and sat there with her until I drifted off also.

I awoke in the morning to find myself alone on the couch. Gwen was in the kitchen cleaning up. I went in and put my arms around her to give her a hug, but she gently shook me off. "Got a lot to do today, Denny, business to take care of. Will you be at the memorial service on Sunday?"

Pausing a moment to adjust, I told her I would. I gave her a quick kiss on the forehead, went into the living room, and put my shoes and coat on. Telling Gwen to send me a Bush Line if she needed anything, I left. From there I drove into town to buy some things I needed before heading back to the cabin.

I felt bad that Gwen had put me off, but I understood. Her mother's death was a major disturbance in her life. She was going to have to take a different tack, and I knew I should try not to interfere with whatever she needed to do. I still had my life in the woods, my cabin was nearing completion, and I was looking forward to moving in. I just hoped we could remain friends.

The whole town turned out for Hazel's memorial. I guess you could say it was a perfect day for it, being cloudy and chilly. Hazel would have thought so, figuring in her way that it was better than wasting a sunny day on a funeral. Monty and his wife were there, as well as Bucky Waters and some shabby-looking woman he had hooked up with somewhere. I noticed that no one was talking to him much. A small group from the Sandals was there, Jeremy included. He nodded when he saw me and I returned the simple greeting. Nothing much to say.

At the service, a half-dozen people spoke of Hazel, her life, and personality. When it was Gwen's turn, there wasn't a sound in the place. She only spoke a few sentences.

My mother was the most solid, loving, and wisest person I ever knew. She was a hard worker and a very smart lady. She loved you all, no matter what. She asked me to tell you to behave yourselves and take care of the town.

Gwen thanked everybody for attending and invited them to come to the Cafe for some food. An Alaska era in our part of the state had come to an end.

My ride home in a light rain was without issue. I was on automatic pilot part of the time, but the trail cut me some slack, and my lack of alertness didn't get me into any trouble.

I turned my thoughts to Hazel O'Mara more than once. She really was a hoot. She always had a strong answer for any remark or question presented to her. When I was first frequenting the Cafe, she would say, "Well, did the Bs and Bs scare you off yet?" She meant the bears and bugs. During my first Alaska winter, she'd ask me if she should turn the heat up in the Cafe, or if I needed a blanket to put around me while I was eating. She really was a character. But, after I'd been at it for a year, she stopped the good-natured chiding and would ask me real questions on how things were going. It made me feel like I had arrived. Though I had only known her for a few years, I knew that, as with the loss of George, things would never be quite the same for me.

Episode

....

35

FALL HAD RETURNED, BUT THIS YEAR IT WOULD BE DIFFERENT. My cabin was done, and I had started to move in. It had taken longer to build than I had expected, more than four years. But it turned out just the way I had planned. It was a sturdy frame structure. I had wanted a good-sized cabin to live in, rather than a small log one such as George had built. A frame home was better because it was insulated and would take less wood than a log structure to keep it heated in winter. If I had built it smaller, it would have been even easier to keep warm, but I wanted the extra room since I planned to live in it permanently.

As I moved all my things from George's old cabin, I reflected on the changes I had gone through while living in the snug little home. I felt as if I had gone through my learning period there and had graduated, moving to my own home. Now, after placing the last bundle on the floor of my new dwelling, there was something I needed to do before spending my first night there.

Walking to the edge of my five acres, I climbed the old spruce I had nicknamed the "Grandpa Tree" because it was larger, and seemed to dominate the other trees on my parcel of land. Climbing up into its thick, rough-barked branches, I continued until I couldn't go any higher, and looked at my new home from that vantage point. I needed to see it in a perspective that I couldn't at ground level, to see its major overall angles and proportions. From the Grandpa

Tree, forty feet above the ground, I saw the cabin more completely. It was all I hoped it would be, my perfect home.

The foundation had taken a while to build because it was my first, but I knew it had to be really level and squared, so I'd built it carefully, to get it right the first time. It was constructed of milled beams set on natural, round spruce foundation posts sunk deep into the ground, which held the cabin several feet off the ground. There were a dozen posts for the main structure, which was sixteen by twenty-four feet, plus several more off the left rear wall for the eight-by-twelve storage room.

Digging holes is an unavoidable chore out in the bush, and I came to dread having to do it. The soil was full of cobbles, so digging by hand was tough going. But, an outhouse needed to have a hole dug, and without a nearby spring a shallow well was necessary, and, of course, all the foundation posts needed them too. But I had stuck with it and got them done.

It was good putting up the actual structure, the walls, and roof framing. It had made me feel like real progress was being made. Putting up the walls was pretty easy, but I didn't forget what it took to make the boards I was assembling. Having to work with raw materials was the way of it out here. It was always satisfying to start a project from nothing but trees and tools, and have it end up as a completed piece. Whether it was a bench, table, shelves, foundation beams, or just a mixing spoon carved with a knife from a hard dry spruce stick, it was a fulfilling process for me. To do it myself required commitment and dedication and the belief that I could accomplish it by myself. I never worked harder in my life or loved it more, sawing and milling, measuring, cutting, and nailing my own home.

I had built a nice little kitchen area in the cabin with a cottonwood slab for the counter top, with cabinets above it and shelves underneath. A large table was in the middle of the cabin for eating, working, and visiting with neighbors. I had cut all its pieces from spruce with natural pole legs cut from straight spruce boughs. It was a fine home for me.

I considered the fact that even if I had known what it was going to take to build out here, physically, mentally and financially before I started, I still would have gone through with it. Working one day at a time, I made or bought all the pieces and put them together to make a snug, solid home. I had been at it for a long time, but it had given me a definite direction for my life, and in a way, I was sorry when it was completed. But, I was sure I could always think of something else to build.

By old time standards, it was a pretty fancy place, having several sliding windows with screens, a small propane range for cooking, and a good wood stove. I kept a large stockpot of water on the woodstove for washing dishes, doing laundry, and bathing. Someday I would have a shower room just like the one Andy Larsen had built, though probably not as finely made.

I would make sure the storage room was well stocked with staples: dried beans, peas, lentils, dry milk, salt, sugar, canned foods, and more. A lot of hardware and equipment would be stored there too, including the pressure cooker and canning jars that helped me survive on the game meat, fish, and berries I harvested.

I had made myself a bed for the new mattress I had brought out in the winter before the place was completed. It had stayed wrapped in plastic and stored until the bed was done. The mattress was three feet off the floor on the bed frame now, which was made of sturdy six by sixes, with storage bins stashed underneath.

The first night I stayed in the new place, I was up late just walking around, studying every corner, beam, and board. I knew every one of them intimately.

I had a fire crackling in the wood stove, the one I'd installed before the walls were up, because it was easier to just slide it onto the open platform than to wrestle it through a door opening later. It had been interesting to arrive at the site and see it just sitting out there, waiting to perform its duties. I'd started fires in it while working on the place in the winter months, but I do believe that the sound of that first fire inside my completed home was the most satisfying sound I had ever heard. I knew with certainty that no matter what else I accomplished here, this snug, strong shelter would always be the major highlight of my life. It might be the only home I would ever build for myself, and it would serve me well.

Sitting near my woodstove that first night, I reflected on Waters, and the way things had evolved between us. It had been quiet for a while, but that didn't matter. There had been too much trouble. I wondered what might eventually happen.

Episode

36

DURING MY FIFTH SPRING IN THE BUSH, I LOST SOMETHING of great importance to me. At the time of year when the warming temperatures of spring begin breaking down the ice and snow covering the land, there had always been a line of huge tracks that cut across the back trail from my homestead about a mile behind the cabin. The trail, at that point, broke out of the thick covering of willows, alders, and stunted black spruce before continuing across a large expanse of open tundra. The paw prints extended in a line across that point as far as one could see in either direction. They were the tracks of a very large brown bear.

In my first four springs living at the homestead, I saw these same tracks. After the second time I saw them, I knew who had made them. The big old bear I'd had several interactions with was the only bruin in the area large enough to leave such impressive tracks. But in the fifth spring they were not there.

Late in my fourth summer, on a day when the dryness of that particular season had diminished the bugs to bearable levels, I was busy cutting firewood in preparation for the coming winter. As I lifted the splitting maul once again to split a round of dry spruce, I heard a shot, then another, and another. I knew, by the time the three rounds had been fired, that they came from the direction of Waters' homestead. Normally, I would just assume he might be shooting at a moose or black bear for food. But, three shots is a universal signal for help. I had broken all ties with Bucky, but it just wasn't in me to ignore the possibility that he might be in some kind of dire straits. I decided it was necessary to take a ride there and check.

Getting my .44 from the cabin, I started up the wheeler and headed to his place. Halfway there, I was confronted with a large, downed spruce tree across the trail. This was the trail Waters had cleared and considered his own. The tree had been cut down intentionally. Maybe he was going to use it for building or firewood, or maybe he had dropped it to block the way. I almost turned around, but instead, worked my way around it and continued on.

When I got up to Waters' cabin, I just sat on the idling wheeler, staring in disbelief. There before me lay my bear, the massive old boar that had connected with me numerous times and had never done me harm. I recognized him immediately by that scar running across his muzzle.

Waters was standing next to the bear with a skinning knife in one hand, and a sharpening stone in the other. I couldn't find any words, but I could feel a hard anger welling up inside me. Waters faced me with a mean look in his eyes, and I stood there glaring back at him, shaking slightly from inflamed anger.
Bucky loudly said, "The S.O.B. was getting into my chicken pen. Damned if I was going to let him kill my birds!"

I got off my wheeler and walked to the pen, Bucky stepping back from me as I passed him. The chickens were clustered inside their coop, but there was nothing wrong with the enclosure, nothing broken, and the chicken wire intact. I turned and looked at him.

"He had his nose against the wire. I knew he was going to get in! I have the right to defend my stuff from these damned animals!"

Walking up to him, I asked the bastard what he was going to do with the knife. "I have to skin him out and take the skull and hide to Fish and Game, so I'm going to do just that. I'm going to take them into their office when I go into town tomorrow."

It was all I could do to keep from taking the knife away from him and using it. But all I did was look him in the eye and say, "You miserable piece of dirt. That bear was worth a lot more than your stinking chickens!"

I had to do something or explode! I gave him one sharp hard jab to the chin. Waters took an involuntary step back and dropped to the ground, sitting there with a stunned look on his face. His expression changed and he started to rise, the knife still in his hand. Putting my hand on the grip of my .44, I shook my head. Bucky must have seen the wisdom of not pushing the situation and slumped back onto the ground. All done, he let go of the knife.

Walking to my wheeler, I turned it around and headed back toward my cabin. It was a difficult ride for me. My emotions were all over the place as

I headed up the back trail, but the feeling that won out over all the rest was anger, pure cold anger. It didn't release me for several hours, rising and falling until it had faded. Though there were plenty of other bears around, the strange special connection that bear had with me was gone forever. The fact that it had been Waters who had ended its life just made it that much worse. My going to his place after the three shots had been a matter of obligation, but never again.

A week or so after Waters killed the bear, I went into town for a small load of supplies and to check my mail. As I came out of the post office, I almost ran right into Monty. After shaking hands and making a little small talk, he asked me if I had seen the latest copy of the *Bugler*. I hadn't yet, so he walked me to his truck and showed me the front page. There was a grainy photo of Bucky Waters, pretending to bite the ear of a dead brown bear, which was loaded into the back of his old pickup truck. A foolish pose probably meant to show his conquest of the great beast. The article read:

> Mr. Waters said he went out into his yard to do some chores and the bear charged at him, scaring him badly. He ran into his cabin, got his rifle and, fearing for his life, shot the bear which was set to charge him again.

Apparently, he had taken the hide and skull over to the *Bugler* office to be photographed and get a little glory out of it. Incredible. I knew it was all a lie. There was no mention of his chickens. I thanked Monty for showing it to me.

"That's not all," he told me.

He mentioned to a couple of people he was going to bid on the hide and skull when Fish and Game has its next auction of confiscated animals hides. When I saw Bucky a couple of days ago, I told him that the person who kills the animal can't bid on the hide. He didn't believe me, but checking at the Fish and Game office, he found out it was true. I know he'd killed the bear out of season just for the hide. He'd seen the bear before, and wanted a shot at him. He can't kill game in season because of poaching charges a couple of years ago, so he thought this was the only way he could get the bear hide.

I was angry all over again, a sour, metallic taste in my mouth. Monty patted me on the shoulder and left. I shopped for what I needed, and headed straight back to my cabin.

I brooded over the loss of the bear and realized that, for me, he had symbolized all that was wild and free. Things would just never be the same. All the other situations with Waters were bad enough, but it felt like the bastard had actually killed something inside me when he took the bear down. I would continue on with my life in the bush doing the things I had to do, but I knew everything would be lessened by this.

It took a while to settle back into my daily routines. I had managed to put the incident behind me. At one point I had even considered leaving, but quickly brushed that thought aside. Finally I decided to accept things as the land itself did, as just part of the cycle, and move on. But, the bear incident had reminded me once again that people can turn something beautiful to ashes and mud, and there was nothing I could do about that.

Episode

....

37

I STOOD LOOKING OUT THE FRONT WINDOW OF MY NEW cabin, a mug of coffee in hand. The view of the glaciered mountains across Long Bay was wonderful and was as fresh in my eyes as the first time I'd seen it.

The woodstove was putting out plenty of heat. I had chosen the right size stove, which, combined with the ample insulation I had put in the cabin, would provide me with warmth through many winters to come.

I had eaten and was ready to begin my day, starting with splitting more firewood. I actually had plenty, enough to last through the winter, but it never hurt to have a little more.

It was a typical late November morning. There hadn't been any real snowfall yet, besides a slight "dusting" several days before, but the land was frozen up hard. I was lacing up my boots to start working outside, when I heard an unexpected noise. It was hard and metallic, a steady clanking, mixed with the sounds of a powerful engine, and it was getting louder. I finished doing up my boots, put my coat, gloves, and hat on, and went outside.

By now, the noise was extremely loud and obnoxious. The smell of burnt diesel fuel lay thick in the cold air, a smell I hated. By the time I got out to the trail, the source of the noise was just passing by. I couldn't believe what I was seeing, and didn't want to believe it. A bulldozer was rumbling down the trail. Lettering on its rear end said CAT D4. The worst part of it was that Bucky Waters was at the controls. Son of a … . He hadn't seen me watching him go by. The dozer continued out across the tundra, leaving a slowly dissipating trail of dark smoke in the air. When Waters got to the beginning of his trail, he paused, lowered the blade to ground level, and continued on until he and the damned machine disappeared from sight. The noise slowly faded to a distant muted rumble.

I just stood there, a knot in my gut. What was Waters up to? Was this his machine or was he just renting it? I decided he was going to do some kind of major work on his place and needed the bulldozer. Knowing there was nothing I could do about it, I just hoped it wouldn't take very long, so it'd go away soon.

The rest of the day, I heard the dozer working away in the distance. I spent some time splitting firewood, but stayed inside the cabin most of the day, where the noise was less audible. In early afternoon, the sound stopped. What a blessing. I relaxed for the first time that day.

It was quiet all the next morning, too. I had almost forgotten the thing was out here. But sometime after noon, it started up again, and soon I heard it coming closer. I really freaked out. It represented everything I had left behind, yet here it was, coming toward me through the trees. I got a little crazy at that point. I took the Winchester and started out the door, but I realized he must be taking it back to town.

Putting the rifle back on its rack, I made myself settle down, put some water on to boil, and put a big pinch of Labrador tea in a cup. But, as I stood waiting for the water to boil, I noticed the dozer wasn't coming any closer. It seemed to be somewhere across from the cabin. I went outside again, to see what was up, leaving the rifle inside this time.

Standing on the edge of the tundra and looking across, I could see the plume of smoke from its exhaust stack in the woods directly in line with where the trail ran across the muskeg. I trotted over, wanting to see what was up. Before I got there, I could hear the sound of a chainsaw revving up. I walked about fifty yards into the trees to a place where I could see what was going on.

There was a man watching a large spruce tree as it fell, while Waters was standing by the running Cat at a safe distance, a chainsaw at his feet. The size and shape of the tree cutter meant it could only be one person, which made me feel even worse, if that was possible. It was Monty Leer. As soon as the tree was down, Waters walked over with his saw, and together they started to limb the tree. I decided they needed the Cat because they were clearing land and would use it to drag the trees off to stack them.

I walked up to Monty, and tapped him on the shoulder. He flinched at that, not knowing anyone else was there. He turned and smiled when he recognized me, but his smile soon faded when he saw the look on my face.

"Monty, what are you doing? I need to know what's going on."

Bucky had just walked up, seeing me talking to Monty. He wasn't smiling either.

"Denny, we're clearing some land here to put up a small lodge. We went in together and bought this five acres from the owner last week."

"A lodge? Right here? Why?"

To make a living, Denny, why else? This is right near the trail, so it'll be easy to bring folks in. The lodge will have two small cabins behind it for the clients to stay in. The people who come can take hikes in the woods and I'll take them on guided horseback rides up in the hills behind Ptarmigan Lake. We'll bring in hunters during moose and bear season too.

Bucky now chimed in, "Yeah, and I'm going to clear some better trails along the ridges to make traveling to and from town easier. That's why we bought this used bulldozer." Seeing the look on my face, he added, "I've got all the state permits I need, so it's a done deal."

I stood there, speechless. There was nothing else to say. Monty knew how I would feel about this. We had talked enough about my reasons for being here. I could appreciate him trying to make a better life for himself, but for heaven's sake, why right here? Turning, I slowly walked away back to my cabin. As I crossed the tundra, I heard the chain saws start up in unison.

Episode

38

FOR THE NEXT TWO DAYS, I JUST SAT IN MY CABIN. THE RECENT events had brought me down, lower than I could ever remember. I sat for hours, tossing wood into the stove once in a while and staring into the flames through the open door. The noises from across the tundra had gone on for hours the first day, but not this morning. Around noon, it started up again.

I couldn't take it anymore. Throwing on my winter trail-riding gear and tossing my pack onto the wheeler's rear rack, I headed toward town. A trail ride had always smoothed out any mental wrinkles I had, but this time I couldn't shake my mind free of what had happened. I was running away from the home I had sweated and frozen over, building it with my own hands and mind. I had to turn away from things I had no control over. After having come all this way and finding a place that suited my needs and dreams, when I thought I had left all my problems behind I found they'd followed me here like evil spirits.

I felt completely undone and like a fool, realizing I had been done in by my own illusions of unending peace and contentment. I managed to slow down my mind and focus, concentrating on the trail ahead of me, following the old familiar landmarks that pointed my way to Hazel. I set my mind toward the Log Cabin Cafe and its familiar, friendly atmosphere.

On the road in my Jeep heading into town, the closer I got to the Cafe, the better I felt. But, passing by George's old home, I was sorry I couldn't stop and talk with him. I was sure he could have brought my spirits up. I'd just have to settle for some friendly company at the Cafe.

The "Under New Management" sign in the front window of the Cafe made me feel physically sick. Gwen had never told me she was selling out. She had mentioned a few times that it was harder to handle the Cafe without her mom, but had never said she wanted to quit.

I knew Gwen had taken up with a local guy, a fisherman she had known most of her life. They had dated as teenagers, but had broken up. His marriage had recently come to an end, and his son had headed down to Washington State for school, so he had been coming into the Cafe alone, and their relationship rekindled. Gwen was still my friend, but I kept an appropriate distance, our history understood and kept discreet.

Now entering the Cafe, I saw only one other customer I knew. I nodded in his direction, and he gave me a knowing little nod in return. I asked the new owner if she knew what Gwen was up to, and was told she was living with her new husband in the town of Coal Bluff, about twenty-five miles north of Hazel. I turned and left the Cafe, no longer feeling any connection to the place.

I don't know why, but I drove out to Gwen's old cabin home. No one was there, and the place was closed up and empty. Just three weeks had passed since I'd last been to town, and an important part of my life had turned upside down. I had nowhere to go.

Sitting in the fast food joint at the main intersection in town, I sipped a cup of their flat commercial coffee and pondered what to do. Watching the people who patronized this place, none of whom I knew or had seen before, realizing they were just like people anywhere else, I knew I would never be able to live a town life again. Tossing the barely drunk liquid in a trash container, I headed to Mary and Walt's place, back out the road.

Walt was home, and he welcomed me in. He looked at me for a moment, and asked what was wrong. I guess my face revealed how I was feeling. I kept it simple and asked Walt if he would still consider buying my place if I ever wanted to sell out. He showed surprise, knowing how much I loved my homestead. I had once told him I would never sell the place, but he said if I ever did, I should give him first refusals. Walt shrugged and asked what I would want for the place. He and Mary had snow machined out the winter before and liked what they'd seen, which is when they had expressed an interest. I offered him the place at a very low price, because they had been very good to me and we had become real friends. They always came out to greet me and offer me a cup coffee when I showed up there.

I told Walt I would let him know if I definitely wanted to sell out, but I realized in my heart that I couldn't stay any longer. I had run every possible scenario I could think of through my mind, and none of them were acceptable to me.

I saw no options. Everything I loved was ruined. But, I decided I wasn't beaten, I had just made a mistake and needed to find a real sanctuary for myself.

I didn't want to return to my place yet. I needed time away from it to consider my next move. I got a room at the motel, and went to the Chinese buffet. It wasn't the Cafe, but I appreciated the anonymity I felt there. Afterwards I just lay in my motel room, my mind racing.

I didn't accomplish much the next day, just wandering around, letting my head run free. It was damned cold, but I took walks on the beach and even drove up to the big hill overlooking the town to enjoy the view of the arm of water outside Long Bay, and the beautiful country on the other side of the water. I considered looking for some remote land over there, but knew there were a lot of people scattered among the coves and inlets.

I was in the post office checking my box, when I overheard two old fellows talking about some land one of them had purchased from the State. I picked up the words "west of Fairbanks," "pretty damned isolated," and "more land available."

Walking up to them, I asked if they'd mind telling me where this land was located. The two of them looked at each other and smiled. One of them told me that the place was a "far piece away from any town" and maybe I wouldn't like being out there. I just smiled and told them I'd manage. The one man looked me in the eyes for a long moment, smiled and said, "Yes, I believe you would."

He told me the State had some sections of land available to the public as "Remote Parcel Leases." "They used to call them homesteads," he told me,

But the rules have changed and so has the name. You don't have to prove up like in the old days. You just pay fifty dollars a year and by the end of ten years you have to have had it surveyed and approved, pay a nominal fee and the land is yours. But I'm telling you, you'd better be committed to the remote life, because that's exactly what you'll be getting. I only grabbed a parcel to use for hunting and fishing, not to live there. It's located on the Nowitna River just outside the southeastern border of the Nowitna National Wildlife Refuge. There are several parcels left.

The man wished me good luck and said maybe we'd meet up there someday.

Listening to this old-timer, I got goose bumps all over, and knew this was something I should look into. The tightness in my gut went away, seeing a possible way to turn my situation into something good. It was a relief to know I had options.

I went to the little state office in Hazel to see if they could help me. They checked on the records, and sure enough there were three parcels left. I would have to go up there and stake out a plot for myself, five acres, and come back and file a document. When I made my interest known, they gave me maps, some paperwork and wished me luck.

I went to the library to do some research on the area I was considering. I'd have to fly in, as there was no other way to get there.

I found out that it was mostly open tundra, but there would be enough trees for building, and plenty of wild game. There were decent populations of moose and bear, and beaver in the numerous creeks. Wolves were there, always ready to take a young or sick caribou from the herd that migrated through the area.

I went to the little Hazel airport and found a bush pilot to talk to about what it would take to get out there. I found one drinking coffee and flirting with the young woman at the ticket desk. I patiently waited until the woman turned away, obviously tired of the lines he was throwing at her. I introduced myself and told him what I needed.

He said he was too tied up to take me, but gave me the number and name of a pilot based out of Fairbanks who could help me.

I called him on one of the airport phones and sure enough, he was willing to take me if I could meet him at the Fairbanks airport in a week. He said the area was already under several feet of snow and temperatures had dipped well below zero and held there, so I should bring the right gear to stay a few days to acquaint myself with the area and stake my five acres. It was all set.

I had plenty of good cold-weather clothing, but needed to get a small sturdy tent and a small liquid fuel stove for cooking. I went to the sporting goods store and found just what I needed. I headed back home, my head filled with all kinds of thoughts whirling around. Halfway back, I got hit with some thick snow coming down.

It was good to get back to my land, but now that I had a chance to get it right, to find a really remote homestead, things were different. I still loved the place, the home I had established, but now it was time to move on. Four days later, I headed out on my snowmobile with the necessary gear and goods in my sled to seek out my new Alaska home.

Episode

39

IT WAS AN EASY RUN UP TO ANCHORAGE AND FARTHER NORTH on the Glenn Highway, into mountainous country I'd never seen before, more rugged and beautiful than the country between Anchorage and Hazel. Passing a sign for a place called Chickaloon, I wanted to explore a location with such an arcane name, but I had more pressing issues. Continuing up the rough, uneven road, I drove past a dominant mass of naked stone, a sheer-faced structure that stood out in great contrast to the forested country surrounding it.

A bullet hole-riddled sign declared it to be Sheep Mountain. Not far past there, the road leveled out as it ran on toward Glennallen.

Stopping for coffee at a place called The Eureka Roadhouse, I saw it was populated with a group of obvious locals, judging from their clothing and the intimate way they were talking together.

They looked like my kind of people, but when I nodded at one of them who kept looking at me, he turned and mumbled something to the others and they laughed. When he turned and looked at me again, smiling, on impulse I flipped him the bird, probably not the best thing since there were four of them. But I had fallen into a crappy mood, my uncertain situation getting the better of me.

The guy got up and came to my table. Standing over me, he asked what my problem was.

Rising, I told him I just did what I figured he'd do if the tables were turned.

He stared at me a moment, smiled and nodded, then asked me where I was headed.

I told him where I was going and why.

He said, "Had a friend go into that country a few years ago and he never came back."

I knew he was jabbing at me, and I told him that if I saw his friend, I'd let him know he was being looked for.

The guy, still smiling, went back to his friends and left me to finish my cup. I bought another coffee to go, before driving up the highway to Glennallen, a wide spot in the road where I spent the night in a shoddy motel that didn't seem to have the heat working. Walking across the highway to a rough-looking Cafe, I had a meal that I was certain came frozen in a box they had heated up and put on a plate.

That night I got little sleep because of the excitement I was feeling, as well as the lousy mattress I was lying on.

The next morning I headed north again, but I hadn't gone two miles when I went around a tight turn and lost traction on the icy highway. Before I could put the Cherokee in neutral and steer into the skid, I was off the side of the road, partly buried in a big snow bank. I was tilted over pretty far and saw that if the snow hadn't been there, I would have rolled down a thirty-foot bank. Swell, just great.

From what I'd heard, when a person was broken down by the side of the road in Alaska, anybody going by would stop to give assistance. I guess that era was over with. Probably a dozen people went by without even looking in my direction, or else looked but kept going.

Finally, a huge state snowplow truck pulled up and stopped. A big man, suited to the truck he was driving, got out of the cab and came over. He looked the Jeep over and told me all his chains were too big to hook onto my vehicle but that he would call Leif in Gulkana on his truck radio and have him come and pull me out. Without another word, he turned and got back into his rig and roared on down the road. There being nothing else to do, I got back into the Jeep and waited for Leif.

It was almost an hour before he showed up, but he went right to work, hooking up a chain to my Jeep's front end from his big one ton dually pickup and told me that when he honked, have the Jeep in low four-wheel drive and give it some gas. He did, I did, and the truck was yanked forward back onto the road again.

When I asked Leif how much he wanted for the help, he said thirty bucks would do it. I pondered this a moment, before asking him how many miles he had come.

He told me about thirty-five. I knew his truck probably got terrible mileage, so I gave him forty.

He gave me a surprised look, said thanks, and headed back north.

I soon followed, continuing on to Gakona Junction, where I would turn onto Highway Four, the Richardson Highway, toward Delta Junction and up to Fairbanks, still many miles away at that point.

I could have reached Fairbanks via the Parks Highway by turning off at Wasilla about forty miles north of Anchorage, passing through Denali National Park on the way. It would have been shorter, but I had heard there were buffalo, American bison, roaming free up in the Big Delta area, and I wanted to see some if I could.

Just after Gakona Junction, snow started coming down, blown around by a turbulent wind. I continued on at a much reduced speed. After about half an hour, the snow let up. The country along the way was beautiful, with varying terrain, mountains and flatland. All the land in Alaska was fine. Though my sliding off the side of the road had dampened my spirits, I started getting excited again, wondering what my new homestead land would look like.

Between Delta Junction and Big Delta further north, I got to see bison. I had just come around a sharp right-hand turn and had to hit the brakes. There, right in front of me on the road, was a huge bull buffalo standing sideways. There were several lesser buffalo walking across behind him. It almost seemed as if the big one was standing guard while the others went across. That bull bison was a very impressive animal, prehistoric in form. He had a massive head with a long "beard" hanging down. I had the feeling that if he wanted to, he could easily flip the Cherokee over. I tried not to convey that suggestion to him. When his partners had crossed, he gave me a look before passing over the roadway after them. The encounter had made it worth the extra driving.

The Delta River kept coming in and out of view to my left. It was one of those meandering, wild-looking rivers that are so abundant in Alaska. Many other areas of the U.S. had the same things, rivers, lakes, and mountains, but in Alaska everything had more energy, more wildness to it. Everything here seemed untamed, even in areas that had been "civilized." Just looking out at the mountains from inside Anchorage gave you that feeling. You couldn't keep the place tied down, that was for sure.

I continued cruising up the highway toward Fairbanks, eager to get closer to the land I might settle. The fact that I would start from scratch this time without any ready-made shelter, wasn't a worry. Plenty of people had gone before me and done the same. I knew it would be a greater struggle creating a home so far out in the bush, transportation and hauling being much more difficult. But, I had confidence, having lived a remote life for years now. I saw creating and living on my homestead as a learning experience that would help me succeed in this new endeavor. It would have been nice though, to have a place to live in while establishing myself again.

I was about ten miles north of Big Delta, when I saw an old pickup truck on the side of the road with its hood up. I pulled up in back of the truck and got out. Standing in front of the old Ford with a disgusted look on his stubbly face, was a skinny old man wearing a large fur hat that looked much too big for his head. He had big insulated boots on and a wool Mackinaw jacket. He didn't look right at me, but went on grumbling something about ungrateful machinery.

I asked if I could help, and he said the engine had started banging loudly, backfired once and died. "I think the thing is gone for good. You headed north? I could use a ride up to Aurora Lodge. Got a friend there who will put me up until I get this squared away."

I told him that was no problem, and so he threw a small duffle bag into the back of my Cherokee, opened the back of the camper shell on his truck, and said, "C'mon dog, let's go."

A big furry dog, a malamute mix I think, jumped out of the truck. The old guy opened the back door of the Cherokee and the dog hopped right in as if he did it all the time, taking up most of the seat when he lay down. He smelled like dog, too.

As we drove north, the old man, named Mitch, and I talked about things in general, the weather, and how Alaska was changing. When he learned I was a homesteader he perked up, a new level of interest in his voice.

I told him where I was going and what I intended to do.

He had been to the general area I would be flying into and suggested I reconsider, because that country was "without conscience" as he put it. He said, "You seem fit enough and probably know the life as well as any, but that area will test you hard, very hard." He smiled and said, "The bears and wolves out there don't have a very interesting diet, so you might just add a little spice to their life." We both chuckled at that one.

He was quiet for a minute, obviously mulling something over, and then asked me if I'd consider settling in somewhere a little less remote.

I told him yeah, if it was still far out enough to be a good distance from other people, and if there were game animals around for food.

He smiled and said he knew of a piece of land that might be available to the right person. "When we get to Aurora Lodge, I'll take you to someone who might be able to help."

When we got to where his friend lived, Mitch talked alone with this other skinny old man who had apparently been his friend for a very long time. I could tell this because of the way they interacted with each other, no formalities, just resuming from where they'd left off. They became embroiled in a quiet but energized conversation about something. The subject was settled, the discussion ended and Mitch introduced me to his friend, George Levine.

"George?" I said.

"Yeah," he responded. "Not a particularly unusual name, is it?"

"No," I said, smiling to myself, "not at all."

Well, it turned out that this George had a piece of remote land along a small branch of the Salcha River called Lanyard Creek.

"It's not too bad getting in there in winter," he said, "but a pretty hard go in summer. It's a half a day's run with a good snow trail. I might interested in letting it go."

Maybe it was because this guy's name was George like my old friend, or just the way this was all playing out, but I was interested.

George asked me all about my homestead, and how I lived out there. He wanted to know if living on the land suited me. I answered him as honestly and clearly as possible.

I stated I wanted to see his land, of course, before making any decisions. George nodded and told me he had an old Skidoo snowmobile I could take and he'd show me how to get there. I agreed, and would come back the next day and head out on the trail.

"You'll know when you get there," George said. "My twelve-by-twelve hunting shack is the only building for miles, and it has a red coffee can over the top of the stovepipe."

There was shelter on the property? This was getting better all the time.

George said he could put me up for the night if I didn't mind the floor and a sleeping bag. I told him that was just fine. Looking around while George cooked us a mess of beans and franks for dinner, I noticed his trailer had lots of memorabilia on shelves and on the walls. On one, two skins, a beaver and a wolverine hung, along with a pair of old but beautifully beaded moccasins. A well-worn pair of long, handmade snowshoes were leaning in a corner. A piece of quartz with definite flecks of gold sat on the kitchen counter. There were a couple of shelves of books, most of them about Alaska, and a stack of James Michener books as well. I felt right at home.

The three of us ate and chatted together. After the meal, we played some three-handed cutthroat cribbage, and I never did win a game with the two old cronies. I felt like the new guy in town, which in fact I was, but I trusted these two.

George didn't have a phone, so I went out to the little gas station/store up the street and called the Fairbanks pilot to let him know I wouldn't be going with him. He wasn't too happy about the last-minute cancellation, and suggested I call someone else next time I needed a flight.

When I got back to George's, he was busy drawing me a nice little map showing the way to his land. I already had all the gear and food I needed to make the run, and stay a couple of days to check out the homestead.

We spent the rest of the evening talking about this part of Alaska. Both George and Mitch had plenty of stories to tell, enhanced by the harsh rye whiskey George had generously been pouring for the three of us. When we finally called it a night, the sleeping bag on the living room floor might just as well have been a featherbed. I enjoyed the first dreamless unbroken sleep I'd had in a while.

The next morning, he took me out to the snowmobile. George had said it wasn't a new machine, and he wasn't kidding. It was old and rough, but started right up and sounded good. The front cowling had been badly cracked and was held together with wire stitches. The seat was split and patched with duct tape, and the cracked windshield was repaired with the same. There was a rear rack that held a full can of gas. I strapped my pack and snowshoes on the back of the seat. We all shook hands, and I took off in the direction of the trail George had pointed out.

George was right about the trail being rough, but it was passable if I took it easy. He told me not to run the river because it had some spots that could be weak all winter long. I stayed to the trail he had marked on the paper. He said I should keep my eye out for blazes on birch trees every few hundred yards, marked with an X. He had put them there many years ago when he had homesteaded the land for a trapping cabin site.

The country was thick with willow and birch. There wasn't much spruce right by the river. It seemed as if George, or anyone else for that matter, hadn't been out along the trail in a while. I had to work my way through willow thickets a few times.

The only bad spot I couldn't handle was where the trail ran along a slope above the river. The right ski dug in and the machine rolled several times down the slope, stopping before it hit the river, and I ended up against a birch tree covered with snow but not badly hurt in any way. It took a while, and I worked up a sweat getting the machine upright and back up the little slope. But it started on the third pull when I got it right side up, and churned its way back up to the trail. No wonder George kept this rig.

Continuing on, I came to a long, smooth, open section that ran for several miles along the river. The easy riding was enjoyable. A short distance further on, I saw some animal tracks and slowed down. There was a set of small moose tracks overlaid with several sets of wolf prints. Just past this area the trees and bushes closed in again, and the trail moved off out of sight from the river. The animal tracks followed this way, and I soon came upon the partial remains of the young moose. The wolves had made their kill, but had left some behind. There was quite a bit of moose meat left on the carcass, and it appeared very fresh, so I hacked off a nice big frozen piece to cook that night, wrapping it in a plastic bag and slipping it into my pack.

I had been riding four or five hours when I finally arrived at George's homestead, so I was glad to have extra fuel along.

The little structure was a simple plywood shack, but the door was solid. Going in, I saw that the one window was unbroken, protected by a heavy shutter covering it on the outside. The roof was covered with snow, but from the inside it looked good. Unfortunately, squirrels had gotten in somehow, and wreaked havoc on the insides, pulling a lot of insulation out of the tarpapered inner walls, and knocking over and chewing on lots of things. At least no bears had messed with the place. The cabin was basically solid, and would do for a start. This place was nothing like my homestead, but it had a good feel to it.

Lanyard Creek was about fifty yards away. George said it was passable in a shallow draft boat, until the end of summer, when the water level was always too low.

I built a fire outside to cook the moose meat, even though there was a nice woodstove inside. The stove seemed large for the small cabin and would probably run me out of the twelve-by-twelve if I cranked it up so I kept the fire low. There was a big Dutch oven sitting on the stove, a lot of shelves on one wall, and some kitchen gear, a typical little cabin set-up. Outside was a small lean-to shed on the sidewall of the cabin. There were some basic tools in it, including a shovel, pickaxe, and splitting maul. This homestead would be a good start.

The nice chunk of moose meat roasted on a green stick over the open fire was delicious, as I sat eating it, warm and comfortable in the little cabin. A kerosene lantern spread a sweet glow, and the night was quiet.

Later it got cold, very cold. I woke up in the wee hours shivering, stirred up the stove, and kept it going the rest of the night. Now the stove's capacity made sense, and I was grateful there was a good stack of firewood behind the cabin. I couldn't tell for sure, but it must have gone down to 20 below that morning. It was good I was prepared for this kind of weather. I had expected the Nowitna River area to be very cold, and had packed the right gear.

When it was light enough, I snowshoed around and found the taped trees marking the boundaries of what appeared to be a five-acre parcel. I also walked over the hill behind the cabin to get a better view. George's land included most of the side of the hill down to the creek. I was glad to have made the climb. The view from the hilltop was truly breathtaking. The land was locked in the grip of winter, with hoarfrost all over the trees. Down the back side of the hill was a lake, maybe half a mile across, and I wondered if it had a good population of fish.

I noticed more taped trees a short distance away and found what seemed to be another parcel, probably another five acres, right next to the one the cabin was on. I wondered if I'd have to deal with neighbors some day. There were many moose tracks along the back side of the hill, so hunting for food probably wouldn't be a problem. I could picture what the place would be like in the warmer, snow-free months, and decided that this land would suit me. There was no evidence of people living anywhere nearby, and I could tolerate anyone passing through. I might meet some interesting people, but wouldn't have to deal with them on a steady basis. George had said that moose and bear hunters came through, but that was acceptable to me. There wasn't much I would be able to do about it anyway.

That second night as I sat close to the hot stove, a cup of instant coffee in my hand, I had time to ruminate on the place, and had a few clarifying revelations. My first homestead, which I had worked so long and hard to create, had taught me many things about myself and the land I lived on. But even though it would always be special, the land here was the same as the land I already had, in feel and potential. It was all Alaska and that made this homestead, in many ways, just as viable a home for me. Just as I was considering this, first one wolf, then another and another started their eerie chorus. Going outside, I listened for a few minutes, feeling the goose bumps rise up on my arms and that familiar little shiver run down my spine. My love and enthusiasm for Alaska, after all these years and through all that had occurred, hadn't diminished one iota. Unless I were forced out somehow, Alaska and the bush would always be my home. The deep cold drove me back into the cabin.

The next morning, the old Skidoo started up after only a couple of pulls in spite of the frigid temperature. I kept tucked in behind the windshield as much as possible on the ride back, but got a little frostbite on my nose anyway by the time I got to George's trailer.

Mitch met me at the door and told me George was feeling poorly and would probably stay in bed the rest of the day. I took George to the gas station where he arranged to have his truck towed in. "That damned old truck and I have traveled together a long time, but I think I'll have to retire it now. Maybe I'll get me one of those neat little RVs and hit the road."

That evening, we towed the old dead truck back to the gas station, and Mitch signed it over to the station owner to use for parts. Back at George's place, I gave Mitch the rest of the moose meat to make a little stew.

George was up and sitting on the little couch at the end of the small trailer. He and I talked about the land. I told him right off that I had liked it and wanted to purchase it from him if he was willing.

He said he was ready to let it go.

When I asked him how much he wanted for it, he and Mitch exchanged a glance. With a dead-serious look on his face, George asked, "How does one dollar sound to you?"

I had no quick answer, and finally asked him if he meant it.

"Denny, I never say anything I don't mean. I have no family and I'm not going to be able to use it any longer, so if you want it, the price is one dollar."

I asked him if the trip out there was too much for him anymore.

George looked at Mitch and said, "You didn't tell him, did you?"

Mitch looked at him and said, "Didn't figure it was my place to, George."

George turned to me and stated:

"Denny, I've got cancer, pancreatic cancer, and I've only got a month or two left. So Mitch and I are going down to Florida where he has family, so I can at least die warm. I don't want to hear any sorries. Just accept what I'm saying. I didn't want to just leave the land alone, but I wanted to give it to someone who can appreciate it like I do. When Mitch met you, he thought you might be a likely candidate and now, I do too, so just give me a simple answer and we can get on with things."

I sat there quietly for a moment, before I agreed to the deal. It didn't seem right to just blurt out yes! without a little time to give such an offer the respect I felt it deserved. George and I had an understanding at that point, and he continued speaking.

"I only have one more question for you, Denny. Will you stay on the land, or just keep it a while and sell it?"

"No, George, I'll live there for as long as the Good Lord will let me. You have my word on that."

"Fine, it's settled. We'll do the paperwork tomorrow and the ten acres will be yours." That was another surprise.

"Ten acres?"

"Yeah, I got the other five acres right next to my cabin land too. Oh, this trailer and the lot it sits on goes with it, so you'll have a place to stay and a parking area for your vehicles when you come in for supplies or whatever. It isn't much, but it's better than nothing. There are very few people here, so you shouldn't have any trouble with vandalism. But these days, you never know."

We spent the evening talking Alaska again and the two old friends told me many stories about their lives there since they had come up from Michigan after World War II. I was sorry they would be leaving soon, especially because of the reason they were going.

The next morning after the post office opened, we went over and the postmaster notarized the transfer of the paperwork. I headed back down to Hazel to get all packed up. As we said our goodbyes, Mitch had told me they were probably leaving soon, but would hopefully see me before they were gone. In case they were gone, he gave me a key to the front door. I told George I was sorry we might not see each other again.

He smiled, winked and told me, "You never can tell, Denny, never can tell.

Episode

....

40

WHEN I GOT BACK TO HAZEL, I WENT RIGHT OVER TO WALT'S and told him I was ready to sell. Walt wrote me out a check on the spot. Shaking hands, I told him I'd bring the deed in a few days.

I drove back toward town, pulling in at Long Bay Used Cars to look at a four-wheel drive long bed pickup truck with a big cap on the bed. I had seen it when I left town, and found it was still there. I struck a deal with the salesman after a long haggle. He was a typical used car dealer, but gave me a reasonable trade-in on the Cherokee. The Chevy truck ran well with its big engine, easily cruising back up the road to Walt and Mary's place. Cranking up the wheeler, I returned to my cabin.

I hadn't expected to feel this much better about things, but I guess once I had resolved to make a change, I was able to move forward with a clear mind. The whole experience with George and Mitch had felt like it was meant to be, almost as if it was planned beforehand without my knowledge. I chose to look at it as the next step in my Alaska life.

As I was riding out the trail I had an epiphany. It suddenly came to me that as much as I loved living alone in my remote home, it wasn't actually living there that was the most important thing, though I loved the life. It was being able to go through whatever was necessary to establish myself there: the building, and the hunting and providing for myself in primitive surroundings. I had proven myself capable of dealing with whatever came.

So, I hadn't failed after all; I had simply settled too soon, and had not gone in as far as I should have because I didn't know enough. Now I could go farther north, deeper into the bush. I had been granted another place more remote, and could feel assured there would be no one close enough to ruin things.

Over the next several weeks, I prepared for my move. This time I knew exactly what I'd need to take with me. I bought an enclosed trailer to hold all my things, including my wheeler and snow machine. When I got back up to George's I would use it for storage. In the meantime, Mr. Harmon let me park it in his lot. I took the time to tell him exactly what was going on. He told me he understood my dilemma and wished me well. He was a good old man whose philosophy about people and life in Alaska I had come to fully understand.

I left Mary and Walt a number of things I felt should stay in the cabin, including the nice little propane range. I could always get more gear.

I was ready to leave. I had packed the final load onto my freighter sled. A new six-inch layer of snow added a cushion to the snow that had already fallen, which would make my passage easier.

I walked around the cabin, examining and remembering just about every piece of wood in the place. I felt sad, but was also filled with excitement to see what would be ahead of me. I'd go up to George's trailer and stay there while getting my stuff out to the new homestead. I'd clear the trail where it had become overgrown. I'd develop my new land and build another room onto the existing cabin, and keep life simple. It would be good, because I would make it so.

I damped the stove down for the final time. Walking out my cabin door, I slowly closed it and put the latch handle on top of the door frame.

I checked the sled load and started the snow machine. As I stood there putting my gloves on, the raucous sound of Bucky's bulldozer starting up across the tundra. All my hard feelings boiled up to the surface. Unhitching the cargo sled, I got on the snowmobile and headed to where a plume of black smoke had risen in the air. I stopped on the edge of the trees, then walked to the clearing. I could see Waters running his Cat over the snowless, barren ground.

Bucky stopped the dozer, climbed down and went to the blade to check something. His back to me, I walked out into the clearing until I was just a few feet behind him. Oblivious to me standing there, he stood inspecting a hydraulic line until, sensing my presence, he spun around. When he saw me, Waters froze in place, just staring at me, a startled look on his face. I stepped forward until my mouth was just a few inches from his ear and said, "We're not over yet."

Turning, I walked out to my machine and headed back to where the loaded sled was waiting. As I hitched it up, I thought to myself: "Now I can move on." That's exactly what I did, and never looked back.

Other Books By Warren Troy

Warren Troy, Alaska wilderness adventure author, continues the Alaska homestead adventures of Denny Caraway. Caraway, long time Alaskan

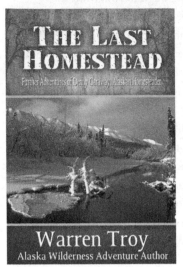

homesteader, is content to live a solitary, rugged and often dangerous life deep in the northern wilderness. After many years alone, however, loneliness causes him to seek companionship on his remote land and he reconnects with a former friend and lover who is willing to share his isolated life.

Denny's world is full and complete until tragedy strikes, and Caraway completely severs all ties with the few people he does know. Leaving his beloved homestead, he leads a totally primitive existence deeper in the forest, hurt and angry, until a loyal friend finds him and Denny realizes it's time to come home.

An inexperienced teenager leaves his suburban California home to visit his brother in San Francisco, and dives into the Hippie Movement of the sixties.

Establishing himself in the Flower Power scene of the Haight Ashbury District, he becomes a bell-bottomed entrepreneur, running a unique used garment business from the back of an old, brightly painted step van, becoming known only as Jester.

Heavily involved in the sex, drugs and rock and roll lifestyle, he meets fascinating characters like Janis Joplin and Timothy Leary and has many amazing experiences, until he burns out on the whole scene. Leaving the bay area, He searches for a different direction.

Jester moves in and out of different lifestyles, becoming a road nomad, traveling, over the years, from the mountains of Big Sur all the way to Alaska, with many stops along the way. In *Jester: Memoirs of a Retired Hippie*, Jester tastes love and loss, joy and deep sorrow, and the magic that still exists in the world, evolving into a unique and wise older man.

Made in the USA
Las Vegas, NV
21 December 2021

39065109R00108